Praise for Mr.

"Readers who can't get enough of Darcy and Elizabeth will find that Reynolds does an admirable job of capturing the feel of the period in this entertaining diversion."

—*Booklist*

"Rarely have I read such sensual, seductive, provocative, yet wholly chaste, love scenes!"

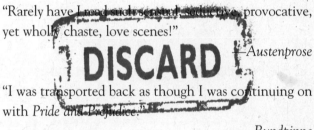

—*Austenprose*

"I was transported back as though I was continuing on with *Pride and Prejudice.*"

—*Rundpinne*

"Another well-written cast and lively variation from Reynolds."

—*Savvy Verse and Wit*

"Abigail Reynolds never disappoints."

—*Books Like Breathing*

"An exciting, well-developed, and romantic novel that stays true to Austen's characters, while being a fantastic unique story of its own."

—*Laura's Reviews*

"The romantic/sexual tension is just perfect."

—*The Calico Critic*

"Abigail Reynolds has created a masterful period novel. The way she weaves romance, tradition, and wit is exciting and fresh. Mr. Darcy and Elizabeth are created here in a way that makes them come to life and live beyond the written page. Austen fans will enjoy the author's unique interpretation of an old love story."

—*Everything Victorian and More*

"I can honestly say that Abigail Reynolds is my favourite writer of this genre. I adore how well she writes Darcy and Elizabeth. She knows their characteristics inside and out and writes their feelings, mannerisms, and quirks to perfection."

—*She Read a Book*

"Excellent writing."

—*Palmer's Picks for Reading*

"A satisfying and compelling novel that you'll wish to read over and over again."

—*A Curious Statistical Anomaly*

"The additional cast adds a completely new dimension to the story and makes it unique."

—*Bookfoolery and Babble*

"Reynolds's love for *Pride and Prejudice* is obvious."

—*Diary of An Eccentric*

"If you have yet to read a book by Abigail Reynolds, you are missing out on something good."

—*To Read or Not to Read*

"I most emphatically recommend!"

—*Austenesque Reviews*

"That we wonder how all will fare, even as we know the ending, is a testament to Ms. Reynolds's fine storytelling."

—*Linda Banche Romance Author*

# MR DARCY'S UNDOING

## ABIGAIL REYNOLDS

sourcebooks landmark

Published by Sourcebooks Landmark, an imprint of Sourcebooks, Inc.
P.O. Box 4410, Naperville, Illinois 60567-4410
(630) 961-3900
FAX: (630) 961-2168
www.sourcebooks.com

Originally published in 2007 by Intertidal Press as *Without Reserve*

Library of Congress Cataloging-in-Publication Data

Reynolds, Abigail.
  Mr. Darcy's undoing / Abigail Reynolds.
    p. cm.
1.  Darcy, Fitzwilliam (Fictitious character)—Fiction. 2.  Bennet, Elizabeth (Fictitious character)—Fiction. 3.  Courtship—Fiction. 4.  England—Social life and customs—19th century—Fiction. 5.  Gentry—England—Fiction.  I. Austen, Jane, 1775-1817. Pride and prejudice. II. Title.
  PS3618.E967M688 2011
  813'.6—dc22

                              2011027392

Printed and bound in the United States of America
VP 10 9 8 7 6 5 4 3 2 1

To
the readers at Austen Interlude and Hyacinth Gardens
who encouraged me to keep writing,
and especially to
Ellen Pickels,
who made my books possible

# Chapter 1

By the time the ladies of the Bennet family reached the Assembly Rooms in Meryton, Elizabeth was already beginning to regret her decision to attend that evening. Her interest had been slender to begin with; she had no desire to be in the company of the officers, particularly Mr. Wickham, and she was not yet recovered from the emotional blows she had received during her recent visit to Kent. Between the persistent complaints of her younger sisters regarding the unfairness of their father's decision not to remove the family to Brighton and her mother's unending reminiscences of the Assembly where Jane had met Mr. Bingley, she was quite ready to be left to her own company. Only the sight of Jane's pallor as Mrs. Bennet continued to hold forth on her loss of Mr. Bingley gave her any sense of purpose. She squeezed her sister's hand reassuringly.

When they entered the Assembly, several of their friends

came up to greet them and to welcome Jane and Elizabeth back to Hertfordshire. Elizabeth was sorry to see that Mr. Wickham was indeed among the crowd; she had seen him twice already since her return. In addition to her other grievances, she had a fresh source of displeasure, for he had made clear his inclination toward renewing those attentions which had marked the early part of their acquaintance. This could only serve to provoke her, and she lost all concern for him in finding herself thus selected as the object of such idle and frivolous gallantry. While she steadily repressed it, she could not but feel the reproof contained in his believing that however long and for whatever cause his attentions had been withdrawn, her vanity would be gratified and her preference secured at any time by their renewal.

As she saw Mr. Wickham approaching her with a charming smile, no doubt planning to ask her for the honour of the first two dances, Elizabeth turned a brilliant smile on the gentleman to her right, an acquaintance of many years' standing by the name of Mr. Covington, who was in possession of a small estate some ten miles from Meryton. She did not know him particularly well, but his native good humour and enjoyment of company rendered him welcome wherever he went, and Elizabeth was not displeased to have his company as an alternative to Mr. Wickham's.

"Mr. Covington," she exclaimed. "It has been quite some time since I have seen you—I dare say it was before Christmas at least."

"You would be quite right, Miss Bennet," he replied. "Owing to my mother's recent illness, I did not have to opportunity to attend events such as these this winter, and by the time I returned, you were off on your travels, and very much missed."

"I am sure," said Elizabeth with an arch look. "With the introduction of all the officers, ladies are now always scarce, so I would imagine that the absence of any lady would be noted."

"The others may speak for themselves, Miss Bennet," he said with an appreciative smile, "but for myself you were missed only for the lack of the pleasure of your company. To make up for my loss, would you do me the honour of dancing the first two dances?"

Elizabeth accepted with a smile; after the stressful nature of her recent interactions with Mr. Darcy and then the discomfort of Mr. Wickham's company, it was pleasant to spend a few minutes in the company of an agreeable and undemanding young man like Mr. Covington. The reassurance that she was still sought out as a partner by men other than the officers did not go amiss either.

She talked happily with him through the first set and afterwards joined him for some refreshments, hearing all the news of his mother's illness and recovery, the effects of the winter on Ashworth House and his tenants; and telling him amusing stories of her journey to Kent and London. She left him without particular regret when one of the officers asked her to dance.

It would have been difficult not to enjoy herself, given the plethora of available partners, and she was successful for the most part at avoiding Mr. Wickham; the one time he managed to catch her and request her hand for a set of dances, she could fortunately plead that she had already promised the dances to another gentleman. Reflecting on the native injustice of the fact that a lady could not refuse to dance with one gentleman without refusing all other partners as well, she made a point of avoiding him after the set of dances were over. Fortunately, Mr. Covington again materialized by her side, offering her refreshments and a hope she would join him for another dance, to which Elizabeth was happy to give a positive response, as it meant one more set where she could evade Wickham.

She was pleasantly exhausted by the end of the evening, and was able to ignore her mother's constant revisiting of the event on the way home and recitals of every officer with whom Lydia had danced.

The first week of Elizabeth's return was soon gone. The second began. It was the last of the regiment's stay in Meryton, and all the young ladies in the neighbourhood were drooping apace. The dejection was almost universal. The elder Miss Bennets alone were still able to eat, drink, and sleep, and pursue the usual course of their employments. Very frequently were they reproached for this insensibility by Kitty and Lydia, whose own misery was extreme, and who could not comprehend such hard-heartedness in any of the family.

"Good Heaven! What is to become of us! What are we to do!" would they often exclaim in the bitterness of woe. "How can you be smiling so, Lizzy?"

Their affectionate mother shared all their grief; she remembered what she had herself endured on a similar occasion, five and twenty years ago.

"I am sure," said she, "I cried for two days together when Colonel Millar's regiment went away. I thought I should have broke my heart."

"I am sure I shall break mine," said Lydia.

"If one could but go to Brighton!" observed Mrs. Bennet.

"Oh, yes!—if one could but go to Brighton! But Papa is so disagreeable."

"A little sea-bathing would set me up forever."

"And my aunt Phillips is sure it would do me a great deal of good," added Kitty.

Such were the kind of lamentations resounding perpetually through Longbourn House. Elizabeth tried to be diverted by them; but all sense of pleasure was lost in shame. She felt anew the justice of Mr. Darcy's objections; and never had she before been so much disposed to pardon his interference in the views of his friend.

But the gloom of Lydia's prospect was shortly cleared away; for she received an invitation from Mrs. Forster, the wife of the colonel of the regiment, to accompany her to

Brighton. This invaluable friend was a very young woman, and very lately married. A resemblance in good humour and good spirits had recommended her and Lydia to each other, and out of their three months' acquaintance they had been intimate two.

The rapture of Lydia on this occasion, her adoration of Mrs. Forster, the delight of Mrs. Bennet, and the mortification of Kitty, are scarcely to be described. Wholly inattentive to her sister's feelings, Lydia flew about the house in restless ecstasy, calling for everyone's congratulations, and laughing and talking with more violence than ever; whilst the luckless Kitty continued in the parlour repining at her fate in terms as unreasonable as her accent was peevish.

"I cannot see why Mrs. Forster should not ask me as well as Lydia," said she, "though I am not her particular friend. I have just as much right to be asked as she has, and more too, for I am two years older."

In vain did Elizabeth attempt to make her reasonable, and Jane to make her resigned. As for Elizabeth herself, this invitation was so far from exciting in her the same feelings as in her mother and Lydia, that she considered it as the death-warrant of all possibility of common sense for the latter; and detestable as such a step must make her were it known, she could not help secretly advising her father not to let her go. She represented to him all the improprieties of Lydia's general behaviour, the little advantage she could derive from the friendship of such a woman as Mrs. Forster, and the probability of her being yet more imprudent with such a companion at Brighton, where the temptations must be greater than at home.

Although he heard her attentively, her father, concerned more with his own domestic peace, was not disposed to agree with her reasoning, nor with her concern for the very great disadvantage to them all arising from the public notice of Lydia's imprudent manner. Elizabeth was forced to be content with his answer, but her own opinion remained the same, and she left him disappointed and sorry. It was not in her nature, however, to increase her vexations by dwelling on them. She was confident of having performed her duty, and to fret over unavoidable evils, or augment them by anxiety, was no part of her disposition.

She was happy to be distracted from both Kitty's lamentations and Lydia's raptures when Mr. Covington and his mother came to call. Mrs. Covington was a contemporary of Mrs. Bennet's, but her nature was quite different, being both eminently practical and tactful; a combination which had served her well during her years of managing the Ashworth estate by herself following her husband's untimely death and before the majority of her son. Elizabeth was not surprised to find that, after greeting Mrs. Bennet cordially, Mrs. Covington chose to locate herself between the two eldest Miss Bennets; she had always had a suspicion that Mrs. Covington found Mrs. Bennet's company to be rather trying, though her manners would never have indicated as much.

Elizabeth expressed her pleasure at Mrs. Covington's

return to health. On this subject Mrs. Bennet waxed lyrical, including referring to every illness she herself had ever suffered as well as those of most of the neighbours. Elizabeth and Jane were finally able to interrupt this flow with a discussion of their recent visit to Town. Mrs. Bennet, with little to say for herself on this topic, spent a rare moment of observation, and caught sight of an unguarded look on Mr. Covington's face as he gazed at her second daughter. Never backward to credit what was for the advantage of her family, or that came in the shape of a lover to any of her daughters, she was immediately delighted. She began to offer him attention, and mark her deference for his opinions sufficiently to catch the embarrassed attention of her daughters.

At this point, Lydia, who had just returned from Meryton, where she had paid a visit to Mrs. Forster, burst into the room with her usual energy, barely stopping to greet their guests before launching into a lively rendition of her adventures in the town and the plans she and her friend had made for her stay in Brighton. She took off a mournful Kitty to see her latest purchases, leaving behind a room that seemed much quieter for her absence.

Mrs. Covington, with the slightest of frowns, asked Mrs. Bennet, "Is your family travelling to Brighton this summer, then?"

Mrs. Bennet explained the circumstances, bewailing a little her husband's cruelty in not permitting the entire family to go.

"I can well understand why you would be reluctant to allow Lydia to go without being there to supervise her in person," said Mrs. Covington decisively, misunderstanding Mrs. Bennet's intended purpose in wishing to bring her family to Brighton. "It is not a place for a young girl on her own; the officers of the militia here seem to be gentlemen, but there are many others who are wild and unmanageable. A girl like Lydia could easily become a target for an unscrupulous man. No, Mrs. Bennet, I fully agree with you that she should not be allowed to go without you."

"That is what I have told Mr. Bennet time and again!" cried Mrs. Bennet. She was not prepared to spoil the mood of a prospective suitor for one of her girls by correcting the misapprehension that she did not approve of Lydia's journey.

"I should agree as well," interjected Mr. Covington, who had been watching Elizabeth's face, and had gathered a good idea of her opinion of the matter. "I would not allow her to go by herself—though I certainly hope for myself that your family will not be travelling to Brighton any time soon. Why, Miss Bennet and Miss Elizabeth have only just returned!" He smiled warmly in Elizabeth's direction.

Mrs. Bennet was delighted by this additional hint as to his intentions. "Well, you need not worry, Mr. Covington. Mr. Bennet has made it clear he will not allow it," she said, with just a hint of testiness. "But Lydia has her heart set on visiting Mrs. Forster there this summer; they are such dear friends, you know."

Elizabeth found it quite astonishing that her mother was being so deferential to the opinions of their guests; and while she could not begin to comprehend why this should be so, she was perfectly willing to take advantage of it. "Could not Lydia visit Mrs. Forster in the autumn instead, at the regiment's winter headquarters, when she would only be with the __shire regiment, whom we know and of whom she is such a favourite?" she asked.

"An excellent thought," said Mrs. Covington firmly.

Mrs. Bennet began to look decidedly vexed; she did not wish to dash the hopes of her favourite merely for Lizzy's sake, but Mr. Covington was quite eligible, and it certainly seemed that Mr. Bingley was never to return. "Well, I am sure Mr. Bennet will give it due consideration," she said querulously.

The visit lasted for over an hour, and concluded with an invitation to dine at Ashworth the following week. Their guests had no sooner departed than Mrs. Bennet's raptures began. "Oh, my dearest Lizzy!" she cried. "Mr. Covington! Oh, why did you say nothing of it to me! He will do very well for you, indeed. You shall be mistress of Ashworth! Oh, Lord! Of course, it is nothing to what Mr. Bingley would have been, but we must learn to live with our disappointments. He will do quite well for you, though I cannot imagine why he did not choose Jane or Lydia instead—but there is no accounting for men's thinking!"

Elizabeth lifted up her eyes. "I must remind you that Mr. Covington has not expressed any intentions at all towards me, nor has he suggested he is calling on me. I suspect he was doing no more than paying a neighbourly call."

"Nonsense, Lizzy!" Mrs. Bennet cried. "Come ten miles just to visit? I think not! No, mark my words, Lizzy, you *will* be the next mistress of Ashworth!"

Elizabeth could see there was to be no reasoning with her, though she remained unconvinced that Mr. Covington's interest in her was anything more than a passing fancy.

She was forced to reconsider this question, though, after their dinner engagement at Ashworth. It could not be denied that Mr. Covington was particularly attentive to her that evening, soliciting her opinion on a variety of matters, and going so far as to offer the party in general, but Elizabeth in particular, a tour of the house and grounds.

Elizabeth felt the compliment of his attentions, but was cautious. She did not wish her liveliness to mislead him, as it apparently had both Mr. Collins and Mr. Darcy in their different ways. Mr. Covington, though, she had known since the days when she wore her hair down, although never particularly well. This was, to her recollection, one of only a half dozen or so times she had been to Ashworth House. It was a well-kept house, slightly smaller than Longbourn, and not particularly well suited to hosting large parties; and since old Mr. Covington's death until his son reached his majority, his mother was less active in the neighbourhood circles than she might have been otherwise.

She felt a little discomfort at the idea of her old

acquaintance becoming her suitor. She had never thought of him in that way, though, as she thought back upon it, he had been more attentive to her than usual for some time now, which she had attributed to his natural affability. She could certainly find no reason to object to his interest in her; he was well respected, amiable, responsible, and she had never heard ill report of him, nor could she recall any instance in which she had been personally displeased with him. If she had not thought of him in the way a woman thinks of her lover, she reasoned, it was likely the result of her unfortunate experiences in the last months, which did not render her likely to look upon any man in such a manner. In some ways it was more surprising that she had *not* considered him as a candidate for her affections—he was certainly more suitable for her than either of the two men who had been her favourites, Wickham and Colonel Fitzwilliam, and he could be very agreeable. Perhaps, she thought, choosing a suitor based purely on immediate liking and attraction was dangerous, since it allowed a scoundrel such as Wickham to take advantage of her; it might be that a sensible match with a man she knew and respected was a better option. Perhaps it was nothing more than his very familiarity that had led her to overlook him.

She refused, however, to allow herself to dwell too much on the matter until such a time as Mr. Covington declared himself. While she was certain of his interest, the truth was that he could do better than her in terms of a match with a woman of greater fortune; hers would be the advantage in a marriage between them. And while his estate certainly was not struggling, it was a small holding, and would benefit by the master choosing a wife whose dowry could enrich the family. Time would tell if his interest was serious, and she would not worry about it overmuch until then.

Her attention, in fact, was elsewhere in any case. Since the loss of the regiment, there had been constant repinings from her mother, Lydia, and Kitty at the dullness of everything around them, which threw a real gloom over their domestic circle. Lydia was particularly loud in her complaints, for she was still angry and disappointed that her visit to Mrs. Forster had been delayed until autumn, and that she would never enjoy the delights of Brighton. Her mother, according to her, had, by taking the advice of Mrs. Covington, betrayed her entire future. Mrs. Bennet wavered between mourning with her favourite daughter as to the opportunity lost and a practical consideration for not offending the only promising candidate for a son-in-law. Once Lydia had determined the true source of her woe, she blamed it fully upon Elizabeth, and did not hesitate to point this out to her sister at every available occasion.

Elizabeth was thus quite in need of pleasant distraction. Her upcoming tour to the Lakes was the object of her happiest thoughts; it was her best consolation for all the uncomfortable hours which the discontentedness of Lydia, Kitty, and her mother made inevitable. The time fixed for the beginning of the Northern tour was now fast approaching. Only a few days remained when Mr. Covington came to call at Longbourn once more.

His primary object in the visit was Elizabeth, and even if he had intended otherwise, Mrs. Bennet, never one to lose an opportunity, would have forced him into a position where it would have been impossible for him to avoid spending time with her daughter. Between the two, there was nothing easier than for him to sit beside Elizabeth and speak with her at length. Elizabeth was honestly glad to see him, as she would have been any caller who did not come solely to mourn the departure of the regiment, and she was quite lively in her description of her hopes for her tour and her interest in the Lakes. Mrs. Bennet was pleased to observe that Mr. Covington seemed to find Elizabeth's enthusiasm quite charming.

"Lizzy," Mrs. Bennet interrupted after a time, "it is such a pleasant day, and the flower gardens are in full bloom. Perhaps Mr. Covington would like it if you showed him the different walks."

Elizabeth was not at all fooled by her mother's stratagem, but obediently made the offer, which was accepted with alacrity. She ran into her own room for her parasol, and then attended her guest downstairs. Outside they proceeded along the gravel path that led to the flower garden; she pointed out several of her favourites to him along the way.

"Do you enjoy gardens, then, Miss Bennet?" asked Mr. Covington.

"Yes, I confess to a love of the outdoors in general, and

Jane and I often will spend our time here among the flowers," she responded.

"My mother has always loved gardens, and it has been a disappointment to her that her health has not allowed her to oversee our gardens as closely as she would have liked in the last few years. They have not suffered overmuch from the neglect, though I think that the gardeners lack my mother's sense for designing plantings."

"It can be hard to match something which is a matter of personal taste, and I can understand your mother's frustration," she agreed somewhat absently.

"Miss Bennet," he said, his voice rather serious, but then he went no further.

She looked up at him. "Yes?"

He took a deep breath, then said, "There is something that I have been… hoping to ask you about."

Elizabeth had a sudden realization of what he was implying, and her pulses fluttered a bit. She had not been expecting this so soon, and had not in truth given the matter enough thought to be sure of her decision, though the arguments in favour certainly seemed to outweigh any against. Nevertheless, she was sufficiently anxious to try to delay matters. "There is?" she asked.

He flushed. "Yes, umm, I have been thinking, umm, of how much pleasure I have had in your company of late, and I know that you are going away very soon, and it will be some time before I see you again…"

She was both amused and a bit vexed by his obvious anxiety. Whatever else might be said against the other two men who had proposed to her, neither of them had any trouble speaking his piece. On the other hand, she thought, there was something to be said for a man who was not so blindly certain of being accepted as to have no worries in the matter. An ardent declaration of love, too, could be a somewhat more embarrassing proposition when faced with someone whom one would continue to encounter regularly even if rejected. She took a little pity on him, and, seeing an opportunity to gain herself some time as well, said gently, "Is there something you would like me to consider while I am away?"

He seemed relieved by her comprehension of the question, though he clearly had hoped for a more immediate answer. "Yes, that is to say, I would very much like it if you would consider whether you would do me the honour of being my wife," he said, the last words rushing out.

Elizabeth, feeling somewhat sorry for his uncertainty, said gravely, "I thank you for the compliment, sir. I confess you have caught me quite by surprise, and while I find I am... favourably inclined, I would appreciate the opportunity to examine my thoughts on the subject more closely, with hopes of giving you an answer to your satisfaction." She smiled at him with a warmth that she hoped would convey her regard for him, despite the delay she was requesting.

"Then I may approach you on this matter on your return?"

he asked. To her relief, he did not seem overly disturbed about the deferment of her response.

Her smile was a bit more free now. "I will look forward to it, Mr. Covington," she said, with just a trace of archness.

He caught her hand and brought it to his lips. "As will I, Miss Bennet."

Elizabeth, feeling suddenly shy, blushed and looked away. Once her hand was free again, though, she looked up at him and saw again the amiable man she had known for years, and was able to exchange a smile with him.

Mrs. Bennet had been quite displeased when she discovered that Elizabeth was not yet engaged despite her efforts, but her vexation was somewhat mitigated when her daughter told her that Mr. Covington had particularly asked if he might call on her on her return. Her mother's frequent lectures over the next few days as to the importance of securing his affections provided yet another reason for her to look forward to her tour.

The trip in every way lived up to her expectations. The company of her aunt and uncle was delightful, and the excitement of seeing places she had only read of in the past occupied her days. The beauty of the Lakes surpassed all her imaginations; she found it to be a landscape that spoke deeply to her. Though accustomed to more level and peaceful terrain, she felt she could happily spend her life among the crags and fells.

Her only vexation was when the question of Mr. Covington would come to her mind. She did not find the thought of *him* vexing, but her own inability to come to a coherent decision about his proposal was a nagging irritant. She was not used to considering herself a dithering miss, yet her usual decisiveness seemed to have deserted her on this issue.

One morning, when they were staying in the town of Glenridding, Elizabeth set off by herself to explore. She was feeling a need to be alone with her thoughts, and even the pleasant presence of her aunt and uncle felt as if it were more than she could tolerate. She struck off onto a path which led above Ullswater, skirting the small woods that clung to the side of the river, and walked rapidly until she felt well winded. Finding herself in a clearing overlooking the water, she settled herself in the grass to admire the dramatic scenery.

For some time she was content just to feel the cool breeze moving over her skin, but soon her thoughts returned to the question she had been avoiding through the entire journey. She could no longer circumvent it; she needed to come to a decision about her future with Mr. Covington. She was not even certain why she was struggling with it; certainly he had a great many of the characteristics she would value in a partner—he was amiable, well-liked and respected, and had a reputation for kindness and generosity. She knew he would never deliberately hurt or neglect her, nor maltreat any children they might have—she found she shied away from thinking of "their children"—and his position in life was one in which she could be comfortable.

It galled her to be forced to consider that very position in life, but the truth was she could no longer afford to ignore it. Her mother in many ways had the right of it—if none of the Bennet girls married well, their position as well as her own would be very precarious after Mr. Bennet's death. Elizabeth had always put this consideration to the side, certain that Jane, with her beauty and gentle disposition, would find an appropriate husband, thus taking the burden from her. Now, though, having seen how little Jane had recovered her spirits after Mr. Bingley's departure, she was forced to reconsider that conclusion. No man would want a wife who was pining for another, and, while Jane was strong enough to continue to put a good face on her sadness, that spark she had owned in the past was no longer present. Her younger sisters gave her even less cause for hope; she doubted that Mary would ever marry, and if Lydia and Kitty found husbands, those men would no doubt be as foolish and impractical as their lady-loves. No, she could not depend on any of her sisters to be able to provide a home and sustenance for their mother or the others after her father's death. Under the circumstances, how could she justify refusing a pleasant, well-to-do gentleman of whom she could make no major complaint?

He certainly was an improvement over her previous suitors, she thought with an ironic smile. Mr. Covington might not constantly challenge her intelligence as Mr. Darcy had, but he was far from the obsequious fool Mr. Collins was; and his manners and conduct were certainly an improvement over the proud and judgemental Mr. Darcy. If he had not the fine countenance and figure of Mr. Wickham, he more than compensated by owning a far greater moral sense than the other ever would. All in all, she had very little to complain of Mr. Covington as a husband—nothing at all, in fact, except that she found herself with no particular urge for his company. She did not miss him when they were apart; she did not look forward with eagerness to their next encounter; she did not remember with delight what he had said at the last. She had hoped to marry for love, but she could go no further than to say she *liked* him. Still, could not that affection develop into more, given time? Was a failure to make her cheeks blush and her pulse run fast a reason to refuse a man who would make a good husband? It was a sensibility she could not afford. There were few enough men who would look at a penniless woman from a family known for ill-bred behaviour.

She sighed. There really was no choice; perhaps that, as much as anything, was what grated on her. She wanted a marriage that went beyond the everyday as much as the spectacular scenery before her outshone the calmer landscape of Hertfordshire, but it was not to be. But it was not realistic to wait in hopes of finding a man who could instantly command her whole heart and devotion. There would not be a husband to open new worlds to her, to continually challenge and stimulate her—that was beyond her reach. But she would not allow herself to be made unhappy by fanciful wishes. She would accept Mr. Covington's offer when he made it, and she would be grateful for it. She resolved that she would think no further on any attributes Mr. Covington might lack, and only to consider the advantages he offered.

The sun went behind a cloud, and she shivered. She should have brought a shawl with her, she thought, rather than rushing out heedlessly without thinking that the weather might change. She took a last look at the peerless view before her before determinedly heading back towards the town.

Darcy had quite enough of his guests for the day. Nothing could please him, neither Bingley's good humour, nor Miss Bingley's condescending witticisms, nor even Georgiana's quiet company. He was restless, and decided to take himself off for a solitary ride before his mood deteriorated any further. He cantered across the familiar and well loved hills of Pemberley until his horse was lathered, then, restive still, slowed him to a walk on his way back to the house. Unwilling to return to company quite so soon, he paused and turned along a favourite path by the side of the water, where every step brought forward a noble fall of ground or a fine reach of woods. In such attractive surroundings, relaxation slowly began to steal over him.

*Elizabeth would like it here*, he thought involuntarily, and a familiar pain rushed into him. An image of her rose before his eyes, the sweetness of her smile contrasting with an arch look in her lovely eyes. *How am I to tolerate this?* he demanded of himself, not for the first time. He had thought this pain would fade with time, but it had not; and coming to Pemberley had brought no relief—if anything, it had worsened his distress and longing for her. *This* was where she was supposed to be by his side, *this* should be her home, and it seemed he could not forget her, not even for a minute.

Then there were those moments when he would see a shadow of sorrow crossing Bingley's face, and know that he was responsible for causing his friend the same sort of agony he now found himself in, and he despised himself for it. But Bingley's loss was the greater; if Elizabeth was to be believed, her sister had truly loved him, whereas Darcy had never been so fortunate as to have Elizabeth's love to lose. It was almost as great a punishment to think of this as it was to recall the bitterness and acrimony of Elizabeth's refusal, and sometimes he wondered that he could still look Bingley in the eye and call him friend. *If only Elizabeth were here*, he thought despairingly.

He gazed unseeingly at the vista opening before him, and the question crept into his mind once more that had been haunting him since the day he had arrived at Pemberley, having ridden ahead of the party so as to have some time in his home alone. Was it possible that his letter had improved Elizabeth's opinion of him? Might it be that, if he were to try to make his suit again, she might be more receptive? Was his pride, his damnable pride, causing him to refuse the opportunity to see if she might yet be won, now that her misconceptions had been laid to rest? *If she ever read the letter,* he thought bitterly, *and if she believed a word you said in it!*

His pride was certainly standing between Bingley and *his* happiness, he knew. He could hardly blame Elizabeth for refusing him when he looked at his own behaviour—giving up on the woman he claimed to love, and allowing his friend to suffer the tortures of the damned on his account. But to confess his insufferable interference to Bingley—what if Miss Bennet had since forgotten him? Would another disappointment not be worse?

Enough was enough, he decided suddenly. He could no longer bear not knowing. He would talk to Bingley, convince him that it was his responsibility to return to Netherfield to collect the quarter-day rents and to enjoy the shooting, and then they would see—see if Miss Bennet still cared for Bingley, and see if he himself had any hope of ever winning Elizabeth's affection. If the answer was no, he would have to accept it, and somehow learn to live with it, but he was damned if he would give up before he knew.

***

Elizabeth kept to her resolution of having no regrets. It was somewhat easier after Mr. Covington finally asked her to be his wife, and she was able to see the joy in his face when she accepted him, and to see the pleasure that their engagement brought to her family. Her mother was delighted that she would be mistress of Ashworth, her father pleased that his favourite daughter would be so near, and Jane, to whom Elizabeth had never confessed her reservations, was as happy for her sister as her spirits would allow her to be.

She felt reassured on another front as well. Mrs. Covington was a woman she respected, and despite her pleasant interactions with her before leaving on her tour, Elizabeth had a very real concern that her future mother would be disappointed in her son's choice. It would have been better for the future of Ashworth, she knew, for him to marry a woman with some fortune of her own, and Mrs. Covington could not fail to be aware of it. Elizabeth disliked the idea of entering the family with any conflict between her and the woman who had managed the household ever since she could remember. It was an agreeable surprise, then, on her first visit to Ashworth after her engagement, to find Mrs. Covington congratulating her with a kindliness which could not be missed.

Touched, Elizabeth thanked her warmly. She was surprised to find herself confessing to Mrs. Covington those very concerns she had worried over, and was for a moment embarrassed to have acknowledged so openly her own consideration that she might not be the best match for her son.

She was immediately reassured, however, by Mrs. Covington's response. "My dear Miss Bennet," the older woman said, "while I cannot deny that I could wish you had some fortune of your own to bring to this marriage, it is not as important a matter to me as some other characteristics you possess in abundance. I am not one to deny harsh facts; I know I almost did not survive my illness this winter, and that my next episode will in all probability be my last. For my own peace of mind, I want to see my son settled, and with a woman who will be capable of managing Ashworth. You are practical, energetic, clever, and unafraid to speak your mind; this is more important to me at this moment than fortune."

"I hope your concerns prove to be quite unfounded," exclaimed Elizabeth, startled by this degree of frankness, "but I will certainly do my best, and I thank you for your kind words."

Mrs. Covington looked at her penetratingly for a moment, then smiled warmly. "I have always been a frank woman, my dear, and now I find myself at a time in my life when I have no patience for arguing the niceties. My son has left this matter of choosing a bride longer than I would have liked, and as a result, I have a great deal which I want to have the opportunity to tell you, and not as much time as I would have wished to do so."

Elizabeth looked at her with a new respect. "I will be grateful for any insights and help you can give me."

"My son is a good man, and will make you a fine husband," she said. "I have much to be proud of in him, but I am not such a doting mother as to think he is without flaw. If you do not know it already, you will discover soon that he is generous to a fault, and dislikes causing unpleasantness. The wrong sort of woman could take merciless advantage of his good nature. You, I think, are too honest to do so, but you will need strength and tact to watch that no one else takes advantage of him either, be it the tenants or the servants or the tradesmen." She watched Elizabeth closely to observe her reaction.

Elizabeth had not truly begun to consider until this moment the changes that were to come to her as mistress of her own home. "I see that I will have a great deal to learn," she said slowly, striving to match Mrs. Covington's directness.

Mrs. Covington looked at her, well pleased with the young woman her son had chosen. She patted her hand, and said, "We shall talk more soon, I hope, but I see a young man coming who is hoping, I doubt not, to take you away from me."

Elizabeth looked up to see Mr. Covington approaching, a pleased smile on his face at the sight of her. "Miss Bennet!" he said. "I was wondering if you would enjoy an opportunity to see the grounds. I would be happy to give you a tour."

"Thank you," she said sedately, with a glance at his mother. "I would like that." She allowed him to lead her outside.

"I hope you were having a pleasant discussion with my mother, Lizzy," he said as they entered the flower gardens.

Elizabeth, not yet accustomed to the familiarity of being called by her name, looked away and reached out to lightly touch a rose. "Very much so," she said. "I like her very well indeed."

He was visibly relieved. "I am glad to hear it. I want you to be happy here, you know."

"Thank you," she said. She was finding this conversation somewhat stilted. "I am sure I will be, Mr. Covington."

"Lizzy…"

She glanced up at him enquiringly. "Yes?"

"Will you not call me James?" he asked. "You used to do it quite prettily, many years ago."

She coloured. "Yes, of course, if you would like," she replied, a trifle uncomfortable with the idea, but feeling his request to be quite reasonable. "James," she added. He looked so pleased by her gesture that she could not help softening a bit towards him, much as she would towards a puppy eager for affection. "The gardens are very lovely—you have many of my favourite flowers. I think I will like it here very much."

To her surprise, he took her gloved hand and pressed it between his. Startled, she looked at him, and found that his gaze held a warmth that she had never seen in him before. His eyes travelled downwards to her lips. She felt a rush of anxiety, but did not move; she understood her obligations to him. Still, she could not help turning her face to the side as he leaned toward her, encouraging his lips to land on her cheek instead of her mouth. The feeling was not unpleasing, and she smiled up at him apologetically. Fortunately, he appeared to be perfectly satisfied with what had occurred, and with another squeeze, released her hand.

She breathed a silent sigh of relief as they continued on, grateful to have that first moment of intimacy past. It would become easier with time, she was sure, and she could see that it would likely even become pleasant as she grew more accustomed to this sort of physical affection. *There is nothing to worry about*, she reassured herself. *Nothing at all.*

# Chapter 2

ELIZABETH DID NOT SEE Mr. Covington overly frequently in the next few weeks; between the harvest approaching and the long ride from Ashworth House, he limited himself to calling on her about once a week. To her relief, she found herself gradually warming towards the thought of their marriage as she had time to become more comfortable with the idea. All in all, she could not complain of dissatisfaction with her lot, apart, perhaps, from the necessity of dealing with her mother's continual overexcitement about the forthcoming wedding.

All that, however, was put to the side, and Mrs. Bennet's mind opened again to the agitation of hope by an article of news which then began to be in circulation. The housekeeper at Netherfield had received orders to prepare for the arrival of her master, who was coming down in a day or two, to shoot there for several weeks. Mrs. Bennet was quite in the fidgets. She looked at Jane, and smiled, and shook her head by turns.

"Well, well, and so Mr. Bingley is coming down, sister," (for Mrs. Phillips first brought her the news). "Well, so much the better. Not that I care about it, though. He is nothing to us, you know, and I am sure I never want to see him again. But, however, he is very welcome to come to Netherfield, if he likes it. And who knows what may happen? But that is nothing to us. You know, sister, we agreed long ago never to mention a word about it. And so, is it quite certain he is coming?"

"You may depend on it," replied the other, "for Mrs. Nicholls was in Meryton last night; I saw her passing by, and went out myself on purpose to know the truth of it; and she told me that it was certain true. He comes down on Thursday at the latest, very likely on Wednesday. She was going to the butcher's, she told me, on purpose to order in some meat on Wednesday, and she has got three ducks just fit to be killed."

Miss Bennet had not been able to hear of his coming without changing colour. It was many months since she had mentioned his name to Elizabeth; but now, as soon as they were alone together, she said, "I saw you look at me to-day, Lizzy, when my aunt told us of the present report; and I know I appeared distressed. But don't imagine it was from any silly cause. I was only confused for the moment, because I felt that I should be looked at. I do assure you that the news does not affect me either with pleasure or pain. I am glad of one thing, that he comes alone; because we shall see the less of him. Not that I am afraid of myself, but I dread other people's remarks."

Elizabeth did not know what to make of it. She supposed him capable of coming there with no other view than what was acknowledged; but from what Mr. Darcy had said to her in April, she thought it possible he was still partial to Jane. She was surprised he should be bold enough to come without his friend's permission, as she could not imagine after her last encounter with Mr. Darcy that he would ever give approval to such a move.

"Yet it is hard," she said one day to Mr. Covington during one of his visits, "that this poor man cannot come to a house which he has legally hired, without raising all this speculation! I will leave him to himself. After all, he has done me the kindness to distract my mother from the matter of our wedding, and I will be forever grateful to him for providing me with a few hours in which I could hear of something beyond lace and the wedding breakfast!"

This remark earned her a light kiss on the cheek, and a reminder that it would not be so long until all the fuss of the wedding was in the past. Elizabeth, by now more able to take this behaviour in stride, agreed, having come to the place where the idea of the independence of her own household was having a favourable impact on her anticipation of her marriage.

She was, however, concerned for Jane in the matter of Mr. Bingley. In spite of what her sister declared, and really believed to be her feelings in the expectation of his arrival,

Elizabeth could easily perceive that her spirits were affected by it. They were more disturbed, more unequal, than she had often seen them.

The subject which had been so warmly canvassed between their parents, about a twelvemonth ago, was now brought forward again.

"As soon as ever Mr. Bingley comes, my dear," said Mrs. Bennet, "you will wait on him of course."

"No, no. You forced me into visiting him last year, and promised, if I went to see him, he should marry one of my daughters. But it ended in nothing, and I will not be sent on a fool's errand again."

His wife represented to him how absolutely necessary such an attention would be from all the neighbouring gentlemen, on his returning to Netherfield.

"'Tis an etiquette I despise," said he. "If he wants our society, let him seek it. He knows where we live. I will not spend my hours in running after my neighbours every time they go away and come back again."

"Well, all I know is that it will be abominably rude if you do not wait on him. But, however, that shan't prevent my asking him to dine here, I am determined. We must have Mrs. Long and the Gouldings soon. That will make thirteen with ourselves, so there will be just room at table for him."

Consoled by this resolution, she was the better able to bear her husband's incivility; though it was very mortifying to know that her neighbours might all see Mr. Bingley, in consequence of it, before they did. As the day of his arrival drew near, "I begin to be sorry that he comes at all," said Jane to her sister. "It would be nothing; I could see him with perfect indifference, but I can hardly bear to hear it thus perpetually talked of. My mother means well; but she does not know, no one can know, how much I suffer from what she says. Happy shall I be, when his stay at Netherfield is over!"

"I wish I could say any thing to comfort you," replied Elizabeth, "but it is wholly out of my power. You must feel it; and the usual satisfaction of preaching patience to a sufferer is denied me, because you have always so much." She was truly worried on her sister's behalf, though. If Mr. Bingley proved indifferent to Jane, it could go hard with her, especially when Elizabeth was no longer at Longbourn to be her consolation.

Mr. Bingley arrived, several days in advance of all expectations. Mrs. Bennet, through the assistance of servants, contrived to have the earliest tidings of it, but as chance would have it, all her machinations proved to be in vain. Sir William Lucas would have the honour of hosting Mr. Bingley first, since the very day after his arrival there was to be a ball at Lucas Lodge to which he was immediately invited.

This intelligence set Mrs. Bennet all aflutter. She had not paid the attention she usually would to the upcoming ball owing to her concern about Mr. Bingley's arrival, and suddenly it was of the utmost importance to have Jane looking at her most beautiful for the occasion. The entire day was devoted to preparing for the event, with Mrs. Bennet's excitement and vexation over anything which stood in her way raising even Jane's normally imperturbable mien to frustration.

At last the time came. As they walked into Lucas Lodge, Jane whispered to Elizabeth, "Promise that you will stay by me, Lizzy! I cannot face all these whispers alone." Elizabeth assured her she would not desert her, but she hoped fervently that Mr. Bingley's appearance would put all these worries aside.

They were among the earliest arrivals, and Jane resolutely took a position with her back to the doors, lest anyone imagine that she was watching for Mr. Bingley. She made a show of chatting lightly with the various acquaintances who approached her, hoping to ferret out a trace of disturbance over her situation that could be widely shared. When at last a stir behind them told Elizabeth that the Netherfield party must have arrived, she looked at Jane in sympathy, noting how her knuckles were turning white as she clutched her hands together. "Come, Jane, let us find some refreshments," she said soothingly.

"Oh, Lizzy, I could not eat a thing!" whispered Jane, but she followed Elizabeth's lead to the table loaded with food and drink.

It was at this time that Mr. Bingley finally came within sight. "Miss Bennet!" he exclaimed, his eyes immediately fixing themselves on Jane. "What a pleasure to see you again!"

Elizabeth breathed a sigh of relief. One look at him made it clear to her that he had never forgotten her sister, and his immediate invitation to Jane to dance the first two dances with him only served as confirmation. She found herself quickly forgotten as the two shyly began to converse. To give them a modicum of privacy, she turned away discreetly to look at the rest of the room, only to discover a familiar figure standing directly in front of her.

"Mr. Darcy!" she exclaimed in surprise, her shock evident as she put one hand to her chest. He was the last person she had expected to see.

He bowed, saying, "Pardon me, Miss Bennet; I did not mean to startle you." His accent held little of its usual sedateness.

"I am sorry, Mr. Darcy; I had not realized you were in Hertfordshire," she said somewhat incoherently, her mind flying back to the discord of their last meetings in Hunsford. What was he doing there? Was he keeping an eye on his friend, to prevent him from any foolish decisions?

He smiled slightly. "It is my turn to be surprised then. It has been my experience that news travels very quickly here, but it seems that is not always the case."

Elizabeth flushed deeply as she realized the news he must be referring to. What must he think of her, to find her about to be married so soon after his own ill-fated proposal? Or was it perhaps a relief, allowing him to put the entire matter behind him to meet her in a more comfortable manner? That must be the case, she resolved, aware of a confusing pang at the idea.

"If you are not otherwise engaged, might I have the pleasure of the first dances with you?" he asked, to her utter astonishment. He seemed to take no particular pleasure in this invitation.

Astonished and confused, Elizabeth scarcely dared lift her eyes to her face, and knew not what answer she returned to his request. Amazed by the alteration in his manner since they last parted, every sentence that he uttered was increasing her embarrassment. She could only think that he was making a point of demonstrating how little the news of her engagement troubled him.

He held out his hand, and without thinking she put her hand in his, conscious of a small shock as she did so. She followed him onto the dance floor silently, trying to somehow understand how she had found herself in the position of dancing with Mr. Darcy. She could read equal amazement that she should be standing up with him in the faces of the other dancers. She could not help recalling with a smile his words at the assembly where she had first met him. Apparently it was no longer a punishment to stand up with her, and at least at one point he had found her more than tolerable. She gave him an arch look as the music began.

She had assumed he would be as silent as he had been when he had danced with her at the Netherfield ball, but this appeared not to be the case as he very civilly commented on how long it had been since he was in Hertfordshire last, how fine the shooting looked to be, and inquired after her father's health. Determined to match him in courtesy, she met his remarks with answers in a light social tone.

The dance began, and they were separated briefly, then came together again. The conversation then threatened to languish. Finding silence to provoke her anxiety, she began to tell him of her tour of the Lakes, a subject on which she could wax eloquent. He asked several thoughtful questions exhibiting a knowledge of the area, then inquired, "Did your entire family travel together?"

"No," she replied with a quick smile. "I went with my aunt and uncle, who were kind enough to invite me to join them." She saw him glance at Mrs. Phillips, who sat talking loudly with Mrs. Bennet, with some surprise. Realizing his thought, she added, "My aunt and uncle are from London; their children remained at Longbourn under the care of my sister Jane during our tour."

"Ah, I recall hearing that you had some family in Town, Miss Bennet," he said.

"Yes, my aunt and uncle live in Cheapside, where my uncle is in trade," she said, stealing a sly glance at him to see how he bore this disgraceful connection, but he sustained it with fortitude, asking her whether she had often visited London.

The entire conversation, as they moved down the set, seemed to be taking place between two people other than the ones who had met that night at Hunsford, and Elizabeth knew not what to make of it. At one point, she looked up at him as they were circling each other, her hand in his, and the reality of it hit her with a shock as she was caught briefly in his dark eyes. A different memory came back to her then, of his saying,

*You must allow me to tell you how ardently I admire and love you.*
A shiver ran through her, and she glanced about the room as
if to ground herself in the present.

She was relieved when the dance ended and he returned
her to the company of her sister. Since Mr. Bingley seemed
disinclined to desert Jane during the interval between dances,
Mr. Darcy perforce stood by her side as well, and an awkward
silence fell between them. Bingley spoke enough for both
men, she thought, and his enthusiasm for her sister was clear.
She was happy to see a sparkle in Jane's eyes that had been
absent for many months.

Finally another gentleman came to claim her hand for
the next set of dances, and Elizabeth bade Darcy a slightly
subdued but quite civil farewell. She could hardly keep her
mind on the dance, though, much less conversing with her
partner. She felt constantly aware of where Mr. Darcy was
in the room, as if there were some kind of silent connection
between them. It was with great amazement that she realized
that he had made his way to the place where Mrs. Bennet
sat accompanied by her friends, and that he was engaged in
conversation with her mother.

Elizabeth felt the compliment to herself, but her aston-
ishment was extreme; and she asked herself continually,
*Why is he so altered? From what can it proceed? It cannot be for
me, it cannot be for my sake that his manners are thus softened.
My reproofs at Hunsford could not work such a change as this.*
She would not allow herself to consider the implications

of his behaviour; she was engaged to be married, and she knew that he understood and would respect that fact just as she would.

Darcy was cautiously pleased with how the evening was progressing. Although the degree of shock with which Elizabeth had greeted him had not been promising, she had agreed to dance with him, spoken with him with an air of comfort, and even teased him a little, if he was not mistaken. He had ached for her from the moment he saw her, standing by her sister with her back to the door, and the exquisite pleasure of touching her hand as they danced had only reinforced his desire to win her. He could not quite bring himself to dance with another woman so quickly, so instead determined to demonstrate his attention to her reproofs by conversing with her family. Unfortunately, the only member of her family then available was her mother. Taking a deep breath, he approached Mrs. Bennet, giving her his compliments and enquiring after her well-being.

Her reception was initially cold and ceremonious, but he persisted in his civility, just keeping himself from rolling his eyes at some of Mrs. Bennet's ridiculous manners. Soon, however, the compliment of having such a man's attention outweighed her former anger towards him, and she began to take advantage of the opportunity to tell him all the news of the neighbourhood.

"My sister Phillips's eldest son married last spring to Harriet Letsworth, and that was quite the occasion," she said.

With pride, she added her coup, "And you have no doubt heard, Mr. Darcy, of my daughter's engagement."

Darcy's wandering attention snapped back to her at these words. Miss Bennet engaged? Bingley would be devastated, especially if the look on his face when he danced with her was anything to judge by. This was a disaster; it would certainly make matters more difficult for him with Elizabeth as well. He cleared his throat, trying to mask his reaction, and said, "Miss Bennet is engaged? No, I have not had the pleasure of hearing the news."

"Oh, no, not Jane!" replied Mrs. Bennet distractedly, her eyes travelling with satisfaction toward the figure of Mr. Bingley. "No, it is *Lizzy* who is to marry Mr. Covington—ah, yes, he has just arrived. My daughter Lydia is unfortunately not with us tonight; she is visiting Colonel Forster's wife in Devonshire."

Darcy was struck by a sharp shock of pain and disbelief at her unexpected words. His Elizabeth, promised to another man? It could not be! The possibility had never so much as crossed his mind that she might look on some *other* man with favour—that she might refuse him again, yes, but marry another, and so quickly? How could this have happened? His eyes sought her out involuntarily where she stood conversing with several acquaintances, and the taste of bile rose in his throat. He forced himself to say, "I do not believe that I am acquainted with Mr. Covington." *But I know enough about him already to wish he had never taken the first breath of life!* he thought darkly.

"Not know him?" cried Mrs. Bennet disbelievingly. "Mr. Covington is master of Ashworth House, and a fine gentleman. Surely you must have met him last autumn, Mr. Darcy? There he is now." With an embarrassing want of propriety, she pointed across the room to a well-built gentleman perhaps a few years younger than Darcy, with a handsome enough countenance though no particular claim to style, but fitting well into the company at hand. As Darcy watched with bitter jealousy, he approached Elizabeth and greeted her warmly, raising her hand to his lips.

Darcy's eyes were fixed on Elizabeth, who welcomed the interloper with a somewhat absent smile, continuing her conversation and apparently including him without particular effort. *Elizabeth*, he thought despairingly.

Mr. Covington's late arrival had not come as a surprise to Elizabeth; she knew he was quite busy at this season, and she was just as happy he had been absent during her dance with Darcy. She could not help but wonder what Darcy was thinking, if he had noticed the two of them together, and whether he was thanking heaven for his narrow escape. As Mr. Covington took her hand for the next dance, she braved a glimpse in his direction.

One look at his face told her something was terribly wrong. She saw her mother chatting away to him while he appeared oblivious, looking directly at Elizabeth. The realization suddenly hit her that he had *not* known of her engagement, that this was news to him; and a sudden wave of nausea passed over her. How cruel he must think she had been with her arch looks and teasing during their dances! She might not care for him, but he had been making a pronounced effort to be civil, and he did not deserve to be treated so. And what would Mr. Covington think if he knew she had been dancing with a gentleman who had loved her ardently and wanted to marry her? She felt heartily ashamed of herself, without quite knowing why.

Mr. Covington noticed her hesitation. "Are you well, Lizzy?" he asked with concern, noting her pallor.

Elizabeth swallowed. "Yes, quite well, sir," she said. "Please, let us continue."

<hr />

It was very late when the gentlemen finally returned to Netherfield. Darcy's mood was very dark, and he had barely restrained himself from snarling at Bingley and his raptures over the charms of Miss Bennet. He said a curt good night to his host, who was far too lost in his own happy thoughts to notice, and retired to his room where he angrily stripped off his cravat and tailcoat before his valet could assist him. "Some brandy, please," he told him brusquely. His valet, wondering at this unusual request from his master, disappeared immediately to do his bidding, leaving Darcy alone with his memories of the evening.

Darcy did not know how he had managed to stay through the end of the assembly. He had hardly removed his eyes from Elizabeth all evening, even when he was mechanically dancing with another woman, and his initial pain and anger had quickly given way to self-blame and loathing. Why had he assumed she would be waiting for him, that she would not catch the eye of some other man? What did she see in Covington that had caused her to accept the man while refusing him? The voice of honesty in him insisted on providing the answer: it would not take much for her to think better of any man than she did of him.

He had somehow forced himself to approach her once more before the evening had ended. "I understand that I should be giving you my congratulations, Miss Bennet," he had said, his mouth dry as ashes. She had looked up at him, engaging in that bewitching habit of hers of biting the corner of her lower lip, and thanked him gravely. Glutton for punishment that he was, he had asked her to dance again, telling himself that it was only to show her he was not so mean as to hold the past against her. He knew, though, that his motivation was more that of an addict seeking his opium—he wanted the touch of her hand, and the opportunity to pretend that her smiles were for him. *Pathetic!* he thought bitterly.

His mind returned like a vulture to the question of why she had accepted Covington. He gathered that he was modestly well-to-do by Meryton standards, but venality was one sin he could not lay to Miss Bennet's door, not after she had refused *him*. The man himself seemed pleasant enough, but he had not struck Darcy as particularly well-educated or witty, but the truth was that if Covington had been the personification of every virtue known to man, Darcy would still have despised him. He had watched Elizabeth carefully when she was with him. The gentleman was clearly overflowing with admiration for her, but Darcy did not notice any signs of particular regard on her part, although she was attentive enough to him.

*What are you trying to prove?* he demanded of himself angrily. *She has made her choice, and there is no going back. You are too late, if you ever had a chance at all—give it up, man!* But he knew he could not—he had tried to walk away from Elizabeth Bennet often enough in the past without success. *Well, you will simply have to learn to do so now!* he told himself sharply. *There are no miracles waiting to happen!*

He downed several glasses of brandy in rapid succession as he brooded over the prospect of his Elizabeth as Mrs. Covington. He knew that his case was hopeless, but as his mind revolved around the whole question again and again, one salient fact kept leaping out at him: he *had* to know, for his own peace of mind, whether she loved Covington or not. It could make no difference to the final outcome; that was already fixed, but if he knew that she was marrying out of deep affection, perhaps he would be able to put her memory behind him more successfully. He was under no illusions, however—even if that would be the best outcome for him personally, he knew he had no desire whatsoever for it to be true. He wanted desperately to believe that she did not care one jot for Covington.

*Well,* he resolved, *I will need to remain here at least a week or two before I can decently make my excuses and leave this place forever—perhaps that will give me adequate time to discover her feelings.* Even as he thought it, he knew that he was only seeking excuses to be in her company once more.

***

The next morning, Bingley was all eagerness to pay a call to Longbourn. Darcy, who was feeling rather worse for wear after the combination of too much brandy and not enough sleep, had difficulty persuading him that it would be better to wait another day, since they had, after all, just arrived. Bingley agreed with visible reluctance, and they went out shooting instead. While the activity provided an outlet for some of Darcy's hostility, his distress was unalleviated.

The next morning he dressed with unusual care, far more than required for a morning call, and when he realized what he had done, called for his valet with a scowl to fetch some more everyday apparel. Bingley's impatience to see Miss Bennet worked to Darcy's benefit this morning—a rapid canter across the countryside allowed him to put his anxiety aside for a short time as he focused on his mount and the uneven ground. No sooner had they arrived at Longbourn, though, that it returned full force. *What is there to fear now?* he scoffed at himself impatiently. *Surely the worst has already happened!*

His eyes flew to Elizabeth the moment they entered the room, watching her as Mrs. Bennet greeted Bingley with an embarrassing degree of civility. *To think I once worried about her manners as an obstacle to having Elizabeth as my wife!* thought Darcy, knowing he would now tolerate far, far worse if it only meant that she were free for the winning. Elizabeth herself was a mystery, saying as little to either of the callers as civility would permit, and attending to her work with a degree of eagerness which seemed out of character. Her cheeks were slightly flushed, and he wondered what she made of his presence.

He was not seated with her, and thus was reduced to occasional glances at her as he practiced conversation with her mother and Miss Bennet. Once he caught her eyes on him, her expression unreadable, but she looked away immediately in apparent embarrassment. It was a combination of pleasure and pain to be in the same room with her, the pleasure of being able to see her fine eyes and her delicate profile, and the torture when he thought of her with her fiancé. *Does Covington kiss her?* he wondered, his eyes resting on her lips. *Has he already taken what should rightfully be mine?* He did not know how much longer he could bear such thoughts, and firmly pushed them away, allowing himself to pretend just for the duration of the visit that there was no such man as Covington, and that he had the right to admire Elizabeth as much as he chose.

Such was his state that, when Mrs. Bennet invited them to dine at Longbourn in a few days' time, he felt a rush of gratitude, and only wished it could be sooner. He chided himself for this as soon as he left—was he trying to arrange for even greater heartbreak?

As soon as the gentlemen were gone, Elizabeth walked out to recover her spirits. Darcy's visit had agitated and vexed her. She could not understand his motives; surely he had not come out of a desire to visit any others of her family but perhaps Jane, and that seemed unlikely. He had conversed more than he had in the past, but not with her. His eyes seemed to rest on her a good deal, but whether it was with greater regret or relief she could not guess. Perhaps he simply did not trust Bingley alone at Longbourn—that seemed the most likely answer.

She could not imagine any good opinion he had of her which had survived her outrageous accusations at Hunsford could remain in face of the news of her engagement. She wondered in what estimation he held Mr. Covington, and why he thought she had accepted him. She could not imagine that Darcy would fail to respect her engagement. Yet if his good opinion of her was lost, or if he thought her lost to him, what had he been doing at Longbourn? She sighed at the seeming perversity of his behaviour. It seemed it was her fate never to understand him.

⁂

Over the next few days Darcy did his utmost to put Elizabeth Bennet out of his mind, with even less success than usual.

Knowing that she was but three miles away was a constant distraction, as he wondered what she was doing and thinking, and more crucially, with whom she was doing it. He had always known that he had a tendency towards jealousy; now he was discovering just how deeply rooted it could be.

He resolved more than once to think no more of her engagement, and just to consider her as a woman who had refused him and was beyond his reach, but these efforts never succeeded for long. If nothing else, he betrayed his resolution in his dreams, dreams of Elizabeth looking up at him with an arch expression in her lovely eyes, Elizabeth accepting his lovemaking, Elizabeth telling him she loved no one but him. Waking was an unspeakable disappointment.

He kept himself busy with shooting, reading, and writing letters, but knew he was but marking time until he saw her again. The days until their dinner at Longbourn seemed to stretch into eternity, but finally the day came.

There was a large party assembled at Longbourn; and the two gentlemen were in very good time. Darcy at first stayed close by his friend's side; he had not anticipated the size of the party, and once he saw it, he realized that it was not unlikely that Mr. Covington would be a guest as well, and this was a circumstance he was not prepared to deal with. Fortunately, he did not make an appearance, and by the time dinner was announced, Darcy was ready to breathe a sigh of relief.

When they repaired to the dining-room, Bingley seemed to hesitate. Miss Bennet happened to look round then, and happened to smile at him, and that was enough. He then took the place by her side which had belonged to him in all their former parties.

Elizabeth, with a triumphant sensation, looked towards his friend. He bore it with noble indifference, and she would have imagined that Bingley had received his sanction to be happy, had she not seen his eyes likewise turned towards Mr. Darcy, with an expression of half-laughing alarm.

Darcy, however, was no longer attending to Bingley; following his friend's lead, he assertively took the place nearest Elizabeth. Now that he knew that she was not partnered for the evening, he had no intention of watching her only from a distance; he wanted to be close enough to see her breathe and to admire the sparkle in her eyes when she smiled. As she turned to him to greet him, he caught a light scent of roses.

"Mr. Darcy, I hope you are well tonight," she said. He wondered how she could make the most banal of statements sound delightfully arch. God, but she was bewitching!—and the oddest part was that it was clearly unconsciously done on her part. She seemed completely insensible to her effect upon him.

She engaged him in a somewhat restrained conversation on the books she had been reading. As always, he found it somewhat difficult to keep his attention on the topic when simply looking at her and listening to her voice filled his senses. It was difficult to watch her leave when dinner ended, and he was frustrated by the length of time the gentlemen spent by themselves before returning to the ladies. His disappointment was only to grow when, on returning to the drawing room, he found Elizabeth clustered among a crowd of women at the table with not a single vacancy near her. He wondered if she had done this on purpose, though when one of the other girls moved closer to her than ever and whispered in her ear, she did not seem to be best pleased.

He walked away to another part of the room, but found himself growing increasingly impatient. Finally, he decided to bring back his coffee cup himself, and he handed it to her in such a way that their fingertips touched for a moment, giving him a sudden flash of pleasure in her touch.

She seemed to start as well, and cast her eyes away for a moment, making him wonder if she was as insensible of his feelings as she appeared. Of course, if she *were* sensible of them, he thought, she would not be able to acknowledge it, nor her own response. He had to wonder again what his own impetus was in thus seeking her out, when any further connection between them was impossible, even were she to regret her engagement; but it was as if he were a lodestone and she the North; he could not prevent himself from drawing as near to her as he could.

When the tea-things were removed, and the card tables placed, he hoped to stay by Elizabeth, but fell victim to her mother's rapacity for whist players, and in a few moments was seated with the rest of the party. They were thus separated at different tables, though he still had the enjoyment of allowing his eyes to rest on the wayward curls at the back of her neck as she bent her head over her cards, imagining how it would feel to caress them with his fingertips and then his lips. He could almost see the desire that would be in her eyes when she looked up at him...

All in all, he had to count the occasion a success, both in terms of Elizabeth, who had favoured him with warm smiles on several occasions, and on his own behalf, in that he had by sheer force of will managed to prevent himself from thinking of her future with Covington.

As soon as their carriage pulled away, Bingley began to praise Miss Bennet. "I tell you, Darcy, she is the most amiable lady of my acquaintance. I had thought perhaps that time had sweetened my recollections of her, but it is not so—she is as kind as she is generous, and you must admit her beauty is undeniable!"

Darcy, who in fact found her rather bland next to the liveliness of her sister, agreed that she was a very beautiful woman. As Bingley rambled on about her virtues, Darcy's mind drifted back to that night in Hunsford, and he heard in his mind as clearly as if it were today—*Do you think that any consideration would tempt me to accept the man who has been the means of ruining, perhaps forever, the happiness of a most beloved sister?* His lingering sense of happiness from being near Elizabeth disappeared instantly. He asked abruptly, "Do you intend to ask her to be your wife?"

Bingley seemed to pale slightly. "I am considering it," he

said, his tone defensive. "I know that it is your belief that she is indifferent to me, but you do not know her as I do, and I do not think her mercenary."

There was silence as several moments elapsed. "No, I think you are correct, Bingley," said Darcy carefully. "I have been given to understand that I was mistaken in that regard."

His friend looked at him in astonishment. "Given to understand? Whatever do you mean by that?" he exclaimed.

Darcy was glad that the darkness of the carriage partially disguised his expression. "I happened by chance to meet with Miss Elizabeth Bennet this spring. When the subject arose, she made it clear that I had misinterpreted her sister's natural modesty and reserve as indifference, and it was her belief that her sister cherished a tender regard for you."

"You learned this in the spring, and you are only now seeing fit to tell me of it?" cried Bingley.

"You are quite right, Bingley," Darcy said levelly. "I should have told you as soon as I learned of it."

"You most certainly should have!" Bingley exclaimed. "I cannot believe you did not!"

It was almost a relief, Darcy found, to face Bingley's ire. It eased his guilt, and perhaps more importantly, it distracted him from regrets about Elizabeth and the opportunity he had missed with her owing to his own foolish pride. "That is not all I should confess," he said, as if impelled. "Miss Bennet was in Town last winter for three months, and I knew of it, and concealed it from you." *If I am truly fortunate*, he thought bleakly, *Bingley will be so furious that I will have to quit Netherfield immediately, and thus rid myself of this impossible situation!* He closed his eyes and leaned his head back against the seat as a sharp pain lanced through him at the thought of leaving. He wanted only to order the carriage back to Longbourn, where he could find solace once more in Elizabeth's laughter and bright eyes.

He was so caught up in his own concerns that he almost forgot Bingley's presence. He was startled, then, when finally Bingley said with obvious anger, "How dare you presume so!"

Darcy shrugged. "Miss Bennet had called on your sisters, and they came to me with their concerns. We judged it best not to risk hurting you by telling you of it." The excuse sounded lame even to his own ears.

"Risk *hurting* me?" Bingley's disbelief was obvious. "Do you have any idea what I have suffered this last year, thinking she did not care for me?"

Darcy experienced a sudden urge to tell him that he knew quite intimately what such suffering was like, but he knew it would be foolhardy in the extreme to let Bingley guess at his improper attachment. "You have my deepest apologies," he said stiffly. "I was completely in the wrong, and can offer no excuse. I should never have interfered."

Bingley did not respond, and the rest of the ride passed in a tense silence. Darcy breathed a sigh of relief when they finally arrived at Netherfield. He did not know what had induced him to make such a confession when he was trapped in the carriage with Bingley—it would have been easier had he been able to walk away sooner. Once they were inside and had handed off their coats and hats, he turned to Bingley once more.

"I do not mean to try your patience," he said. "I will depart in the morning. Again, I apologize for my misjudgements." He made a slight formal bow, and headed to the stairs. He was nearly to the landing when he heard Bingley's voice call after him.

"Darcy, wait!" he said loudly. "You at least owe me more of an explanation than that!"

With a sigh, Darcy said, "Very well." He returned downstairs and followed Bingley into a sitting room where he helped himself to a generous serving of brandy. "What is it you would like to know?" he asked tiredly.

"All of it—tell me *all* of what happened!"

Briefly, Darcy recounted the history of Miss Bennet's visit to London. "I thought no more of it after that," he continued, "until I happened by coincidence to meet Miss Elizabeth Bennet in Kent, when I was visiting my aunt there. During the course of… a conversation, she gave me to understand that her sister had been quite unhappy since your departure from Hertfordshire, and that she herself was aware of the role I had played in the matter. Whether or not she has confided any of her suspicions to her sister, I cannot say. This was the reason I suggested we return to Netherfield for the shooting—I hoped it would allow you to meet her once again, and, if you were both still so inclined, to return to the point where you were November last."

Bingley stood and began to pace the floor. "I do not know where to begin! That you and my sisters should conspire so against my happiness! That you were so inclined as to not mention this to me for *months*! That you went so far as to discuss this with my Jane's own sister! I cannot understand what inspired you," he said bitterly.

"At the moment, neither can I," said Darcy wearily. "It was done with the best of intentions, though, if not the best of understandings."

"Tell me again—what exactly did Miss Elizabeth say of her sister's sensibilities?"

Darcy closed his eyes. That was not a moment he cared to return to in memory, but he at least owed Bingley the truth of what was said. "We did not *discuss* you," he said. "In a moment of anger, she accused me of destroying her sister's happiness. That is all I know of her thoughts at the time."

Bingley looked shocked. "She must have been very angry indeed to say such a thing!

Darcy grimaced. "She was. I had said some… ill-considered things, and she was quite right to object to them."

"*She* seems to have forgiven you, at least," said Bingley accusingly.

With a bitter smile, he stood and put down his empty glass. "Yes, she seems to have *forgiven* me. Good night, Bingley, and good fortune in your wooing of Miss Bennet."

"You are not still planning to leave, are you?"

"I fear I must—it is best that I do," said Darcy, thinking of Elizabeth.

"Darcy, I do not deny being angry with you, but that is no reason to run off!" exclaimed Bingley. Ruefully, he added, "Besides, I may need you as a witness to my innocence if Miss Bennet does not forgive me for failing to call on her in London."

"Somehow I suspect she will forgive you anything," Darcy said dryly, the relief of knowing that he would be able to see Elizabeth again outweighing all else. "Well, if it is your wish, I will stay a bit longer, to see you settle matters with Miss Bennet."

"And I shall!" said Bingley happily. "I most certainly shall."

The gentlemen arrived early at Longbourn the following morning, and were welcomed effusively by Mrs. Bennet, who was certain that this third visit in as many days was a declaration of Mr. Bingley's intentions. She was determined to find a way for him to be alone with Jane, and when Bingley, who was of a similar mind, proposed walking out, Mrs. Bennet announced that she had need of the younger girls at home, but that Lizzy and Jane were free to go if they wished. Elizabeth shot a quick glance at her mother at this, wondering if she had any inkling of Mr. Darcy's attention to her, but she knew it to be false—not even her mother would condone such a thing, now that she was engaged.

Her mother approached her as she was donning her bonnet. "Lizzy, you must keep Mr. Darcy out of Mr. Bingley's way—you will know how, but Mr. Bingley *must* be alone with Jane," said Mrs. Bennet. "You need not put yourself to any inconvenience; there is no occasion for talking to Mr. Darcy, except just now and then."

Elizabeth was not inclined to inform her mother that, regardless of whether Jane and Mr. Bingley should have some private discourse, she herself had no intention of being alone with Mr. Darcy. They seemed to have a silent pact not to mention his proposal and letter, but she did not wish any opportunity to challenge it.

They started out, Mr. Darcy setting a good pace with Elizabeth by his side, while Mr. Bingley and Jane soon lagged behind. There was indeed little conversation among the pair in the lead; Darcy seemed in a somewhat grim mood. Elizabeth had no intention of leaving Jane in an uncomfortable position, however, and they had not gone far before she stopped and said, "Mr. Darcy, we are leaving my sister behind; pray, let us wait for them to catch up to us."

To her utmost surprise, instead of complying, Darcy took her hand and placed it on his arm, making it clear he had no intention of stopping. Elizabeth, displeased with this forwardness, was about to open her mouth to protest when he said, "Forgive me; your concern is, of course, laudable and proper, but Bingley needs a few moments with your sister—he has something particular to discuss with her, and the least I can do is to provide him with the opportunity to do so. They are well within our sight—there can be nothing to object to."

Darcy had turned his eyes straight ahead as soon as he was done speaking, leaving Elizabeth looking up at him in shock. Being told so bluntly of Mr. Bingley's intentions was surprising enough, but to see Mr. Darcy with a rather grim countenance at the matter brought unpleasant memories. "You seem less than pleased, sir," she said tartly.

He turned to her with a look of dismayed surprise. "Not at all, Miss Bennet," he responded. His gaze softening as he looked at her, he added, "I must ask your forgiveness once more; I am not in the best of humours today, but it is my hope that Bingley will receive a satisfactory response from your sister."

Elizabeth, quite unsure how to respond to this, simply dropped her eyes. She was not quite comfortable with how physically close he was to her, nor with her hand on his arm. His presence seemed to loom quite large.

Darcy sighed, apparently reading her dissatisfaction. "Very well, if you would know, Bingley and I had words last night, and it is still somewhat in my mind. I made a confession to him, telling him of my interference in his affairs. I could not allow myself to conceal that your sister had been in Town three months last winter, that I had known it, and purposely kept it from him. I told him, moreover, that you had… that I had known for some time that she was not indifferent to him. His surprise was great, and he was understandably quite resentful."

She had forgotten Darcy's tendency to discuss surprisingly intimate matters openly with her. Feeling something of the danger of this, especially on a topic so closely related to their unfortunate encounter, she responded cautiously, "I see. It seems, though, that you and he are reconciled."

His mouth twisted, and he did not look at her. "Bingley is a forgiving soul; and I do not doubt that his anger will pass completely once he is no longer in any doubt of your sister's sentiments."

Something in his tone raised her concern, and she looked at him searchingly. If he was not concerned with Bingley's judgement, it must be that he had not forgiven himself—or perhaps he felt *she* would not forgive him. With a unforeseen urge to reassure him, she tightened her hand on his arm momentarily, and said quietly in a voice of sympathy, "I am sorry—that must be difficult."

Her warmth was unexpected, and almost proved his undoing. Darcy had known he was playing a dangerous impromptu game in confiding his feelings to her, but had not gone so far as to anticipate how she might respond. Now he turned to face her, barely holding in check his desire for her, and his longing to tell her what he felt. Their eyes caught and held, his with an unspoken need, and as he looked into her lovely eyes, he saw a new awareness dawn there which made his heart race.

*This cannot be!* he chastised himself desperately, fighting his spirit's desire to celebrate. *She is not free!* He cleared his throat, hoping his tension would not be apparent in his voice. "Do you suppose Bingley has had adequate time? Perhaps we should walk back to meet them."

Elizabeth, her mind whirling in confusion, murmured her assent. She did not know what to say, or how to look, and was relieved to quickly cross the distance to join the others. She was grateful for the distraction when she saw Jane's face shining with happiness. No words needed to be said—Jane instantly embraced her and acknowledged with the liveliest emotion that she was the happiest creature in the world.

"'Tis too much!" she added, "by far too much. I do not deserve it. Oh! why is not everybody as happy?"

Elizabeth's congratulations were given with a sincerity, a warmth, a delight which words could but poorly express. Out of the corner of her eye, she saw Darcy shaking Bingley's hand warmly and offering his own felicitations.

Both Jane and Bingley were anxious to return to Longbourn. Jane was all eagerness to tell her mother, and Bingley to ask Mr. Bennet's consent. They could not restrain themselves from reassuring one another as to the depth of their happiness, which fortuitously helped to cover the silence of the other pair, each of whom was deep in thought.

Darcy was struggling with a profound sense of envy for his friend's situation. As his initial euphoria wore off, he remembered nothing had changed, nothing at all—even if there had been a brief moment when Elizabeth had wanted him, she would still be Mrs. Covington all too soon. It was hard in face of Bingley's joy to face the fact that he would never be in that same position. He glanced at Elizabeth, who appeared unwontedly serious, and wondered what she was thinking.

*It is less than two months till my wedding,* thought Elizabeth, as if by sheer dint of repetition she could forget what had occurred. *I have no right to be thinking of any other man, especially not that man!* She did not understand what had taken place; the feelings her encounter with Darcy had aroused in her were as yet unknown to her. That they were dangerous was clear, and likewise that she would need to forget they had ever occurred. She firmly resolved she would not make herself unhappy over Darcy, and she would not think of this again. With a sigh, she began to enumerate to herself once again the advantages of her upcoming marriage.

## Chapter 3

SHE CAME INTO THE room, her form light and graceful as always, the curves of her body exposed by the lines of her dress. He stood politely, and said, "Miss Bennet, this is a most pleasant surprise."

She looked at him boldly, a smile playing about her tempting lips, saying, "Surely you knew I would come, Mr. Darcy."

Involuntarily he took a step towards her, and as he drew nearer, he could see her fine eyes filled with that look of awareness they had held earlier. His breathing became more rapid, and he knew she could read his desire in his stance. "No, I did not," he said, distracted by the knowledge that she was no more than an arm's length away from him. "I never seem to know what to expect of you."

She moved closer, the restless movement of her hands betraying her nervousness. Her eyes darted away from him, a delicate blush rising in her face. He could not help himself; he reached out and touched the soft skin of her cheek with his fingertips, and *a powerful surge of desire overtook him. She looked up at him through her lashes, her lips slightly parted.*

*He could not refuse her unconscious invitation; slowly he lowered his lips until they touched hers. She did not protest, and her hand stole around his neck to prevent an escape for which he had no wish. Deeper and deeper he tasted her, until he knew beyond a doubt that she was his for the asking. In exultation, he caught her hips in his hands, then drew her towards him until he felt the shock of her supple body against his, her need for him expressed in the manner in which she arched against him and gasped as his lips travelled over her face, across her neck, and down into the exposed soft skin of her shoulder.*

*"Please," she begged, and he was only too happy to oblige.*

⁂

Darcy opened his eyes to discover light streaming in the window. With a groan he buried his face in his pillow, willing sleep and his dream to return. He hated the abrupt shift from the warmth and happiness of his dreams of Elizabeth to the cold reality that all he would ever have of her was a few memories of visits, watching her play and sing, and being teased by her sparkling eyes. Another man would discover the reality of all his dreams. But it made no difference; for months, there had been dreams almost every night, and he doubted they would stop now.

There was a new poignant sense of loss this morning, though. In a way it was a comfort to know that Elizabeth could feel some attraction to him, that there could be in this sense some truth to his dream, but knowing what *could* be only added to the pain of knowing he would never experience it.

He thought back to the previous day. It became evident when they returned to Longbourn that Elizabeth was taking advantage of the excitement over Jane's engagement to avoid private conversation with him. He knew she was only behaving as she ought, how she *must* behave even if her feelings for him had been far stronger than they were. He would never have wanted her to do otherwise—no, that was a lie; he was far beyond caring what rules of propriety were violated if it meant that any part of her could be his. It was irrelevant, though, since she would never go so far herself.

He rose from the bed, realizing these thoughts were bound to continue to torture him until he could find relief in her presence again. Bingley was no doubt going to Longbourn this morning, if he was not already there; it was enough of an excuse for Darcy to go there too.

A pattern was thus begun. Bingley from this time was of course a daily visitor to Longbourn, and almost always came accompanied by his friend. Elizabeth, who was usually left in the somewhat uncomfortable position of being chaperone to the two lovers, gradually grew to be more comfortable in Darcy's presence, mostly by refusing to allow herself to consider any of their past interactions or the reason for his presence in Hertfordshire, and more specifically in her company. He proved in general an engaging companion, which was rather useful since neither Jane nor Bingley had any attention to bestow on anyone else in the other's presence. His behaviour was always completely proper; and if her engagement was a subject which was completely avoided by both of them, the rules of it were forgotten by neither.

"So, Mr. Darcy," said Elizabeth one morning after a week or so of these visits, a hint of a smile lurking around her mouth, "tell me about Pemberley—I heard so much praise for it last autumn from Miss Bingley that it has quite taken on legendary status in my mind."

Darcy raised an eyebrow, well aware he was being teased. "Legendary, Miss Bennet?"

She seemed to be paying great attention to her embroidery. "Well, from Miss Bingley's description, I understand that Pemberley is altogether larger and grander than Blenheim and Chatsworth put together, and that Kew has nothing compared to the gardens of Pemberley."

The corners of his mouth twitched. "Then she no doubt told you that the park is of a natural beauty unparalleled in England, and covers in extent almost half of Derbyshire."

"Only half?" Elizabeth turned eyes full of laughter up at him. "I do not know, then, how there would be room for all the marvels she mentioned, the peacocks roaming the grounds, the tame deer…"

"Oh, the tame deer are nothing," he responded gravely. "The tame tigers patrolling the grounds are more unique, not to mention the unicorns and the phoenix that inhabit the woods."

"Tigers? I am not certain that I would care to meet one of them, tame or not," said Elizabeth teasingly. "And I suspect that very little at Pemberley is truly tame, in any case."

"Miss Bennet, you dismay me with your doubts! Of course they are tame—we have hereditary gamekeepers whose sole employ is to tame the tigers, and only very rarely is one of them eaten alive."

"Do not the tigers eat the unicorns, as well?"

"Not at all," he said, his voice suddenly taking on a more serious note. "The tigers protect the unicorns."

Something in his air caused a shiver to go up Elizabeth's spine. Bingley, rolling his eyes at their foolishness, encouraged them all to walk in the garden "despite the absence of leopards, unicorns, and whatnot." Elizabeth was agreeable to this distraction from the increasingly intense look in Mr. Darcy's eyes, but just at that moment, Mr. Covington was announced.

Elizabeth felt a moment of confusion, but collected herself to greet him warmly. She had a distinct consciousness of Darcy's eyes upon her.

"Lizzy, it is a pleasure to see you—you are looking quite lovely today," said Mr. Covington gallantly, then greeted the others.

"We were about to take a stroll in the garden, sir," said Jane. "Perhaps you would care to join us?"

"Mr. Covington has just ridden in," objected Elizabeth, who was eager to separate her fiancé from Mr. Darcy, "and I am certain some refreshment is in order. Let me see to that while you walk out, and perhaps we will be able to join you later."

Mr. Covington, his eyes on Elizabeth, acknowledged that he would rather stay within. Bingley, hoping to give the two some privacy, prevailed upon Jane to continue with their plan, and said, "Darcy, you must come, too—the fresh air will do you good."

"Not now, thank you, Bingley," said Darcy dryly. "I would enjoy some refreshment myself."

Elizabeth shot him a glance as the other two departed. "Of course, Mr. Darcy, as you wish," she said neutrally. "I hope your mother is in good health, Mr. Covington."

"I am glad to say she is continuing to do well, and sends you her compliments," he replied. "She would have liked to have joined me today, but the carriage is under repair."

"What a pity! I should have enjoyed seeing her," said Elizabeth with real regret.

He inquired after her family as Darcy looked on sardonically, wondering what Elizabeth could possibly see in this dull fellow. It grated on his nerves every time Covington called her by her name or allowed an admiring look to rest upon her. Nevertheless, he gave no thought to leaving; as vividly unpleasant as this might be, nothing would induce him to leave Elizabeth alone with Covington while he had a choice in the matter. There was a certain ironic humour, he reflected, in finding himself as her chaperone.

"It has been quite busy at Ashworth. Part of the road washed out in the rains last week, and we have some men working on that, but of course with the harvest coming in, the timing could not be worse," said Covington. "I am glad to be able to say that we did lay hands on the poachers who had been troubling us, though, and I wager they will not be doing it again!"

"Were they local men?" inquired Elizabeth, who was growing increasingly uncomfortable with the dark silence emanating from Darcy.

"No, fortunately—that always makes it so much more difficult. Then we have to deal with the problem of the families, which is always painful."

Elizabeth turned to Darcy, determined to draw him into the conversation. "Do you ever have problems with poachers at Pemberley, Mr. Darcy?"

He looked directly at her, and said, "No, Miss Bennet; the tigers take care of them." He was pleased to see the corners of her mouth twitch.

Mr. Covington looked disconcerted. "Tigers, Mr. Darcy?" he asked politely.

"A joke, sir," Elizabeth said quickly. "We were spinning stories earlier about the wild creatures of Derbyshire."

"I see," he said, looking baffled.

Elizabeth quickly shifted the conversation to a new subject. She could sense Darcy's eye on her, and once her guest was suitably distracted, she gave him a quick glare. He responded with a slow, mocking look that made her feel hot inside, and she quickly turned her attention away from him.

She made no further attempts to include him in the discourse between her and Mr. Covington, but his presence could not be forgotten for a minute. Even when they finally walked out to join Jane and Bingley in the garden, he did not allow her to walk alone with Mr. Covington, but instead walked on her left side, close enough to her to be skirting the boundaries of propriety.

It seemed as if he were almost issuing a challenge to her, and Elizabeth found it agitated her in ways both pleasant and irksome, but became increasingly more vexatious as the afternoon wore on. *After all, how dare he behave as if I have no right to enjoy the company of my betrothed! He has no rights over me, none at all*, she thought in exasperation. *It is fortunate that Mr. Covington is good-natured; otherwise there might be trouble!*

He did not leave her alone even for a moment, and finally, as it drew time for Mr. Covington to depart, she walked him out to his horse after giving Darcy a heated glare which could not be misinterpreted. It earned her a short distance of freedom, enough that she could converse in quiet tones with Mr. Covington without being overheard. "Thank you for calling, James," she said, feeling oddly as if she should apologize for Darcy's behaviour.

He smiled widely at her use of his name. "It was my pleasure, dearest one," he said. "I could have wished for a little time alone with you, though—has your father appointed Mr. Darcy as your watchdog?"

Elizabeth could not help laughing at the idea of her father working in concert with Darcy on such a matter. "I doubt it," she said. "I fear it is his own idea of being responsible; he has a younger sister whose guardian he is."

He stepped a little closer to her and raised her hand to his mouth. Kissing it lightly but lingeringly, he said, "Poor girl! He must watch over her like a hawk. Well, perhaps we will have better luck next week."

She smiled obediently, but dropped her eyes, and knew that her blush at his implication was more out of concern for what Darcy thought of what was happening between them than for his actual words.

"Until next week, then," she said lightly.

"I will look forward to it, sweet Lizzy," he said softly. With a sharp glance at Darcy which said this was no concern of his, he leaned over to kiss her cheek, then mounted and was off, pausing to wave from the gate.

She took several deep breaths to calm herself before turning to walk the dozen steps that separated her from Darcy. She would not be intimidated by him, she resolved—having made in the past a proposal she had refused conferred no special rights on him now.

"Miss Bennet," he greeted her quietly as she made an attempt to walk past him into the house.

She turned and gave him a sharp look. "Well, I hope you enjoyed yourself, Mr. Darcy," she said tartly.

"Not as much as I might have," he replied enigmatically, then added with a mocking inflection, "Lizzy."

Her eyes flashed with anger. "You forget yourself, sir," she said icily.

He said nothing but bowed slightly. To Elizabeth's relief, they were joined then by Jane, preventing any further discourse in this dangerous direction.

❧

*He was galloping pell-mell over the countryside, driving his stallion with his fury as if by doing so he could erase any trace of that man from the world, when his eye was caught by a surprising sight. He reined in abruptly and turned back to see if his eyes had deceived him. It was Elizabeth, sitting at the edge of a brook, her dark hair tumbling down over her shoulders and her bare feet dabbling in the rushing water. She looked up at him for a moment as he approached her, then back at the brook, her expression unreadable. He dismounted and strode over to kneel beside her.*

*"Elizabeth!" he said, quietly demanding. She looked up at him silently, as if unaware of the impropriety of her position, and her silence only fed his anger and his desire. Why was she here, as if*

she were waiting for him? It was intolerable; he would no longer allow her to toy with him. He caught her face in his hands and kissed her fiercely. To his surprise, she met him with an equal passion, and he knew then that she had indeed been waiting for him. Their mouths encouraged each other as his hands began impatiently to explore her body, taking possession of her waist, her breasts, her shoulders. She did not protest, and in fact seemed with her movements to be inviting more, enticing him to even greater ardour. She sighed against his lips as his fingers discovered her curves and she slid her arms around his neck.

It was not enough. He had to claim her, every inch of her in every way. Almost roughly he pushed down the sleeve of her gown, freeing her hand and allowing him to draw down the rest to expose her creamy breasts to the air and to his hungry eyes and hands. She still said nothing, only pressed her nakedness against him.

He took advantage of her embrace to press her backwards until she lay upon the grass, her hair spilling around her. Covering her legs with one of his, he kissed her fiercely again, caressing her until her body began to move involuntarily beneath him. He began to feel satisfaction—it would not be enough merely to have her; she had to want him as impossibly much as he wanted her, and he needed to own all her pleasure.

It would never be enough. Without releasing her, he removed his leg long enough to draw up her skirts, then trapped her bare legs again with his, his hardness pressing urgently against her hip.

Not enough, never enough. He pulled away just long enough to dispose of his trousers. With a sense of triumph, he lowered himself between her legs, reclaiming her mouth with the passionate demands of his own. She arched against him, and he pressed his arousal into her until he met the expected resistance, and then with a sharp thrust he took what should have been his so long ago.

The pleasure of her flesh around him was exquisite, and his hunger was great, but as he moved within her he continued to encourage her with his lips and his tongue and his fingers until she shook with waves of fulfillment around him. Then at last he held back no more, and thrust himself into her time and again, hard and demanding and unrelenting until he exploded in a fiery burst of ultimate satisfaction.

He collapsed into her arms, his need finally sated and his anger dissipated. "Now you are mine," he said, their bodies still joined into one. "You will never so much as look at him again."

"But I must," she said softly, speaking her first words since his arrival. "I must marry him—you know that."

Darcy sat up in bed, his forehead beaded with sweat. *What a dream!* He could still almost feel the sense of her body against his. Then those nightmarish words coming out of her sweet mouth…

He was aware he had behaved badly that day at Longbourn, and Elizabeth had every right to be angry with him. He had not shown her the respect she deserved, and he had spoiled their hard-won myth that he had accepted her status. What had he been thinking?

He knew all too well what he had been thinking, unfortunately. He had been thinking of how much he had wanted to tear Covington limb from limb to keep him away from Elizabeth. On the other hand, he considered what he had *not* done—he had not challenged Covington to a duel, he had not insulted him to his face, he had not tried to take Elizabeth away by force, he had not—as he had been tempted at one point—announced that she was his mistress. No, he merely had stayed close by her, had been something less than civil, and been overly familiar with Elizabeth that once. Seen in that light, it seemed hardly unreasonable; but it was unacceptable.

He had not been spending his days with her by her invitation; he had been imposing upon her in order to feel the relief and pleasure that only her presence could bring him. He had been selfish, just as she had accused him of being all those months ago, taking what he wanted without thought for her. He had not been thinking of what was best for her—what kind of love was that, which put his needs and desires ahead of hers? And then to behave as if their time together gave him some sort of claim on her, when she had never indicated any desire for his company—what a fool he had made of himself!

It would not do. Yet he knew that it had taken all of his control to stay as calm as he had, and that, should he again be in company with Elizabeth and Covington, he would likely do no better. He cursed himself. What was he hoping to achieve, after all? The benefit of seeing her was a temporary relief from pain, but it was predicated on the absurd invention of forgetting Covington's existence. It would do him no good in the long term, and soon it would no longer be possible, because she would be living at Ashworth, and he knew that he would not be able to bear to see her there, knowing she belonged to Covington.

He lay back in bed with a curse. He should be accustomed to this by now, the ripping pain that went through him whenever he thought of her marriage, but it injured him anew each time.

What was he to do? The sensible thing would be to put an end to it, to go back to Town and try to find a woman who could help him forget Elizabeth Bennet. But sense never had any role in his feelings for her—when it came to Elizabeth, he lost his rationality completely. She deserved better, though, and he needed to find some way to give it to her, no matter how unpalatable it might be to him.

He would stay away from Longbourn tomorrow, he determined. He would not trouble her with his demands, and would prove to himself that he could resist temptation for a day, at least. Then, perhaps, he could determine the best course of action, and how to separate himself from her, for her sake, if not for his own.

❦

Unfortunately, the next day provided him no answers, nor the following day as he continued his lonely vigil at Netherfield.

Bingley was understandably puzzled by his choice, but accepted it with his usual good cheer and went off on his own to visit his beloved, never guessing how sick with jealousy it made his friend to watch him go. They had been two of the longest days in his memory—he could find no distraction in books, billiards, or letters. Riding became a constant battle not to turn his mount toward Longbourn, hoping against hope to encounter her somewhere along the way.

He was no nearer to a resolution, either. He missed her with a violence even greater than he had anticipated, her laughter, her wit, her sparkling eyes, all the many facets of her he loved. *But why go back?* he argued with himself. *Then it will just begin again, and you cannot avoid this separation.* But each time he tried to convince himself to leave Netherfield, he would think of how he would never see her again, and his desire to steal as many moments with her as possible would raise its head anew.

He was still undecided as to what to do when he appeared at breakfast the next morning. He was inclining towards going to Longbourn, with the feeble excuse that it would look suspicious if, after so many days of regular visits, he suddenly disappeared for days on end. He wondered if she had missed him at all, then cursed himself for being an idiot. She had no doubt found it a pleasant reprieve.

Bingley entered a few minutes later, greeting him cheerfully and helping himself to a heaping serving of food. He had only just seated himself across from Darcy when a servant appeared with a letter. He opened it carelessly and began to scan it, and Darcy saw his face go pale.

"Good God!" Bingley muttered as he read.

"What is it?" asked Darcy calmly, having seen his friend overreact on many occasions in the past.

"It is from Jane—her sister has eloped. The youngest one, Lydia. I must go to her immediately!" He dropped the letter on the table and went to the door, calling for his horse to be saddled immediately.

*My poor Elizabeth!* thought Darcy, reaching for the letter as if reading his friend's correspondence were the most natural thing in the world. Skipping past the greeting, he read:

*An express came at twelve last night, just as we were all gone to bed, from Colonel Forster, to inform us that Lydia was gone off to Scotland with one of his officers. Imagine our surprise. To Kitty, however, it does not seem so wholly unexpected.—But I am willing to hope the best. My poor mother is sadly grieved. My father bears it better, but Lizzy has gone off and will speak to no one. They were off Saturday night about twelve, as is conjectured, but were not missed till yesterday morning at eight. The express was sent off directly. Colonel Foster gives us reason to expect him here soon. Lydia left a few lines for his wife, informing her of their intention. I must conclude, for I cannot be long from my poor mother. It would probably be best for you to remain at Netherfield today, but I will send you word as soon as any arrives.*

Bingley returned for a moment. "I am off to Longbourn, Darcy—I doubt I will see you before tonight."

"Wait," said Darcy, his earlier indecision forgotten. "I will come with you."

His friend looked at him unhappily. "Darcy, do you think that a good idea? I cannot imagine they will want anyone but family there today."

The image of Elizabeth, alone and in distress, cut through Darcy's usual reserve on the subject. "Nonsense," he said, brushing past him. "Someone must look after Elizabeth, and no one else will."

<hr />

He found Elizabeth in the garden, her arms wrapped around herself, pacing back and forth silently. His heart went out to her as he saw the blank look of pain on her face, and he wanted nothing more than to take her in his arms to comfort her.

She did not see him until he was almost upon her. *So he has returned, under these impossible circumstances!* she thought, looking away lest he see too much in her eyes. She had missed his company these last two days more than she cared to admit, and found the idea he might have given up on her oddly painful. She had chided herself more than once for the impropriety of these thoughts, and tried to throw herself anew into her wedding plans, resolving to think of him no more.

Now, though, the situation could not be worse. Once he knew what had occurred, he would certainly never want anything to do with her again. She wished she could disguise it, but that would only delay the inevitable. Gathering up her courage, she said, "Mr. Darcy, I am afraid you do not find me at my best. My family has received some dreadful news, and I do not think any of us will be suitable company today, I am sorry to say."

"I have heard," he said gently. "Your sister sent a note to Bingley, and he is presently inside with her and your mother."

His kindness almost proved her undoing. She swallowed hard, resolved to keep her composure. "*They* still believe that they are gone to Scotland," she said bitterly.

"And you do not?"

"Of course not! She has no money, no connections, nothing that can tempt him to—she is lost forever. *You* know him too well to doubt the rest."

A dark foreboding filled Darcy. "I do not know of whom you speak," he said.

She looked up at him in pained surprise. "I thought you had heard," she said, heartsick at having to reveal this last shame to him. "She has eloped with Mr. Wickham."

Darcy was fixed in astonishment. "When I consider," she added, in a yet more agitated voice, "that *I* might have prevented it!—*I*, who knew what he was. Had I but explained some part of it only—some part of what I learnt, to my own family! Had his character been known, this could not have happened. But it is all, all too late now."

It was a moment before he could take in her words. "I

am grieved, indeed," said Darcy compassionately, "grieved—shocked. But what has been attempted to recover her?"

Elizabeth shook her head bitterly. "Nothing at all—they all believe her gone to Scotland. We are awaiting the arrival of Colonel Forster with more further intelligence, but I cannot, I *cannot* go inside and pretend there is any hope!" Her voice cracked on the last words.

Darcy did not know how he kept himself from touching her at that moment. "I wish to heaven that I could disagree with you and say they were gone to Scotland, but we both know that I cannot," he said, in a tone of gentleness and commiseration. "But it is not impossible that this could be mended; please do not give up all hope."

"Nothing can be done to mend it!" she cried. "I know very well that nothing can be done. How is such a man to be worked on? How are they even to be discovered? I have not the smallest hope. It is in every way horrible!"

Darcy's face twisted into a grimace of distaste. "There is but one way to work on him, and that is with money—Wickham will do *anything* for money."

She looked at him with eyes that spoke only too eloquently of her despair. She knew that her father had no resources of the necessary magnitude, but she would not say that to him; she would prefer that he not know yet how certain was the shame her family would suffer. *Let him believe for a little while longer that we are not completely disgraced!* she thought, knowing it could not be for long.

"Miss Bennet," he said in a voice that bespoke his concern, "let us walk a little through the garden while we wait; it benefits nothing to dwell further upon it until we know more."

"There is no need for *you* to wait, sir," she said, her eyes not meeting his. She had no desire for him to know how much she longed for the support and understanding she had no right to expect from him. "This is no concern of yours; I am sure you would be far more comfortable at Netherfield."

"There is *every* reason for me to wait," he said, almost violently, not caring how improper it was. He held out his arm, and, though she would not look at him, she took it and leaned a little upon him as they walked, taking a kind of comfort from his nearness.

After a time she began to shiver, more from the shock of her distress than from any chill, and he insisted on leading her inside. When she refused to join the others, he took her to a back sitting room, and fetched her a glass of wine. He talked to her quietly of whatever came to his mind— Pemberley, Georgiana, Bingley, neither expecting nor receiving a response.

Finally a stir was heard at the front of the house, and Elizabeth leapt to her feet. "Excuse me, Mr. Darcy; that may be Colonel Forster."

"Yes, let us see what he has to say," said Darcy.

She caught his sleeve. "Mr. Darcy, I appreciate all you have done, but you cannot afford to be publicly associated with our family at this juncture. You should not be seen here."

He looked down at her hand on his arm, eternally damning the fact that he did not have the right to comfort her as he would wish. "Thank you for your concern, but I will judge that; at present I find there is reason for me to be here."

She did not argue further; she was too grateful for his presence. She only hoped he would not regret it later.

The new arrival was indeed Colonel Forster. After a brief greeting to the ladies, he disappeared into the library with Mr. Bennet, Mr. Bingley, and—to Elizabeth's surprise—Mr. Darcy. It was some time before they emerged, leaving the ladies in a state of high anxiety as to the outcome. The grim look on Mr. Bennet's face did nothing to reassure Elizabeth, and she immediately glanced at Mr. Darcy, who looked more thoughtful than anything else. She wondered what he was thinking.

"I wish I had better news to deliver," said Mr. Bennet bleakly. "It appears there is reason to suspect they are not gone to Scotland after all." Mrs. Bennet gasped in dismay, beginning to sob as her husband shared the remainder of Colonel Forster's information. The intelligence that Lydia was not in fact married, nor likely to be, came as a devastating shock to Jane, who would not have believed so much evil could exist in the world. It was far too much for the nerves of Mrs. Bennet, who was finally taken to her rooms in hysterics by her second daughter. It was much later when Elizabeth returned downstairs, and she was surprised to find Mr. Darcy still there, apparently waiting for her. Mr. Bingley and Jane were sitting close together, talking quietly; signs of tears still showed on Jane's face.

She managed a small and weary smile for Darcy as he stood to greet her. He was glad to see it; he had spent her absence reminding himself that he had no right to offer her consolation in the way Bingley could with Jane. It was more difficult than ever to accept it after spending so much of this trying day together, and being treated by her family almost as a member.

"I hope your mother is better," he said cautiously.

"She is asleep; we gave her a sedative," said Elizabeth tiredly, knowing that as soon as her mother awoke, her demands and wails would begin anew. "Has Colonel Forster gone?"

"Yes, he left almost immediately, hoping to reach London tonight. Your father is in the library making preparations to follow him in the morning."

She gave him a quiet smile for his efforts, knowing he had gone well beyond the duties of friendship for her, and too exhausted by the effects of the day to try to deny what this implied about his feelings for her. A knock came at the front door, and she looked up eagerly, hoping for news.

She was destined for disappointment, however, for a moment later Mr. Covington appeared unannounced, having clearly ridden hard. He came straight to her and knelt beside her chair, taking her hands in his. "I am so sorry, Lizzy," he said with obvious concern and solicitude. "I came as soon as I heard."

"I…" Elizabeth stammered, staring half-bewildered at him. She could not comprehend Mr. Covington's presence; it was as if a total stranger was before her. Looking at his earnest expression, she finally admitted the truth to herself: it was not *his* comfort she wanted. With dismaying clarity, she faced the reality before her—she was to marry one man when it was another she wanted and needed, and it was no one's fault but her own. There was nothing to be done for it—it was already too late. The tears she had been barely managing to hold back all day suddenly escaped as she faced the bleakness of her future, and she began to sob uncontrollably.

Darcy reacted to Covington's arrival as if he had been slapped. *He* had been taking care of Elizabeth, *he* had been planning solutions—and now he was totally put aside. He watched as she started to cry, she who had struggled so hard to be in control of her emotions all day with him, apparently waiting for this moment when she could let down her guard. She covered her face with her hands, crying even harder now, and Darcy winced as Covington put his arms around her.

He knew then that his game of make-believe was over—he could not look at this tableau and imagine it meant anything but that Covington was the one she loved and trusted. She might have felt an attraction to him at some moments and enjoyed his sense of humour, but in a time of crisis, it was not to him she turned, not even when he was the only one available. It was agony even to breathe as the scene in front of him burned itself into his memory.

Perhaps he had been able to offer her a slight comfort earlier, but now his presence could make nothing but trouble for her. It was her love he wanted, but that was a hopeless cause; all that was left for him now was to give her the best chance of happiness she had. His face set in grim lines, he silently turned and left her to her future with Covington.

Elizabeth remained lost in helpless tears for some time, both for her sister's lost hopes and her own. How had she found her way into this dilemma? And her position was as hopeless as Lydia's—even if she were ever free, Darcy could never ally himself with her, not after her sister's disgrace by a man whose name was punishment for him to speak. She could only be grateful that he had not decamped immediately on hearing of it. She forced herself to breathe more evenly until Mr. Covington released her gently from his unwanted embrace. It was Darcy's arms she wanted around her, his voice offering her words of comfort. It could never be, of course, but just this once, she wanted to look at him with honesty in her heart; but when she turned to where he had been, he was gone.

It was nearly a fortnight later that Bingley arrived for his morning call on his betrothed with Mr. Darcy once again in tow. Elizabeth, in a whirl of embarrassment, could hardly bring herself to look at him when they made their greeting. Since she had seen him last, it seemed her every waking moment, apart from those taken up with worry for Lydia, had been spent trying to reconcile herself to a future without him. There had been a great many such wakeful moments in which to think, since many of her nights were spent in sleepless preoccupation with the feelings she had denied so long.

She had given up hope of seeing him again, at least not for a long time. She had not been in his company since that moment she had recognized the truth of what lay between them; Bingley had brought news the next morning that Darcy had departed for Town and was not expected to return. It had been an acutely painful blow, though she soon realized it was for the best. She needed to make her peace with her upcoming marriage, and it would have been impossible to do so in his presence. Still, she could not stop herself from missing him, and longing for his company.

Now he had reappeared completely unexpectedly, and she did not know what to make of it. She stole glances at him from under her lashes as she sat at her work, but his attention seemed elsewhere, directed to her mother, her sisters, and occasionally on no less an object than the floor.

"Have you heard, Mr. Darcy, that my youngest is to be married next week?" said Mrs. Bennet with great satisfaction.

Darcy replied that he had, and made his congratulations. Elizabeth, humiliated, dared not lift up her eyes. How he looked, therefore, she could not tell.

"It will be a delightful thing, to be sure, to have a daughter well married, and two more soon to come, but at the same time, it is very hard to have my youngest taken such a way from me. They are to go to Newcastle, a place quite northward, it seems, and there they are to stay."

"Very hard indeed, I would imagine, to have one so dear to you far away."

"How suddenly you went away, Mr. Darcy!" continued Mrs. Bennet.

Darcy looked grave. "Yes, it was unfortunately sudden; urgent business called me to London. In truth, I am leaving again this morning; I came last night only to settle some matters with Bingley. I cannot stay long, but since I was unable to call to make a proper farewell before my last departure, I hoped to make it up to you now, and to thank you for all the hospitality you have shown me."

Elizabeth froze at his words. She had somehow assumed that his reappearance meant their old pattern of daily meetings was to resume.

"Leaving again, Mr. Darcy? So soon?" Jane asked.

"Yes, I must be back in London tonight, and next week I will be undertaking a longer journey, and do not expect to return to England for some time."

Elizabeth looked up at him in shock at this statement. His eyes met hers in a serious look, and she bit her lip, trying to fend off the loss she felt already. She understood his presence now; he had come to say a final goodbye to her. He too must have acknowledged that what was between them must end. A lump formed in her throat, and she looked away suddenly before tears could begin to appear in her eyes.

Mrs. Bennet inquired as to his destination. He replied, "I will be going to Vienna—I have not been there since my grand tour, and I always intended to return there to acquaint myself with the city properly."

Now that she knew she had lost the small hope of him she had, Elizabeth could not decide whether she more wished him to stay longer or go immediately. It was an acutely painful pleasure to sit across from him, able to look at him but nothing more, and to know there would never be anything more.

She did not have long to think of it, as in fact it was only a brief interval before he said he must go. When he rose to leave, she boldly seized her moment to see him to his carriage, hoping that no one would notice her agitation. She did not know what she wished to say to him, if in fact she wished to say anything, or if she just hoped to be in his company a few minutes longer. His eyes thanked her, however, and that was enough.

She found, though, that she must say something, or stand in uncomfortable silence as the maid brought his hat and coat. "I hope you enjoy Vienna, Mr. Darcy," she said.

The corners of his mouth quirked in what was almost a smile. "It is a place to go," he said. Their eyes met again for a long moment, and she looked away first. He moved towards the door, then stopped again just at the edge of the vestibule. "Before I go, though, Miss Bennet, I must beg your forgiveness."

"My forgiveness? For what?" she asked. *For engaging my affections when I was already bound to another man?*

"For this," he said. Before she realized what he intended, he leant towards her and kissed her, a brief, tender touch of his lips to hers. "There is no need for you to come any further. Goodbye, Miss Bennet, and please accept my best wishes for your marriage."

She could not help herself; her eyes clouded with tears, and by the time she had blinked them away, he was already out the door and stepping into his carriage. He did not look back, and she watched with stinging eyes as the carriage disappeared down the lane, still feeling the sensation of his kiss.

# Chapter 4

THE TRIP TO THE Longbourn church seemed to take forever to Darcy. He could see the breath of the horses steaming in the cold air; in March the promise of spring had not yet arrived in Hertfordshire. The leaves had been falling when he had left five months earlier, and it seemed as if winter were not prepared to loosen its grip on the countryside this year. His mouth twisted into a frown as he saw the spire of the church ahead.

The occasion was merely a meeting with the rector to review the order of the ceremony, and as such, the focus would primarily be on Bingley and Miss Bennet, but Darcy could not help but wonder what other members of the Bennet family might also be present. It did not seem likely Elizabeth would be there—presumably one of her younger sisters would be serving as Jane's bridesmaid, since Elizabeth would be married herself now—but the mere possibility made him tense with anticipation. He did not know whether he more longed for or dreaded the prospect; he ached to see her, but it would be crushingly painful knowing she was Covington's wife now. The very thought made his chest grow tight in a now familiar feeling of distress.

This occasion was unlikely to be a pleasant event in any case—if he did not have to face Elizabeth, it would no doubt mean dealing with some of the more difficult members of her family in her stead. At least he need no longer concern himself with the possibility of those connections becoming his own, but somehow this thought was of no consolation whatever.

He sighed as he drew up at the church. The sooner this farce began, the sooner it would be over. Bingley had not even waited for him, but had gone in on his own. *No doubt anxious to see his beloved after the long separation of a night*, thought Darcy sardonically. *Try five months, my friend, and see how that feels. Try forever.*

He removed his hat and strode into the church. As his eyes adjusted to the dimness of the midwinter church, he saw Bingley and Miss Bennet standing near the altar with Mr. Roberts, the rector, who was gesticulating some instruction. It was only then that he made out, off to the side, a shape he knew intimately from his dreams. He caught his breath at the sight of her. Time had changed nothing. He walked up the aisle to meet the others, mechanically greeting Miss Bennet and the rector, but his attention was all for the figure he could see only from the corner of his eye. She acknowledged him with a nod and a curtsey, but came no closer.

He listened to Mr. Roberts with only a fragment of his attention; the rest was on Elizabeth. As soon as he could reasonably look away from the others, his eyes fixed on her. She was not oblivious to his presence; her lips were curved in a subdued version of that familiar arch smile in response to his look.

He could not understand why she was standing apart; he could hardly go to her when she was obviously keeping her distance, but it made no sense. She was not making any effort to ignore him, and in fact seemed as inclined to watch him as he was her, albeit with more amusement. With good reason, he thought—everyone in Meryton was going to guess his feelings about her if he could not stop staring at her like a damned soul seeing his only hope for salvation!

The rector droned on, far longer than Darcy thought necessary, but finally brought the discussion to a close. Elizabeth at last joined the group, and as they made their way outside, Bingley said, "We are all invited back to Longbourn; will you come with us, Darcy?"

As if he had a choice in the matter! He accepted the invitation courteously.

"Good!" said Bingley energetically. "I will take Jane in my carriage, then; will you bring Lizzy?"

"It would be my pleasure," he murmured, glancing at Elizabeth to see how she took this suggestion. "You are for Longbourn as well, then?" he asked her, not yet able to bring himself to pronounce her new name.

She raised an eyebrow and smiled. "Yes, of course. Thank you, Mr. Darcy."

Bingley, eager to be alone with Jane, was already halfway to his carriage, while Darcy and Elizabeth set a more sedate pace. She seemed to have recovered from her unusual reticence, and began to ask him about his travels. It was a blessed relief to have the distraction of a simple conversation as he handed her into the carriage, a surge of desire racing through him simply from the light touch of her gloved hand.

Darcy climbed in on the other side, and spurred the horses on with a quick flick of the reins. He glanced sideways at her, relieved to discover that his behaviour at their last meeting seemed to have joined the rather long list of events regarding him that she was pretending had never occurred. She seemed to relax and smile more freely as they spoke of insignificant matters. He had observed her for months, however, and he could sense her underlying tension, and finally heard it put to words when she asked, "How long do you plan to remain in Hertfordshire, Mr. Darcy?"

So his presence did make her uncomfortable. With a sardonic smile, he responded, "Not long, Mrs. Covington. I have a sister I have neglected far too long."

Startled, she looked up at him. "It is still Miss Bennet, sir," she said, her voice a trifle unsteady.

He felt a moment of shock, and then violent embarrassment as he realized his error. "My apologies, then, Miss

Bennet; I had not realized that your wedding had been delayed as well as your sister's."

She smiled with just a trace of her old mischievous look. "My wedding is not to take place at all. Mr. Covington and I ended our engagement some time ago; I thought you would have heard." She drew her arms more tightly around herself against the chill in the air. Her distress at the position in which she found herself was substantial; this meeting was quite trying enough for her, and it was an unhappy surprise to discover he was unaware of all that had transpired.

Darcy did not know what to think, or even how to think. At first the incredible rush of relief was overwhelming, but then he looked at her drawn face and realized what must have occurred, and felt a sudden violent urge to strangle Covington with his bare hands for hurting her. What a fool, to break off his engagement simply because of the disgrace of Lydia's hasty marriage! For a moment he did not feel sufficiently in control of himself to speak, then he said savagely, "I am sorry—it had never occurred to me that he would not honour his promise to you."

Elizabeth winced; this was worse than she had imagined. She did not look at him this time as she answered. "You mistake my meaning, sir. *I* was the one who broke off the engagement, not Mr. Covington."

She had done *what*? He could not credit what he had heard. She was no longer engaged, and by her own decision? It was all he could do not to halt the carriage that minute and take her in his arms. *It will not help matters if you insist on behaving like a lunatic!* he scolded himself. *Control yourself!* Unfortunately, it seemed he very much wanted to behave like a lunatic. "My apologies," he said quietly. "This news is quite surprising. I am… sorry for any pain it occasioned you."

She smiled as if at something only she could appreciate. "It is old news here, sir; there is no reason to be concerned."

No reason to be concerned! No reason, after the hell he had been through these last months, haunted by images of her as Covington's wife? Even Vienna had not been far enough away to keep the spectre of Elizabeth Bennet from his mind and his dreams. His only consolation had been the thought that she would be happy with Covington. He would not have returned now, had it not been for the hope that the sight of her as a married woman would at last prove the cure to his obsession. A pathetic hope, but neither time, nor distance, nor force of will seemed able to change his feelings, and he had been desperate.

Now all his suffering proved to have been for naught. She was free once more, free, and not objecting to his company. Free, and she had allowed him once before to kiss her without scolding him for it now. Free, and by her own choice—was it too much to hope for that he might have played a role in her decision? It was more than he could comprehend all at once. He reined in the horses, bringing the carriage to a stop at the side of the road, so as to be able to give her his entire attention.

He took a deep breath. "I am clearly behind the times. May I impose upon you to help me understand what has occurred in my absence?" Although his words were courteous enough, he had no right to ask such a question—he could simply not bear to remain in ignorance.

The intensity of his interest was palpable as his dark eyes seemed to bore into her. She did not know how to understand him; there had been no word of him at all for months, and now suddenly he appeared, feeling entitled to ask her deepest secrets. She had forgotten how easily he had always spoken to her of matters no one else would dare broach, and she knew she must be cautious with him. In such a case as this, there could not be too little said.

"You have the greater part of it already, sir," she said in a light, social voice. "You know of my youngest sister's elopement. Mr. Wickham, as you will have heard, was eventually prevailed upon to marry her, but it was too late to hush it up; all of Meryton was already talking. I terminated my engagement, and Jane's wedding was delayed to allow both scandals time to pass."

He did not fail to notice she had neatly sidestepped his unspoken question. "Miss Bennet," he said, his voice tight, "it is not my desire to force your confidence; however, I do find myself very much wishing to understand what led you to take such a step. I cannot believe you would undertake such a course of action without extreme provocation."

She closed her eyes, realizing he must think she had

expectations of him. It was understandable enough, she supposed; she would have to make clear she recognized just how hopeless her position was. "Mr. Darcy, the rules for a woman in making a marriage are much like those at a dance. A woman may not choose her partner; she has only the right of refusal, and even that comes at a price. If she refuses to dance with a gentleman who has invited her, she must then refuse to dance with anyone else who asks, or be thought ill-bred and improper. When I chose to break my engagement, I did so with a very clear knowledge of the price I would pay. I knew it would mean I would be a scandal, that I would *never* marry, never have children of my own. It was not a decision I entered into lightly." She was being far too serious, she thought, and in a lighter tone, she added, "I am quite resigned to my lot, Mr. Darcy. My sister and Mr. Bingley have invited me to live with them after their marriage, an offer which I have accepted. I will always have a home with people I love, and I will grow old helping to care for Jane's children and grandchildren. There are far worse fates; I have no complaints to make." She prayed that he would not press her further.

He was silent for a long moment. Did she honestly think he would just let her go, now that she was free? If so, she had a few things yet to learn about him, and about his feelings for her. He said determinedly, "*You* may be resigned to that fate, Miss Bennet, but I am not. I can understand it is too soon for you to accept another suitor, but a few months will remedy that. I can wait."

She felt a treacherous surge of joy at his words, at the knowledge that, in defiance of everything, she was still dear to him. Yet it was a joy that carried pain in its wake, because its culmination could never be. She did not dare look at him, for fear she would weaken. "You would wait in vain, then. I will accept no suitors, now or ever," she said flatly, answering his directness with her own.

There was a tense silence, long enough for Elizabeth to feel the regret for chances lost. Oh, why had he come to disturb her hard-won equanimity?

"Why?" he asked finally, his voice clipped.

She took a deep breath. "Mr. Darcy, I am unmarriageable. When you have had time to reflect, you will know this as well as I. Even were it not for the matter of my sister's marriage to Mr. Wickham, you cannot ignore the disgrace I brought upon myself by breaking my engagement."

"I care nothing for any of that," he said fiercely.

"It is perhaps easier not to care when you do not have to live it," she retorted with unexpected bitterness. "*You* do not have to ignore the silences when I walk into a shop in Meryton, *you* do not have to endure my mother's anger and constant reminders of what my decision has cost not only her but my entire family. *You* are not the one who has to walk into that church, knowing that Mr. Roberts, who baptized me, now views me as little better than a fallen woman. You would care more for it then, I assure you, so please do not torment me by suggesting it is of no consequence!"

He paled at her anger. "I am very sorry you have been put through such a trial," he said, wanting nothing more than to kiss away her pain.

Elizabeth, looking at his face, realized she had said too much, and strove to lighten the air between them. "Do not pity me too much, sir," she said with a forced smile. "I have avoided the greater part of it, spending the last months visiting my aunt and uncle in London, waiting for the scandal to die away. It will be forgotten—mostly—when some other outrage gives the gossips something new to harp on. So, shall we not continue on to Longbourn?"

"No," he said firmly. "You have not yet told me why."

She could not bring herself to pretend she did not understand his meaning. "I believe that is something which should remain between Mr. Covington and me," she said steadily.

To her mystification, she saw a smile beginning to grow upon his face. *I will never understand this man*, she thought impatiently. "Well, Mr. Darcy," she said tartly, "perhaps you would care to share what you find so amusing about all this."

He shook his head with a bemused look. He had just experienced the startling revelation that what Elizabeth had *not* said was more important than what she had. It would have been simple enough for her to say her broken engagement was the result of her sister's disgrace; the mere fact that she had not done so suggested there was more to it. She had not said a word to suggest she did not welcome his affection, just that his suit was not acceptable. The rapid shift from months of despair to the very near reality of happiness was like strong drink on an empty stomach, and he was intoxicated by it. "I am more amazed than amused, my dear Miss Bennet—oh, yes, *quite* amazed," he said, reaching out with his fingertip to stroke her cheek.

Elizabeth felt a shock of sensation at his touch. "Mr. Darcy!" she protested.

He laughed, the laugh of a man who has been released from prison. "I am afraid you have betrayed yourself," he said. He knew his behaviour was outrageous, but he could not bring himself to care.

She raised an eyebrow. "Betrayed myself? How so, sir?" she asked suspiciously, finding his mercurial change of mood both incomprehensible and unsettling.

Exhilarated, he caught her hands in his. "You forget, Miss Bennet—my dear Miss Bennet—that I am not inexperienced in the manner in which you reject an unwanted suitor, and today you have told me only why *I* should not want to marry *you*. You have not," he said, pausing to kiss her hands, "indicated that I am the last man in the world whom you could ever be prevailed upon to marry. You have not even," he continued, turning her hands over to press more light kisses into her palms, "addressed my arrogance or conceit—though perhaps you will be tempted to do so now—nor so much as shown surprise at my declaration."

Elizabeth, stunned by this unexpected frontal attack on her defenses, and undermined by the flashes of exquisite sensation caused by his caresses, could not even think to pull her hands away. In weak protest, she exclaimed, "You assume a great deal, sir!"

"Oh, yes," he replied, looking deep into her fine eyes, and not displeased with what he saw. Moving closer to her, he bent his head to caress her lips with his own, then whispered, "I assume a very great deal." Before she could respond, he captured her mouth once again with a kiss that tugged at her senses with a mixture of tenderness and passion.

It was a combination she could not resist. His nearness stole away her power of thought—even though nothing touched but their lips and hands, the very intensity of the forbidden act sent tremors of pleasure through her in ways she had never imagined. Without conscious intent, she yielded to her own deep need, allowing her most private self to emerge to meet his kiss with an honesty and directness she had not known she possessed. She had missed him for so long, and despaired of ever having more than a casual meeting with him again, and now he was here, declaring himself and kissing her with an ardency that left her awash in the intense exhilaration of love long denied. It was her first taste of the delight a lover's touch could give, and she could not immediately bring herself to turn away from the captivating pleasure of his kiss.

Darcy felt the shift in her as her desire rose to meet his own. The physical pleasure of tasting her lips was as great as he had imagined so many times, but to feel her response, her acceptance of the power of the bond between them, exhilarated him in a way he had never dreamed. He felt the danger of it, too—he had spent far too long hoping for any crumb she might toss his way, and to suddenly have the entirety of her was enough to undermine the strongest self-control. Long before he was ready, he pulled away, his heart pounding as he gazed into her passion-darkened eyes.

"Oh, my dearest," he said, his voice laden with emotion. "You cannot know how happy you have made me."

He could not have said anything that would have returned Elizabeth to painful reality with greater force. She knew all too well that she had no choice now but to make him very unhappy, and she wondered at her own lunacy in breaking through her reserves to give him hope that could never be fulfilled. She could feel for herself the bitter taste of the loss of the closeness they had shared so briefly, and before her courage vanished, she pressed her fingers to his mouth before he could say anything more. "Please do not," she entreated him. "Let us not make this any harder than it already is."

He looked at her in disbelief. Surely she could not be denying him now? He was not such a fool as not to recognize her response for what it was. "What do you mean?" he asked with deep unease.

She smiled sadly. "Nothing has changed, my dear—except perhaps that I now know my own weakness better than I did a few minutes ago. My situation is no different."

His mouth went dry. "I will not allow you to deny this,"

he said, a feeling of desperation beginning to make itself felt. He grasped her hands again, willing her to listen to him.

"I must remind you, sir, we are on a public road, and my reputation is in sad enough condition as it is, without further provocation," she said, averting her eyes. "Please, take me home now, I beg you."

Nervelessly he released her hands and picked up the reins, but could not bring himself to use them. He looked at her once more, hoping for some kind of softening, and saw instead a kind of misery he had never perceived in her before. It occurred to him that while he had indulged his sorrow in Vienna in near complete freedom of circumstance, she had made greater sacrifices and been subject to the cruel whims of society, without the power to choose whether she might see him again or not. Was it such a surprise that even her resilient spirit was a little bowed and weary? Was he not being selfish, to focus on his own pain and feelings of rejection when she was suffering?

"Miss Bennet," he said gently, "I will take you home, but I would prefer to do so without this conflict between us. Can we not find some common ground?"

She glanced up at him, the ghost of a smile appearing on her face. "I fear that would require great skill at legerdemain, Mr. Darcy."

He smiled back cautiously. "Let me propose this for now: I will cease pressing you on the subject of marriage, if you will not deny what there is between us."

She raised an eyebrow, and he was glad to see she still had enough spirit to question him. "And what will that accomplish, sir?"

He looked at her thoughtfully. "A certain honesty, perhaps? A little peace? I am not suggesting that you need tolerate my attentions; you are welcome to slap my hand if I try to kiss you, though I cannot promise not to try."

To his relief, this produced a genuine smile. "I shall hold you to that, Mr. Darcy; I have never struck a gentleman, but I am a quick learner," she teased.

He gave her a self-deprecating smile, then barely touched his fingers to the back of her hand. "Just let me love you—you might as well give in on that, since all your best efforts have failed to stop me from doing so," he said softly.

"You are very persistent, I will grant you that," she said amusedly. She could not dispute that it felt like a reprieve to return to friendlier terms with him, though she questioned her wisdom in making such an agreement. She was far too susceptible to him, especially when he leveled his rare, devastating smile at her. *Still*, she thought, *I will never capitulate to his request for marriage, for the simple reason that it would grieve me more to see him suffer the life-long consequences of such an unfortunate union than to bear the pain of doing without him.* She was sobered by a familiar constriction in her chest at the notion, but forced herself not to acknowledge the feeling, and instead to look at Darcy with a smile. "Very well, sir; I accept your terms for the present," she said, recognizing how very much she longed to let him address her with affection as he wished.

"Thank you; you are most generous," said Darcy. Relieved to have won so much so easily, he decided not to press his luck any further, and slapped the reins against the horse's back. Silence seemed safer than conversation at present, so he limited himself to occasional glances at her which conveyed his sentiments clearly. She wore a beguiling look of resigned amusement which could not help but make him smile in return.

They arrived at Longbourn. As she went past him into the vestibule, he took the opportunity to murmur seductively in her ear, "Incidentally, Miss Bennet, you need not feel *obligated* to slap my hand if I try to kiss you."

She gave him a sidelong look. "I had never realized you were such an eternal optimist, Mr. Darcy," she said impudently as she moved past him toward the sitting room.

Just as she reached the door, she heard her mother's querulous voice. "I do not know why you must vex me so, Jane! You have no pity on my poor nerves. I cannot see why you cannot have Mary or Kitty as your bridesmaid—it is still not too late. No one will pay any attention to you if Lizzy is standing up with you."

Elizabeth impulsively caught at Mr. Darcy's wrist to stop him from entering. He looked at her in surprise, and she gestured with her eyes towards the sitting room. She wished he were not there to hear this, but it would be worse if they went in—her mother would only carry on even longer. Realizing she was still holding his arm, she released him embarrassedly. He responded by silently moving closer to her, as if to protect her.

"I will not change my mind, as I have said often enough already," they heard Jane say in a pained voice. "I have always planned to have Lizzy as my bridesmaid, and if anyone is shocked, I am sorry, but that is not my concern."

"I agree with Jane wholeheartedly!" said Bingley warmly.

"She will embarrass us all, acting as if she has done nothing to be ashamed of!" cried Mrs. Bennet. "I will not have it!"

Elizabeth closed her eyes and took a deep breath. These attacks by her mother were still painful, but at least this might convince Mr. Darcy of her earlier point. She ignored a traitorous little voice inside her which whispered that she did not want him convinced of it. She could feel Darcy's rising tension as he listened.

"Come, now, Mrs. Bennet, this is all settled," said Mr. Bennet. "Besides, my dear, you will look so lovely yourself that not a soul will notice Lizzy."

Knowing that her father's compliment would, as intended, cause her mother to subside, Elizabeth chose that moment to go in, smiling pleasantly for all the world as if she had not heard a word of the previous debate. Darcy followed with a more stormy expression, and merely nodded curtly to Mrs. Bennet's effusive greeting. Remembering how civil he had been to her mother this summer, Elizabeth only hoped that her mother would think this no more than a return to his earlier proud ways. She did not dare to contemplate how much her mother could embarrass her were she to engage in words with Darcy.

To her surprise, her father came forward and welcomed Mr. Darcy warmly, and invited both him and Mr. Bingley into the library for a drink. *Of course,* she thought with sudden understanding, *he is trying to prevent a scene.* Darcy assented courteously to the idea, with a quick glance at Elizabeth.

Once the gentlemen had made their escape, Mrs. Bennet seemed prepared to return to her previous topic of conversation. Wanting to spare herself the discomfort of it, Elizabeth decided to retire to her room. The fire had not been laid, but it was still preferable to remaining downstairs. She wrapped herself in blankets against the chill, and had a sudden poignant memory of the warmth of Darcy's kiss.

Darcy felt in a daze as he drove back to Netherfield. Once he had the opportunity for quiet reflection, the shock of what had occurred began to set in. The situation had changed so drastically so quickly that it was almost impossible to grasp. He was pleased beyond measure that Elizabeth seemed willing to allow him to express his feelings, at least to a certain extent. He had trapped himself neatly, however, by agreeing not to press her about marriage—how on earth was he to win her consent if he was not to raise the issue? *Well*, he thought, *our agreement will simply have to be renegotiated periodically, and there is no need to hurry—we could not announce an engagement for some months yet in any case.* He had to acknowledge, however, that with his own longing for certainty, he wanted to have that commitment from her now.

How quickly he had moved from giving up on her to being her determined suitor! To think that he had been suffering needlessly for months, thinking her married! He wondered why Bingley had never told him of her broken engagement, then answered that question himself. Bingley had always been a poor correspondent, and recently, no doubt owing to his preoccupation with his betrothed, his letters had deteriorated to the point of being little more than a few sentences long, and rare as well. He had no reason to suppose Darcy particularly interested in Elizabeth's marital status in any case. Still, he could have mentioned it, and not only saved him a great deal of pain, but also prevented him from being ambushed by the unexpected news. *On the other hand,* he thought, *there is something to be said for being ambushed.* A slow smile crept over his face as he thought of their carriage ride, and the sensation of her lips against his.

# Chapter 5

THEY WERE ONCE MORE in the curricle, driving back from the church, and he was tasting her delectable lips, which were answering him with an uncertain and innocent ardor; but this time he had no intention of stopping before he had her consent. Gently, he teased her lips apart with his tongue, and felt her surprise followed by the unmistakable pressure of her response. It was just as he had always dreamed it would be—he was awakening in her a passion to match his own. And there was so much more he planned to teach her, now that she was free again, and wanted him…

He let his fingers drift along her neck, enjoying the discovery of the smoothness of her skin. He could sense the tremors of desire in her, and as their kiss continued to increase in intensity as she gained in confidence, he felt her delicate hands slide inside his coat. Her touch aroused him beyond anything he had ever imagined as she explored his chest until stopped by the limits of his clothing. He could tell she was aware of how much he wanted her. He moved to put his arms around her waist, not hesitating to explore the curves of her hips as he did so, and pulled her against him, her soft body yielding and molding itself to his. Ah, he had to have her; there was nothing else for it.

His voice was hoarse as he whispered, "We cannot continue this here—let me take you back to Netherfield."

"Oh, yes, my love," she replied, sprinkling his face with the lightest of kisses. "I want to be with you."

He felt an overwhelming surge of desire at her words, and expressed himself by a brief but thorough ravaging of her mouth. He had to be alone with her. Quickly he spurred on the horses to a brisk trot, but even then he could not wait; he laid his hand lightly upon her skirt, feeling the shape of her thigh beneath it. Her gasp of pleasure only enflamed him further, and he began to move his hand until he was stroking her leg through the fabric, moving slowly upwards and inwards until his hand rested between her legs, just below the spot he most desired. There he allowed his fingers to brush lightly against her inner thighs, hearing her rapid breathing. "You never loved him," he said, his words a command more than a statement.

"No," she said breathily. "Never. Only you."

"There will never be anyone but me," he said.

Finally, they were at Netherfield, and he led her into a small sitting room with a lively blaze in its fireplace. He locked the door behind him, and hungrily drew her into his arms, taking possession once more of her mouth, drowning himself in her taste and her scent and the feeling of her willing body within his arms. She responded to his every touch, and, after he paused to strip off his coat and cravat, her hands began to explore his body with as much eagerness as his did as he discovered her hips, her waist, her breasts, and all her most sensitive places.

"Only you," she whispered again and again, her voice smoky with desire, as he stripped her of her clothing, feasting his eyes on her. Gently he settled her on the thick carpet in front of the fire, attending carefully to her comfort.

Only then did he find the place meant for him from the beginning, and he thrust himself into her again and again as she clung to him with cries of pleasure, taking possession of her until he found his bliss. As he spent himself within her, he said in her ear, "You will never leave me again."

⁂

Darcy did not have the opportunity to see Elizabeth again until the wedding two days later. He had spent the time impatiently thinking of what to say to her, how to behave when he was with her, and wondering how she would act towards him. His concerns were not alleviated by the arrival of Bingley's sisters. Miss Bingley, who had not seen him since the summer, was embarrassingly attentive, and his attempts to discourage her were as unsuccessful as ever.

It was a relief when the waiting was finally over and he could be with Elizabeth again, or at least stand across the aisle from her as the marriage service was read. She kept her eyes downcast through most of it, but occasionally looked up to find his gaze upon her. Her face showed only a trace of warmth at those times. Darcy had to remind himself repeatedly of the delicacy of her situation; her behaviour needed to be above reproach, as she would be a target for many curious gazes owing to the recent gossip.

He intended to give her no cause for concern in public; he was impeccably correct with her as they walked down the aisle together and gave their congratulations to the bride and groom. No sooner were the happy couple surrounded by family and friends, though, than Elizabeth began to sidle away. She was nearly at the edge of the churchyard before he caught up to her.

"Miss Bennet, you are not leaving already, I hope?" he asked, wondering at her behaviour.

"I fear that I am," she said, but with a charming smile which eased his anxiety. "I am ready to return to Longbourn."

He glanced at the crowd by the church door, knowing that his place—and hers—was there. "May I have the honour of accompanying you, then?" he asked.

With an arch look, she said, "If you wish; but it is hardly a long walk."

"But in the right company, even a short walk is pleasant." They set off together, and, still curious about her decision to depart early, he asked, "Are there further preparations to be made for the wedding breakfast?"

She shook her head. "Everything is well in hand, I

believe; I simply prefer to arrive home before the guests do." She stole a quick glance at him. "I will not be attending the breakfast—I will be remaining upstairs."

He looked at her in concern, and was silent for a few moments. Finally, he had to ask. "Are you attempting to avoid my company, Miss Bennet?"

She was obviously surprised by his question. "No, indeed, sir; you are one of the very few people whom I am *not* attempting to avoid. You need have no concerns in that regard. I simply have no desire to attend an event at which half of the guests will be too embarrassed to speak to me, and the other half will be talking about me behind their hands, while I stand by myself pretending it does not matter."

"I cannot believe it will be so bad as that," he said reassuringly.

"You underestimate the ladies of Meryton, then."

"*I* will speak to you—and I will not leave your side if you will attend," he offered.

She looked down. "Thank you, sir; I appreciate your offer, but I fear it might create problems of its own. It is best that I stay away." She paused for a moment, then decided to address directly what she imagined his true concern was. "You will have other opportunities to see me, Mr. Darcy. You may even name a time, if it would make you happier."

He smiled dryly. "You may find this difficult to believe, Miss Bennet, but that is *not* my only concern. You have done nothing you need be ashamed of; will you allow this talk to chase you away on your sister's wedding day? That would seem to be practically an admission of guilt."

Her mouth set in a straight line. "Whether I have done anything to be ashamed of is a matter of opinion." Her tone made it evident that she was among those who believed in her guilt.

Darcy, troubled by the turn of her countenance, said, "There is no reason to feel shame for following your conscience."

"I am not troubled by my decision to terminate my engagement, Mr. Darcy. I cannot say the same for some of what came before. I have made misjudgements from which others have suffered, and it is not unreasonable that I should suffer for them as well."

"In that case, perhaps *I* should hide myself away as well—*you* know, perhaps better than any other, how grave some of my own errors have been. One of them has only been put to right today."

She smiled mirthlessly. "Perhaps, but you *have* put it to right, and our society is notoriously more lenient on gentlemen than ladies in these matters."

Her comment led a different matter to the forefront of his mind, and he turned a look of some intensity on her. She could feel her cheeks growing warm. His voice low, he said, "There is one matter you could put to right with no more than a word."

"Only if I were willing to solve one problem by creating a host of others," she responded gently.

He sighed. "Well, I have said I will not press you. But it does grieve me to see you hold yourself to an impossible standard. Why can you not forgive yourself, when you seem to have little difficulty in overlooking the fact that I was very nearly responsible for ruining two of your sisters' happiness?"

She gave him a questioning look. "*Two* of them?" she asked, in a voice almost teasing. "Is there something I am unaware of?"

He flushed. "Surely it has not passed your notice—it was owing to my misguided pride that Mr. Wickham's character was not more generally known. It was my unwillingness to expose my actions to the world that allowed him to deceive your sister, and I fear she may yet suffer for it, given his character."

She looked at him gravely. "I can hardly blame you, sir, for doing everything you could to protect your sister's reputation."

"At the expense of other people's sisters and daughters."

"Well, Mr. Darcy," she said with laughter in her voice, "I do not think I shall believe you when you tell me not to blame myself, since you do such an impressive job of taking responsibility for matters beyond your control."

He bowed slightly, looking amused. "Your point is well taken."

Elizabeth allowed a smile to play about her lips. It was odd that she seemed able to confide her feelings to Mr. Darcy when she had declined on more than one occasion to speak even to Jane on the matter. His interest and concern for her were undeniably gratifying, and she knew she could rely upon his secrecy, but she could not justify her choice. It seemed, she thought with unwonted seriousness, as if his very intentness upon her made it natural to put her confidence in him—but it was more than that as well. Even when she had disliked his manners, she had known him to be a man of profound loyalties, one who was responsible and steadfast. She bit her lip, realizing how difficult it might prove to hold herself aloof from him.

Darcy's thoughts had apparently been running in not dissimilar lines. "Why did you break off your engagement?" he asked in a voice that betrayed his emotion.

It was as if she could suddenly sense his presence with her entire body. Her arms tingled with an awareness of him, and it became unexpectedly difficult to breathe. "I realized I was marrying him for the wrong reasons," she said quietly. She *would* control this vulnerability to him; she was determined.

"What were those reasons?" He knew how improper it was to ask, but he could not stop himself.

She bit her lip again. "So as not to disappoint either my family or his."

This seemed to be enough to satisfy him, at least for the moment, since he did not ask further; or perhaps it was just that they were arriving at Longbourn. She knew she should be relieved, and could not explain a small feeling of discontent that this should be so.

"Will you attend the breakfast with me, at least for a

little?" His voice held a certain humble supplication she was not accustomed to from him, and it discomposed her.

"Is it so important to you?" she asked, feeling herself wavering.

*Important, that she would have the courage to appear in public with me? What does she think?* he asked himself, but aloud he said only, "Yes, it is."

She thought for a moment, then responded with that twist of humour which so enchanted him. "Very well, sir," she said archly, "if only to demonstrate to you how very perilous it can be to face the ladies of Meryton."

He felt a surge of relief, not so much for her decision as for the fact that she had decided it in his favour; in some ways, this was a far greater concession than allowing him to kiss her. "I will do my best to mount a defense against such formidable opponents," he said dryly.

She raised an eyebrow knowingly. "The tame tigers, perhaps?"

It took him a moment to connect the reference to their conversation months earlier. "The tame tigers would be an excellent choice," he agreed, his tone light but with underlying meaning. "They can be quite ferocious in guarding their own."

The manner in which he was looking at her sent shivers of anticipation down her spine. She *knew* he would not kiss her, not in the house with servants wandering past to set up the breakfast, but she also knew he was wishing to do so, and were the circumstances different, he would. She touched her tongue to her dry lips and said, "It is perhaps fortunate for the ladies of Meryton, then, that I belong to no one but myself."

He looked at her intently. "You always will belong to no one but yourself; but there are some who choose to bind themselves with silken cords of love."

"And some find themselves so bound whether they choose it or not," she said with rueful amusement.

His eyes flared. Elizabeth, abruptly realizing the damning admission she had just made, coloured deeply, and frantically searched for some way of lessen its import. If only she could think clearly! But her mind seemed to lose its usual quickness when he looked at her in that manner. Fortunately, she was rescued by the timely arrival of Mr. and Mrs. Bingley and the wedding guests.

More alarmed by the prospect of remaining in Darcy's immediate company than of the gossip and possible shunning she might receive, she made her way quickly to the table where she busied herself with making tea. Having a task to perform seemed her best defense, she thought. She kept her eyes on her work as she poured out the tea, her insides churning, wondering what Mr. Darcy was thinking. She glanced up to see him engaged in conversation with Miss Bingley.

What was she to do? She seemed to betray herself at every turn, no matter how firmly she was resolved to keep her distance. Her difficulty lay, she decided, in the fact that she did not *want* to stay away from him; she needed to accept the existence of these traitorous impulses if she was to have any success in controlling them. What was it he had asked of her—not to deny what lay between them? Well, he must be satisfied in that regard now, she thought philosophically. He had known precisely what to ask of her to obtain what he wanted; it was only in her denial of the reality of his love for her that she had remained safe to keep her own impulses towards him in check.

She handed out cups of tea mechanically. *At least he found a way to distract me from worrying over whether I will be ostracized!* she thought, her lips curving in amusement.

"Miss Bennet!" A voice broke into her reveries, and she turned to face Mrs. Covington. She flushed; in her concern over Darcy, she had completely forgotten the Covingtons would likely be present. Apart from a moment in passing at the church, she had not seen either of them since the painful day when she had gone to Ashworth to break off her engagement. She had seen his mother first that day, and, although she had not disclosed to her the purpose of her visit, the change in the older woman's demeanour had been clear. *She* would never have tolerated behaviour like Lydia's in one of her children, and it had been evident that the taint of the Bennets' disgrace clung to Elizabeth in her eyes. Elizabeth had felt this rebuff quite keenly at the time; she had come to feel a certain closeness to Mrs. Covington over the months of her engagement. That, as much as Mr. Covington's look of bewilderment and pain when she announced her purpose, had been the reason Elizabeth had left Ashworth House in tears, feeling all her bridges had been burnt. His mother's coolness had the benefit, however, of saving Elizabeth from feeling something like regret when she considered the implications of her decision.

"Mrs. Covington," she said politely, conscious that they would be the object of much scrutiny on the part of the other guests. She noted that the older woman appeared more frail than when they had last met, and recalled with a twinge her prediction that she would not live out the winter.

"This must be a very happy day for you," she said, looking over at Jane.

"I am very happy for Jane," she replied quietly, wondering at her purpose in bringing up the obviously tender issue of marriage.

"I imagine she will do quite well," Mrs. Covington predicted in her decisive way. "I hope you will as well. I never had the opportunity to tell you, my dear, that I admired the way you handled yourself when that business arose. I am sorry matters had to turn out as they did; it just demonstrated that I had been right in thinking you had the courage and determination to meet the task of being mistress of Ashworth. It is a pity it was not to be." She paused to catch her breath, then added, "I hope you have not been unduly troubled by petty gossip." She tilted her head towards where a group of women were sitting.

Elizabeth, stunned by both her communication and her

extreme frankness in such a setting, could only say, "No, not unduly."

"I am glad of it. Well, my dear, I wish you well in whatever the future brings you." She reached over and, to Elizabeth's astonishment, gave her a light embrace.

Elizabeth had time only to murmur her thanks before Mrs. Covington left her to rejoin the other guests. She found herself grateful once more for the business of pouring tea, which allowed her a few moments to compose herself. It was gratifying to know that Mrs. Covington did not think really ill of her—*only of my connections*, she thought, with a glance at Darcy. The unexpected encounter had moved her beyond what she would have anticipated; she suspected Mrs. Covington had deliberately staged it as something of a farewell gift, aimed at demonstrating to those who might have assumed otherwise that she still thought well of Elizabeth.

She felt a shiver travel down her arms, and knew without looking that Darcy had materialized by her side. She turned and held out a cup of tea to him. "Tea, Mr. Darcy?" she said.

He accepted it with thanks, his gaze fixed on her. He could tell she was disquieted, and wondered whether he was the cause. She had seemed to flee from him earlier after her astonishing and clearly unintended disclosure, yet surely she must know that he could do nothing to act upon it in this company. It did not seem to be the case that she was being shunned—certainly the woman she had just been speaking to had seemed happy enough to see her. Perhaps she was upset he had not followed her immediately? "I apologize for failing to remain at your side, Miss Bennet; I was… waylaid," he said, glancing at Miss Bingley.

With a small smile, she said, "Yes, so I observed. You need not worry, sir; I have been managing tolerably well on my own."

His look showed that he was pleased she was doing well, but he teased her by saying, "Pity. I had been hoping to prove indispensable to you."

He was quite dangerous to her peace of mind when he flirted playfully like this, she reflected. "I am sorry to prove again a disappointment to you, sir," she said impishly. "I release you from your pledge to stay by me today, in any case—I fear it might cause some talk."

The smile that played about his lips somehow produced a sense of heat within her. "Only if I may then claim the right you offered earlier to name another time to enjoy your company," he replied, his eyes promising he would take full advantage of such a time.

She coloured, but saw no choice but to agree. He said, "Tomorrow morning, then, before I leave for London?"

She raised an eyebrow quizzically to cover an odd sense of disappointment. "You are leaving so soon, then?"

His lips quirked. "It seems only polite to give the newly-weds a little privacy," he said. His eyes travelled slowly down her figure in a manner which made her flush. "You may depend upon it, Miss Bennet, I will return soon."

She watched as he took his tea and went over to join her father, who welcomed him into a conversation with Mr. and Mrs. Gardiner. She was again surprised by his agreeable air—he looked comfortable enough that, had she not known better, she would have thought he was well acquainted with the Gardiners.

There was a lull in the need for her services, and she took the time to look about the room. Ordinarily she would have mingled with the guests, but under the circumstances she thought it best to wait for others to approach her. Finally Maria Lucas came over and asked her about her time in London, a gesture Elizabeth appreciated; then some other girls joined in, and she breathed a little easier.

She was distracted from the conversation when Mr. Covington brought his cup back himself. She knew him well enough to recognize his look of trying to perform an unpleasant duty with as much grace as possible. "Good day, Miss Bennet," he said formally. "I hope you are well?"

She felt a surge of guilt. "Well enough," she said softly, wishing she could somehow ease the pain she had caused. "And you?"

"Well enough," he echoed. "I understand you have been in London. I hope your stay was pleasant."

"My aunt and uncle were most kind. I did not go out much; I preferred to spend my time with my nieces and nephews, or in quiet reflection." She hoped he could hear the unvoiced concern in her words. "I was glad to see your mother still in good health," she said a little awkwardly. She wished their first meeting could have been at any occasion other than her sister's wedding; it must have been bitter for him that Bingley, far less tied to Meryton society and with the greater freedom his wealth gave him, had failed to accept Jane's offer to release him from their engagement following Lydia's disgrace. He could not have known there was nothing he could have said that would have swayed Elizabeth from her course.

He thanked her and took his leave, leaving Elizabeth somewhat downcast. Since the termination of their engagement she had made an effort to think as infrequently as possible of Mr. Covington. It had all seemed so very clear at the time; while she had not objected to marrying a man for whom she felt no more than fondness, it became quite a different prospect when she faced doing so knowing she loved another. She had decided it would be better to be alone than to live such a lie, and she had the excuse of Lydia's disgrace to mask her deeper reasons.

Her reaction to seeing Mr. Covington now was enough to convince her she had been correct—though she had felt an active concern for him, her feelings were not those of a wife for her husband. Why then, she wondered, was she troubled by the loss of him? Perhaps it was more the loss of the life she had expected to lead with him she regretted. Throughout the previous summer, she had expended significant effort to accustom herself to the idea of being his wife, taking her place as mistress of Ashworth, and accepting his mother as hers. It had become a familiar and easy picture in her mind, at least until her unforeseen response to Mr. Darcy caused her to question it. Giving up that future was more than the loss of an abstract idea to her; it felt more like losing a part of her family. She had particularly looked forward to knowing his mother better—she had a good deal of respect for Mrs. Covington, and more than a little fondness. Now they were both lost to her—no matter what the future brought, there could be nothing between them, not even friendship.

As she turned back to Miss Lucas, attempting to disguise her low spirits from any watching eyes, she caught sight of Darcy, his gaze fixed on her with an expression of displeasure. Suddenly impatient with his single-minded focus on winning her, she did not acknowledge him, but resumed her conversation immediately. *Life, and affairs of the heart, are far more complicated than that*, she thought with a certain bitterness.

She was not in the least surprised to discover him at her side again almost directly. Boldly she turned to him and said somewhat brusquely, "Is anything the matter, Mr. Darcy?"

He raised an eyebrow at her tone. "I was merely contemplating the attractive idea of sending to Pemberley for the tigers," he said.

She was in no mood, after seeing Mr. Covington's discomfort, to hear Darcy's banter about his jealousy. "Why, surely we have no need of tigers in Hertfordshire," she said with deceptive sweetness.

ABIGAIL REYNOLDS

He smiled, a half-teasing look on his face. "Is that so? I am relieved to hear it," he said.

It was no different than a dozen other playfully insinuating remarks he had made to her that day, but for some reason it felt intolerable. She felt a surge of irritation rising at his evident expectations of her, and his teasing in face of Mr. Covington's pain seemed almost cruel. Her eyes flashing with feelings she could no longer contain, she said emphatically, "Good day, Mr. Darcy." She brushed past him to leave the room and the assembled guests, and did not stop until she reached the privacy her room.

The tumult of her mind was now painfully great. She sat in a chair and for some time held her hands over her face as tears ran down her cheeks. She was not even certain why she was crying, or what she regretted; it seemed so much had gone awry as to leave no hope of finding her way out.

It was all too much—seeing Jane's happiness in contrast to her own confusion and distress, all her sister's hopes and dreams coming true while her own were in ashes; then being taken so off guard by Mr. Darcy as to admit far more than she ever intended. And to come full face with the mistakes she had made in terms of Mr. Covington—no, it was intolerable.

She was not at all reconciled to the manner in which her decision had affected Mr. Covington. She knew now from hard experience how painful it was to love hopelessly, and could not forget she had caused him to feel that same pain. It was owing to a long series of misjudgements on her part that he was injured, starting with her cavalier acceptance of Wickham's story and continuing to her misjudgement and refusal of Mr. Darcy, and not least her failure to attend to her own sensibilities in choosing to accept Mr. Covington. She could not quite forgive herself for that, especially since she could not deny that mercenary sentiments had a role in her decision. She was not unaware that this sword of practicality cut both ways; along with the pain and confusion she had seen in his face when she broke off their engagement had been a certain relief. Just as she could not ignore his position, he could not overlook the effect Lydia's behaviour would have on the reputation of their family if he persisted in his plans to marry her. She did not blame him; it was only sensible. She supposed she should be grateful he had allowed her to end it rather than disgracing her further by jilting her.

Nor could she feel happy about Darcy's return to Hertfordshire. Was love not meant to include a desire for the beloved's presence? She could not deny feeling a thrill whenever she saw him, nor an answering response in herself when he gazed at her with passion in his dark eyes. It was not the sort of pleasure which led to contentedness, though, and therein lay her difficulty.

She had laboured hard to find a kind of peace after he had left Hertfordshire and she had broken her engagement. She had never been under the illusion that there could be anything more between them, and facing her feelings for him was only the beginning. She had ached for him night after night lying awake in London, missing him, missing his dry sense of humour and the familiar look in his eyes, and remembering the sensation of heat that had stolen through her when he had kissed her. It was a long time before she learned to master this pain, to set it aside so as to be able to enjoy the everyday pleasures of life again. Finally, she had reached the point of acceptance. Her lot in life, while not what she would have chosen, was one she had learned eventually to face without being unduly burdened by grief.

Then he had returned, bringing back all her longings, and refusing to acknowledge they could be nothing more than friends. With each approach he challenged her hard-won equanimity, tempting her to believe in a future that could never be, and then she must face all the pain of loss again.

She blamed no one but herself for part of it; she wanted so badly to believe in his fantasies, to believe she could marry him without irreparable damage to his reputation. He seemed unable to imagine he could ever face society's disapprobation. She knew differently—the blow to her pride caused by her fall from grace in the eyes of the community had undershored her natural resilience. He would see it differently once he found suitors shunning his beloved younger sister owing to the disgraceful match he had made. And if the pain of doing without him now was excruciating, she could not imagine how much worse it would be to see him withdraw his affection later, and to spend the remainder of her life knowing he regretted marrying her. She had seen the results of such an inequity of status and reputation clearly enough in her parents' marriage, and knew she could never bear that.

At the same time, she wished she *could* make him happy—oh, what a miserable dilemma it was! She recalled the look on his face when she had left him—why had she taken her anger at a situation of her own making out on him? So many people had been made unhappy owing to her misjudgements—Darcy himself, Mr. Covington, Mrs. Covington, and her own mother, not to mention her. She did not know how she was ever to forgive herself.

She glanced out the window, and her gaze was arrested by a familiar figure, seeming to be looking over the gardens. He was bare-headed and without his overcoat, but he did not seem to notice the chill. He was clearly unaware of her observation, and she took the rare pleasure of allowing herself to gaze her fill at him, feeling her affection and admiration for him wash through her. She imagined being held in his strong arms and laying her head upon his shoulder, and coloured as she remembered the shockingly pleasurable sensation of his kisses.

She could tell by the set of his shoulders that he was unhappy. *Why would he not be?* she thought sadly. She wanted nothing more that the chance to make him happy, to see the startling brilliance of his rare smiles. She wondered how he looked when he was truly content; she suspected she had never seen him in that state. If only she could offer that to him! But that would only be trading present joy for future unhappiness.

But was there any reason to deny herself his company and

the unique sense of being fully alive she experienced in his presence? She rationalized that as long as she remained clear as to her position, it could do no harm.

❦

Darcy had been staring at the gardens for some time, but if asked, would have been unable to name a single item he had noticed. He was wishing, not for the first time, that he could go back in time and behave differently. *He* had been so filled with happiness from Elizabeth's admission of loving him that it barely occurred to him she might *not* be happy, though she could not have said any more directly that this event would be painful for her. He had been at least feeling solicitous of her welfare up to the moment when she had started speaking with Covington. A blind rush of jealousy had taken him then, and instead of feeling concern for her sensibilities, he had gone charging over to demand reassurance, of all things.

A rustling noise behind him alerted him he was no longer alone, and he attempted to school his features into a semblance of calm. He was surprised to discover it was Elizabeth coming towards him, carrying his greatcoat and hat.

She held the items out to him. "It is too cold to be outside unprotected," she said, her musical voice quiet. "I would not have you take a chill, Mr. Darcy."

"You are most kind." He donned the proffered garments, thinking that he could quite easily accustom himself to the idea of Elizabeth being solicitous of him. "Thank you for coming down again, and thus giving me the opportunity to apologize for my insensitivity earlier."

She looked up at him and shook her head slightly. "You did nothing, sir; I should not have taken my anger out on you."

He had no desire to pursue the matter further, since if she had not been angry at him, it followed that it was talking to Covington which upset her. This was not an implication he wished to consider, yet for Elizabeth's sake he was willing to do worse. He steeled himself, then said, "It must have been difficult for you to see Mr. Covington again."

She sighed. "I know he is very disappointed, and that troubles me. I know it is my fault, and I would never have agreed to marry him in the first place were I not fond of him, so naturally I do not like to see him in pain." It occurred to her this was a very odd conversation to be having with Darcy under the circumstances.

Darcy was in fact wrestling with himself. He did not want Elizabeth even to be fond of Covington. *At least it is only fond!* he thought. It was the look on her face which finally convinced him of what he needed to do; she was clearly distressed, and alleviating her distress had to come before his own selfish desire to hear nothing further of Covington.

Carefully he said, "I can see why that would be difficult."

She glanced at him in surprise. "It was his mother who upset me more," she confessed.

"Was she unkind?"

"Not at all; she told me how much she respected me for what I had done, and that she was sorry..." Elizabeth was horrified to hear her voice tremble. What was it about Darcy that could so undercut all her defenses?

"You are fond of her as well?" he ventured.

She nodded. "I have a great deal of respect for her. She is not in good health, and has not long to live. I had assumed I would be the one caring for her through her last illness, and as it is... I shall most likely never see her again."

The tears she had fended off before would not be denied any longer. She turned her face away as she began to cry in earnest.

Darcy, acutely aware that they could be seen from the house, could do no more than give her his handkerchief and observe her in compassionate silence. He wished he had some comfort to offer her, but he knew there was none. He hated the helplessness of watching her pain, but could not deny a certain relief in discovering Mrs. Covington's importance to Elizabeth. What had she given earlier as her reason for wanting to marry Covington—*to please my family and his*? Yes, he could see how it would hurt her, and he could muster more sympathy for this grief than for any pain she felt over losing Covington.

Gradually Elizabeth regained her composure. Dabbing at her eyes, she exclaimed with guilt, "I am truly sorry, Mr. Darcy. You are the last person I should be troubling with these matters."

He looked at her intently. "Do not apologize—I *want* to

be the one you turn to with your troubles, no matter what causes them, and regardless of my like or dislike of the subject. As it happens, in this case I am… not uninvolved."

The level of emotion in his voice moved her, and she raised her eyes to his. The intensity she found there shook her deeply, and she felt helpless as though before an onslaught. Unconsciously she bit her lip, trying to prevent tears from recurring.

He seemed to sense her discomfort. His voice was gentle as he said, "But you do not need me to add to your troubles today, Miss Bennet. Suffice to say I hope you will always feel able to confide in me."

Dropping her eyes, she thanked him in a quiet voice. She suggested they return inside then, having made the discovery that his gentleness and sympathy were a far greater threat to her resolve than his jealousy and anger.

Darcy made his appearance at Longbourn the following morning just as Mrs. Bennet, Kitty, and Mary were preparing to leave for Meryton to visit Mrs. Phillips for the pleasure of dissecting each moment of Jane's wedding. He was surprised by the alacrity with which Mrs. Bennet consigned him to Elizabeth's care, leaving them unchaperoned.

Elizabeth herself did not appear to be in spirits, and he cautiously thanked her for staying at home to receive him.

"I had told you I would," she replied, "but you give me

credit where none is due. I was not invited to accompany my family to Meryton." From her tone of voice, it was evident that her mother's disapproval of her had not abated, nor had her distress in it.

"I am sorry for your sake," he said gently, "although grateful for my own—it is an unexpected pleasure to be granted the privilege of being alone with you."

"It is not so difficult to achieve. I am not thought to be worth the trouble of chaperoning any more since I have no reputation left to protect," said Elizabeth with more than a little bitterness.

He could not bear seeing his vivacious Elizabeth reduced to this state. He caught her hands in his, waiting until she met his eyes directly. "You must stop this. Your mother's is not the only opinion in the world. Your sister and Mr. Bingley do not agree, nor do I, and I would imagine your aunt and uncle did not treat you thus when you were in London," he said forcefully. When she did not respond other than to drop her eyes, he added, "Did they?"

"No, they were very kind," she said quietly.

"Your father—I know he would not reject you," he said insistently.

"No, he has not," she said, a trace of a smile beginning to appear.

"I hope you do not consider your mother to be an expert on propriety," he said, with such an obvious effort to hide his distaste with the very idea that she could not help but laugh.

"She is more angry with me than shocked by my behaviour," she admitted. "It was a great disappointment to her that I did not marry Mr. Covington. And I know she was trying to do her best for me in her own way by pushing me into the marriage."

"That," he said rather savagely, "just proves her lack of judgement."

"Well, I know you have a completely unprejudiced view of the matter," said Elizabeth with the absolute solemnity which indicated she was teasing.

"Perhaps I *am* a bit biased," he acknowledged. "Hopefully your mother will consider me an adequate substitute for Mr. Covington."

The look of dismay on her face was not feigned. The idea of her mother realizing Darcy's intentions towards her was not a happy one. "Mr. Darcy, I have not changed my mind," she said quickly.

"I remain the eternal optimist," he said softly.

She could not help but smile at how he used her own words against her. "I would not wish for you to be hurt in any way."

"The only way you could hurt me would be by telling me you do not care, and I do not believe you could say that truthfully," he said.

She looked away, embarrassed, not knowing what to say.

"Your honesty is one of the many things I love about you," he continued softly. "Although you may in jest profess opinions not your own, I know that in matters of importance you would never deceive. I know very few women who would be so honest as to face the consequences of terminating an engagement rather than live a lie. Quite apart from my personal interest in the matter, it only makes me admire you more."

Elizabeth's eyes remained on the floor, her cheeks flushed. She could not think how to tell him it had not been a matter of virtue in her mind, but a matter of necessity, that her love for him would have haunted her every day and stood between her and her husband forever.

Darcy, seeing only that she was allowing him to speak his heart to her for the first time since he had taken her by surprise at Hunsford, continued. "Do you not know why I could not give you up, despite everything that stood between us? There is no other woman for me than you; no other with your bewitching combination of liveliness of mind, kindness of heart, honesty, and willingness to speak your mind. You captured my heart so long ago I can hardly remember what it was not to love you, and giving you up when I thought you loved Covington was the hardest and bitterest thing I have ever done. I would do more than that, though, if I believed it would make you truly happy, but you cannot ask me to give you up now that I finally know you care."

She did not know how to maintain her distance in face of his tenderness. Numbly she said, "I cannot see my way clear to it, Mr. Darcy."

He tipped her chin up with his finger until her eyes met his. She saw a gentleness there which went beyond her expectations. "Then take your time, my dearest; you have been through far too much difficulty of late. Is it too much to ask for you to think about it while I am away, remembering that I see no impediment?"

She shook her head wordlessly, mesmerized by the depths of his dark eyes. He was so close, her skin tingling where his thumb caressed the back of her hand. She recognized the look of desire on his face, and wondered absently if he could see it in her as well. The aching for him which had haunted her nights returned to her in force. *I have let him kiss me twice; will a third time matter?* she thought, her mind floating dizzily on a current of longing. Almost as an extension of her thought she tilted her face toward him slightly, and that was all the invitation he needed.

Their lips met with the tentativeness of those who know they are risking hard-won self-control. For Elizabeth, it was almost unbearably sweet, the sense of completion she felt when they joined so, and the pleasure it produced deep within her. How was she to refuse when her own body delighted so in his kisses? It seemed that in his touch he spoke so deeply to her that she had no choice but to be honest in return.

It required great strength of will for Darcy not to move beyond light kisses when her scent was washing over him and she was being so sweetly responsive. It did not help knowing that once he stopped taking his pleasure of her lips, she would return to refusing him—who could resist the temptation to take, and keep taking, the part of her which was giving him the answer he so much desired?

He moved his hands to touch her cheeks lightly as they continued to kiss, the silken softness of her skin tantalizing him with all it promised. Giving in to the temptation to caress the lines of her neck which he had so often admired from afar, he allowed his fingers to explore freely down to her shoulders. When her soft moan of pleasure against his lips tempted him to taste all the delights her mouth had to offer, he had to force himself to draw back.

Feeling somehow bereft without his touch, Elizabeth abruptly gained recognition of her unconscionable behaviour. What was he to think, when she refused his hand but permitted such liberties? She coloured and looked away.

He seemed to read her thoughts. "Do not regret it, my sweetest Elizabeth," he said. "I have only two regrets—first, that I lacked sufficient self-control to continue, and then that I have not the right to do it in the first place. For my part, if you find my kisses persuasive, I have no complaint to make. I am not averse to employing such arguments." He smiled at her, then brushed his lips lightly against her own once more.

*You must stop this before it goes even further!* she thought anxiously, worried by how easy it was to allow him touch her at will. Aloud she said, "Perhaps we might discuss something else, Mr. Darcy."

"Why do I assume you are not referring to the question of whether you might call me by my name?" he teased.

She gave him a baleful glance. He added with a smile, "No, I did not think so."

It was hard to remain vexed with him when he was being so charming. His behaviour was at least superficially correct for the remainder of his visit, though the warmth of his glances, had they spoken in words instead of looks, could not have been considered proper. Elizabeth found she could not keep her inner self from responding to these looks, nor from desiring more of them.

When he finally rose to leave, she found she was more disappointed than she had anticipated, but was determined to keep it hidden. "I hope your journey is an easy one," she said lightly, then undermined her own position by looking up at him through her lashes. "Please do give my regards to the tigers. I hope they are in better spirits now."

He gave her a look of amusement which spoke volumes. "The tigers are quite content now, I believe—apart from being very, very hungry," he said meaningfully.

She could not stop herself from raising an eyebrow. "Why, then you should feed them better, sir," she said impudently.

His eyes darkened. He pushed the sitting room door closed with his shoulder, and in the same move, put an arm around her waist and pulled her to him. She gasped, but made no struggle, and the manner in which she put her hands to his shoulders and held them there did not bespeak rejection.

When he saw her fine eyes looking up at him questioningly, her body against his, he could no longer hold back; his mouth caught hers and took advantage of her surprise to deepen the kiss, expressing all the passionate need for her he had denied himself earlier.

As her shock at his action gave way to comprehension, the excitement he stirred in her grew until she met him halfway. How her arms had found their way around his neck, she could not have answered—she only knew that the feeling of his hard body pressed against her filled a void she had never known existed, even while it created new and even deeper needs in her.

It ended as abruptly as it had begun, and they were both breathless when Darcy released her. He could not believe what he had done—how could he have lost control of himself in such a manner? What would she think of him? He had to remember that this was the real and innocent Elizabeth, not the seductress of his dreams, to whom he could do so many intensely pleasurable things. If she knew the kind of thoughts he had of her, she would no doubt never let him in the door of her house—but what a temptation she presented! In an attempt to keep his hands from returning to her lovely body, he raked one hand through his hair. Dismayed at his conduct, he quoted ruefully, "'What the hand dare seize the fire?'"

"I beg your pardon?" asked Elizabeth, quite baffled.

"No, I should beg yours," he said contritely. "I am not

normally a barbarian." His grimace demonstrated how cha-
grined he was by his own actions.

She discovered that his discomposure somehow made it
easier for her to regain her own equanimity. Determined to
make light of what had occurred, she cocked her head to one
side and said judiciously, "No, for the most part, you are not.
It is likely just the influence of the tigers."

It took him a moment to realize she was teasing him;
then he smiled slightly and shook his head. "Do not see me
out, Miss Bennet—I do not want to get myself into further
difficulties." He reached out and traced her lips lightly with
his fingers, wishing he dared propose to her again. Despite his
intention, he leaned down to taste her lips gently once more.
"We will continue this…" he said, pausing to kiss her lightly
yet again, as if he could not deny himself. "We will continue
this conversation when I return." Finally he forced himself to
step away from her.

Her mouth quirked with amusement. "Good day, then,
Mr. Darcy," she said.

He opened the door, then turned back for a moment just as
he was departing. In a solemn voice, he said, "It is not always
wise to feed tigers—sometimes it only makes them hungrier."

Elizabeth blinked in surprise at his tone, but was reassured
when his devastating smile appeared. Without a further word,
he was gone.

She collapsed into her chair, feeling as if she had been
running hard. Despite her concern over what had occurred,

though, it was only a moment until she laughed at the thought of what her mother's attitude would be if only she knew. Now Elizabeth could truly say she had disgraced herself and her family by her behaviour, and yet if Mrs. Bennet had been aware of it, she would have been nothing but delighted by the news. *It is a pity she will never know!* mused her daughter.

# Chapter 6

ELIZABETH'S LAST FORTNIGHT AT Longbourn proved as distasteful as she had expected. She was beginning to doubt whether her mother's vexation with her would ever abate. Mrs. Bennet's want of propriety and inclination to complaint led her to be more vocal on the subject than another woman might have been, and her daughter could only do her best to turn a deaf ear to it. Her father's occasional gestures and words of support warmed her, but she still could wish he might do more to rein in his wife's behaviour in regard to her.

She was naturally relieved when the time came for her to remove to Netherfield, though there was a certain sadness attached to leaving her childhood home forever, especially under these circumstances. Although Bingley and Jane welcomed her warmly to their household, Elizabeth, conscious that they were still newlyweds and she had been invited to live with them as an act of charity only because it was untenable for her to remain at Longbourn, made an effort to leave the couple to their own devices as much as possible. She began to feel more comfortable as she realized that Jane was reassured by the familiarity of having Elizabeth with her, and that she could offer support and assistance as her sister took over the management of Netherfield House.

The thought of Darcy was a constant undercurrent during this time. She wondered where he was, what he was doing, and whether he was thinking of her; or whether, with more distance and time to reflect, he had come to acknowledge the seriousness of her reservations. The memory of his look and his kisses left her lying awake more than one night longing for him.

While she was still at Longbourn, her thoughts had been full of unhappiness and doubt, but gradually, once freed of the constraint of her family's disapproval, her usual sense of humour began to emerge once more. It did not hurt that winter was turning to spring, and she could resume her habit of long walks, although she now never went in the direction of Meryton except when absolutely necessary. She could even be in good spirits if she avoided the painful question of how she was to face life without Darcy. She was tired of self-pity, and did not want him to think her to be grieving. She decided that if he returned to Netherfield, he would meet with her wit this time instead of her sorrow, and she ignored the qualm which came with the thought he might *not* return.

But it was only a month or so until Bingley received a letter from his friend announcing his plans to arrive the following week, accompanied by his sister and Colonel Fitzwilliam. Bingley, who enjoyed the lively company of the latter gentleman, exclaimed with pleasure over this addition to the party. Elizabeth, however, was silent; the traitorous surge of excitement she felt at the thought of seeing him tempered by the knowledge that their struggle was not over; he would not be bringing his sister were he not still resolved on changing her mind.

As the day of his arrival approached, Elizabeth began to admit to herself just how much she had missed him. It was almost as if he were a part of her which had been lost, and was now returning. The depth of these emotions worried her, and caused her to revisit her decision more than once.

She could not find another solution, though. She remembered his words at Hunsford about his connection to her being a degradation, all Wickham had said of his pride, the descriptions of Pemberley she had heard from her aunt and Miss Bingley, and she knew it to be impossible. It had been unlikely at best before the events of the autumn, but the Mistress of Pemberley and wife of Mr. Darcy must not be touched by any hint of scandal, much less be sister to the steward's disreputable son and have a past with another man. Darcy might now, in the heat of passion and infatuation, be prepared to overlook it, but she could not imagine he would not eventually come to feel the shame and degradation of it.

It would break her heart to see him suffer it, and to know she was responsible for it.

Yet she knew she would weaken again in his presence, especially if he was as unrelenting as she rather suspected he would be. Flight seemed her only option. *I will stay a week, but no more,* she thought. *Surely I can manage one week.* Feeling a complete coward, she quickly penned a letter to her aunt Gardiner, asking if she could again pay them a visit.

On the day the guests were scheduled to arrive she found herself unaccountably nervous, and decided to walk out to calm herself. She was longer returning than she had expected, for when she reached Netherfield, Darcy's carriage was already being unhitched and the guests were inside. She took a deep breath before entering.

They were situated in the large sitting room. Elizabeth's eyes flew immediately to Darcy, where they were met with a gaze of such intensity as to make it impossible for her to turn away. His eyes told her everything he wished to be doing, and it did not stop at kisses; he looked at her as if he wanted to strip away every secret she possessed. She found herself becoming aroused in response, and quickly turned her attention to greeting Colonel Fitzwilliam, who seemed delighted to see her again.

Darcy presented his sister to her, and Elizabeth was astonished to see that Miss Darcy was at least as embarrassed as she. Mr. Wickham had described her as very proud; but the observation of a very few minutes convinced her that she was only exceeding shy. She found it difficult to obtain even a word from her beyond a monosyllable.

Miss Darcy was tall, and on a larger scale than Elizabeth; and, though little more than sixteen, her figure was formed, and her appearance womanly and graceful. She was less handsome than her brother, but there was sense and good humour in her face, and her manners were perfectly unassuming and gentle. Elizabeth, who had expected to find in her as acute and unembarrassed an observer as ever Mr. Darcy had been, was much relieved by discovering such different feelings.

"So there we were, making our annual pilgrimage to Rosings," said Colonel Fitzwilliam, who had clearly been in the midst of a tale when she had entered. "You cannot *imagine* how dull it was, and one day I was saying to Darcy how much more agreeable it had been last year, when you, Miss Bennet, and Miss Lucas were also in Kent. Imagine my surprise when Darcy told me he had just seen you again! It has been an age since I had seen Bingley here as well, so when he told me that, I could not resist the opportunity to join him."

Jane and Bingley both expressed their delight in his presence. Elizabeth, conscious of her position as a poor relation, said nothing, limiting herself to a smile of welcome.

Darcy could not take his eyes from her. She seemed more in spirits than when he had left, though her sober reaction on seeing him suggested she had not changed her mind about him. Well, he had been expecting that; he knew she was not

ABIGAIL REYNOLDS

a woman to be won over by a few kisses, and he had spent six weeks marshalling his arguments. For now, it was enough to be in her company and to see her smiles. Once he found a time to be alone with her, it would be different.

He was constantly aware of her presence, feeling alive in the way only she could make him, but had no opportunity even for guarded discourse until after dinner. When the gentlemen rejoined the ladies, Elizabeth without a word rose and moved to a corner of the room where she began to work on some embroidery. Jane cast a concerned glance after her, but said nothing.

Darcy was less than happy about Elizabeth establishing so clearly that she was not one of the hosts of the occasion, but he was not averse to taking advantage of the situation. He excused himself, then returned a moment later with a book in his hand. He sat in the chair nearest Elizabeth and said, "Miss Bennet, I hope I am not disturbing you."

She glanced up with a quick smile. "Not at all, sir."

"I brought you something from London." He handed her the volume.

Looking down at it, she said carefully, so that no one could overhear, "You know I cannot accept this, Mr. Darcy."

"Certainly you can. I will not tell a soul," he said with an engaging smile which wrought havoc on Elizabeth's equanimity. "Or you could consider it a permanent loan."

"It is not proper," she insisted.

"You could make it perfectly proper by accepting me," he

continued lightly. "Or you can refuse it utterly, but I will feel obliged to make a scene if you do."

A glance at his face was enough to reassure Elizabeth that he was teasing her. She narrowed her eyes and replied, "Very well; if it is that important to you to have me read it, I shall be happy to accept the *loan*. Thank you."

His smile broadened fractionally. Every concession from Elizabeth was one more step towards victory. "You are very welcome. I must mention there is little point in returning it, as I already have a copy in my library, and I did purchase this specifically with you in mind."

"You are quite incorrigible, Mr. Darcy, but you are not a whit more stubborn than I." Elizabeth opened it to the frontispiece and raised an eyebrow when she saw the title. "*Songs of Innocence and Experience?*" she asked dubiously. "I have never heard of it."

"Mr. Blake is not as well-known as he ought to be," allowed Darcy. "You might not want to admit to receiving it from me; he holds some rather scandalous religious and philosophical views. His poetry should not be missed, though."

"Interesting reading material you are choosing for me," she murmured, glancing at him teasingly from under lowered lashes. She flipped through the first few pages, noting the appealingly childlike illuminations accompanying each verse.

Darcy took the book from her hands for a moment, opened it to a page marked with a silken bookmark, and handed it back to her. She took one look at the drawing of a tiger at the bottom of the page and laughed delightedly, reading aloud,

> "Tyger! Tyger! burning bright
> In the forests of the night,
> What immortal hand or eye
> Could frame thy fearful symmetry?
> In what distant deeps or skies
> Burnt the fire of thine eyes?
> On what wings dare he aspire?
> What the hand dare seize the fire?"

She paused. "Is this meant to be a warning for me, Mr. Darcy?" she asked impudently.

"Merely a reflection, my dear Miss Bennet," he said with a sidelong glance.

> "And what shoulder, and what art,
> Could twist the sinews of thy heart?
> And when thy heart began to beat,
> What dread hand? and what dread feet?
> What the hammer? what the chain?
> In what furnace was thy brain?
> What the anvil? what dread grasp
> Dare its deadly terrors clasp?

"A valid question, sir."

"Read on," he requested.

> "When the stars threw down their spears,
> And water'd heaven with their tears,
> Did he smile his work to see?
> Did he who made the Lamb make thee?
> Tyger! Tyger! burning bright
> In the forests of the night,
> What immortal hand or eye
> Dare frame thy fearful symmetry?"

She looked at him with raised eyebrows. "And which is it, Mr. Darcy? Are the tigers of Pemberley creatures of God or of the Adversary?"

He gave a low laugh. "Surely that is for the reader to decide."

"But you must have some thoughts on the matter," she said mischievously. "After all, I am not so *experienced* with tigers as you are."

He gave her a look full of meaning. "Not for want of trying," he said.

They were interrupted at that moment by Colonel Fitzwilliam, who came to request that Miss Bennet favour them with some music. Elizabeth, covering with a mocking glance the disturbance which Darcy had created in her sensibilities, readily agreed. Darcy watched her walk off with his cousin with a mixture of satisfaction at how their encounter had gone and vexation with his cousin for interrupting and for having the presumption to smile at his Elizabeth.

The next day Darcy hoped to find some time with Elizabeth when they could be alone, but his hopes were doomed to frustration. While he likely could have stolen her away from Mr. and Mrs. Bingley easily enough, it was a different matter altogether with Georgiana, who did not expect to be dismissed, and was overwhelmed enough by being in an unknown place. Colonel Fitzwilliam also seemed to gravitate to Elizabeth's presence, making what seemed to Darcy to be a rather intolerable crowd. It was rather ironic, he reflected on more than one occasion, that he should be wishing two of his dearest relations far away, even though he had specifically brought Georgiana to Netherfield to become acquainted with Elizabeth. This endeavour had not had much success so far either, since Georgiana hardly said a word to anyone but him, and Elizabeth insisted on deferring to Jane as Georgiana's hostess in terms of spending time with her.

In the meantime, he found consolation in being the frequent subject of Elizabeth's teasing, which he interpreted as a sign of affection. There were a few intimate looks exchanged between them, and on one occasion, when everyone's attention was distracted, he managed to catch her hand in his own for a few minutes. While she did not acknowledge his action overtly, neither did she draw away. Still, he had hoped for much more; and staying under the same roof as Elizabeth was exciting both his fancy and his desire.

It was the third day of his stay before he saw his opportunity. Stealing away while Bingley was showing his cousin his prized collection of hunting rifles, and able to hear the distant sounds of his sister practicing the pianoforte, he sought out Elizabeth, hoping fiercely she would not be with Mrs. Bingley. It seemed he was in luck; he discovered her alone in the dining room, standing by the table with her head bent over an arrangement of flowers. He stopped a moment in the doorway to admire the picture she made as her hands moved deftly through the blossoms. Her back was to him, and his eyes were drawn to the nape of her neck where a few tiny rebellious curls escaped the tight confines of her hairstyle.

A surge of desire overcame him, and his intention to speak with her slipped to the recesses of his mind. Without any plan, he moved silently towards her and, putting his hands lightly on her hips, he placed a light but lingering kiss at the point where those tempting curls met her flesh. She stiffened, apparently in surprise, but made no move or protest, which he took as invitation enough to continue to explore her tender skin with his lips.

After the first shock of being taken unawares, Elizabeth felt paralyzed by the exquisite agony of desire his caresses were causing. How could he, merely by moving his lips against the back of her neck, cause her entire body to ache for him? Against her wishes, she had found herself waiting for his touch since his return, and it had been a long time in coming. She closed her eyes and her breathing came faster as he explored her shoulder, then followed a line up to her ear. She felt him nibble her earlobe, sending a shock of sensation through her until, unable to resist the temptation any longer, she turned her face to his to meet him in a kiss of desperate longing.

She had not believe it was possible to want a man's touch so badly. Nothing had prepared her for it; her response to Mr. Covington had been only lukewarm. It was as if she were a completely different woman with Darcy, one without shame, who could not have enough of the intense pleasure and arousal his touch afforded her.

Their mouths clung together passionately, meeting again and again as they sought to assuage the pain of their parting. Elizabeth sighed as she felt him slip his hands around her waist. As he drew her back against him, she felt a profound shock at the sensation of his body against hers. It was as if her entire body were coming to life in a new way, yet it also seemed so natural and so right. She pressed herself against him as if seeking more, but knew she could never have enough.

He whispered against her mouth, "Have you any idea how I have ached for you, my best beloved?"

His words opened a new well of need within her, and she kissed him as if wanting to draw his essence into herself. It seemed whenever he touched her that nothing else mattered in the world—not society, nor propriety, nor any rules or limits—only this conflagration burning between them.

Her need for his kisses was by no means sated when he heaved a sigh and buried his face in her hair. She attempted to still her breathing, but his arms were still around her, his thumbs caressing her body in a manner which sent shivers of fire through her. She could not concentrate on anything but those slight movements and the profound reaction they were eliciting from her, igniting a desire which came from her most secret self.

Darcy had hungered for her for too long; though he was able to force himself to stop kissing her, it only drew his attention that much more to the feeling of her soft body against his. He wondered vaguely how much longer he would be able to stop himself at kisses, and even whether Elizabeth wished him to or not. The thought itself was so provocative as to make his lips return to hers.

He murmured, "Please tell me you have reconsidered," though he knew within his heart she had not.

"I cannot," she said, her conflict evident in her voice.

He could not stop himself. "How can you kiss me like this and still refuse me?" he asked.

She could hear his frustration with her. It was a question she had asked herself repeatedly while he was away—how could she allow it, and be so shameless as to wish to do it again when she knew there could be nothing more between them? She could not be his wife, and would not be his mistress. "I do not know," she whispered. "I do not know!"

"You cannot deny you want to be with me," he insisted.

It was unanswerable, so she avoided the point. "Passion is a poor predictor of felicity—I must listen to my rationality,," she said. "Kisses are simple. Life is not."

"No, life is not simple, but that is no reason to let past errors dictate future mistakes! I have considered it time and again, and each time the answer is the same—having you is worth far more than any potential loss from social consequences."

"So it seems now," she said tiredly, removing his hands from her waist and stepping away. She hated this conflict between them. "It may seem very different in a year or two."

He looked at her with distress in his eyes. "Do you really distrust me as much as that?"

"If you call it distrust of you to fear the impact of society's judgement and past sins coming back to haunt me, then yes," she said in deep frustration. She wanted only his love, his embraces, and his kisses, yet all she could do was quarrel with him.

Their eyes battled, then he gave a sigh of defeat, and held his arms open to her. She did not even stop to think before she went into them, laying her head upon his shoulder and taking the momentary comfort she could in his embrace.

"Can you give me something—anything?" he asked quietly, his voice ragged.

*So this is heartbreak,* she thought. She looked up at him and said gently, "We both want the same things, my dear—we disagree only as to whether they are possible." She could feel his chest rising and falling with each breath.

An edge of determination entered his voice. "I am still resolved, you know."

She could not help laughing. "I would be a fool to think otherwise," she said ruefully.

They heard the voices of Bingley and Colonel Fitzwilliam approaching, and sprang apart guiltily; but Darcy's eyes continued to assure Elizabeth that he was far from giving up.

❧

Darcy was not slow to recognize the error he had made by pressing Elizabeth too hard. He determined that his best strategy lay in wearing down her resistance, and realized one of his strongest weapons lay in the pleasure he could give her by touching her. She could refuse him with words and looks, but when he kissed her, the truth of her feelings seemed inevitably to come out. *He* could not change her mind, but perhaps with enough time and enough familiarity with him, she would change it for herself.

Having determined there was no reason to deny himself, especially since he had every intention of marrying her, he seized every opportunity to steal kisses from her, and when this was not possible, at least to find a way to unobtrusively touch the back of her hand. He did not raise the subject of marriage again, concentrating as much as possible on being agreeable to Elizabeth. He was civil when her family called at Netherfield, even to Mrs. Bennet, whose appearance inevitably led to a rapid disappearance on the part of her second daughter. Once he was even fortunate enough to discover Elizabeth during one of these times of flight, and was able to offer her the solace of his embrace. He was encouraged that she no longer fought off his comfort in times of distress, and pleased he could give it to her.

Elizabeth would not have disagreed with his assessment that her resistance was weakening. Although she made every effort to disguise it, her resolve seemed to flag each time they were together. Her strongest defense came from knowing she would leave soon, and so need not resist long. But as the days passed without a response from her aunt, she began to worry.

Finally a letter came, but not with an answer to satisfy her. Mrs. Gardiner was very apologetic, but confessed it was not the best time for a visit; her brother and his family were staying with them for a time, and the house on Gracechurch Street was not large. She suggested perhaps Elizabeth might come to them in the autumn, if that were convenient for her.

Elizabeth was taken aback by this; it had not occurred to her that her request might be denied. As she considered it further, though, she came to the guilty realization that a great deal had already been asked of the Gardiners in terms of care for wayward nieces. First Jane had spent months with them the previous winter, pining over the loss of Mr. Bingley, then they were forced to deal with the vexation and very real financial stresses of Lydia's elopement and wedding. By the time they had taken in Elizabeth, fleeing from the effects of her broken engagement, and apparently grieving over it, they must have already been feeling the stress, although they never let it be known, any more that they had admitted to laying out money to bring about Lydia's wedding. With four young children of their own, they could not have avoided feeling the burden.

In a paroxysm of guilt, Elizabeth immediately wrote back to Mrs. Gardiner, making light of her own request and thanking her for all she had already done. She painted as rosy a picture of her life with the Bingleys as she dared, and sent it off, hoping for the best.

This left her, however, in a position of having nowhere to go. She considered her other alternatives—Longbourn hardly seemed a viable option, and Darcy would not let three miles stop him in any case. She even debated the possibility of writing to Charlotte, but the words of the condemning letter Mr. Collins had sent Mr. Bennet on the occasion of the ending of her engagement still remained fresh in her mind. No, she would not be welcome at Hunsford for quite some time, if ever.

Finally, with resignation, she accepted that she had no choice but to stay and somehow manage to deal with Darcy. She had no answers as to how she might do this; none but the treacherous one which drew her more each day she spent in his company. She had by this time given up any pretense that she was not hoping for more of his kisses, and it went hard with her because she felt the fundamental hypocrisy of her position, and was disturbed to acknowledge her own weakness.

Her distraction was evident the rest of the day. Darcy was solicitous, going so far as to ask if she had received any distressing news. Lacking time alone with her, though, he could not discover anything.

By the next morning, Elizabeth had resolved to put the best face on her disappointment. She determined that she could only proceed one day at a time, and fretting about the future benefited her not at all. Her improved spirits were apparent, and she had lively discourse with the others at breakfast.

Later that day, Darcy returned from a ride to discover her playing and singing for a clearly enchanted Colonel Fitzwilliam. Darcy's usual pleasure in Elizabeth's performance was muted by his unhappiness over discovering this tête-à-tête, and he took a moment to school himself into calm before entering. Just then he heard Elizabeth's delighted laughter ringing out in response to some comment his cousin had made.

Without further consideration, he walked in wearing a cold look Elizabeth remembered well from his first visit to Hertfordshire. She raised an eyebrow, then turned to Colonel Fitzwilliam and said with a conspiratorial air, "Mr. Darcy looks quite fierce today—I hope we are not in his bad books!"

Colonel Fitzwilliam laughed and leaned closer to her. "Have no fear, Miss Bennet; he is never so fierce as he looks when the mood is upon him, but soon he will deign to smile on us mere mortals again."

Darcy, who would have cheerfully strangled his cousin at that moment, only scowled more fiercely. Elizabeth, perceiving that he was in truth offended, but not knowing why, said with concern, "Come, Mr. Darcy, will you not join us? Your cousin has been quite negligent in failing to select a new piece for me to play; perhaps you can do better."

"Nonsense, Darcy, it is my choice!" cried the colonel gaily as Darcy silently moved to the stack of music by the pianoforte.

Darcy's temper, already strained by the long days of uncertainty over Elizabeth and concern over the meaning of her withdrawn mood the previous day, reached the breaking point. "No, the lady says the choice is mine," he said with an edge to his voice, and deliberately placed his hand on Elizabeth's shoulder, encompassing both the top of her sleeve and the exposed skin above it.

She looked up at him in embarrassed surprise at this flagrant and uncharacteristic breach of propriety, but his attention was apparently on the music he was rifling through with his free hand. He chose a piece and placed it on the stand in front of her, directing a challenging look to his cousin as he did so. He then finally glanced down at Elizabeth's frowning visage. As if suddenly realizing what he was doing, he tightened his hand on her shoulder momentarily before releasing her.

Elizabeth was far too mortified to even look at Colonel Fitzwilliam. She could only imagine what he must be thinking of her, but between the grim look on Darcy's face and her natural disinclination to draw any more attention to his lapse, she saw no better course than to begin playing as if nothing had happened. She was nonetheless roused to silent resentment by his action, and when Colonel Fitzwilliam politely excused himself after her performance had ended, she turned on Darcy with anger.

"What, pray tell, was that show about? Or dare I guess that, having lost patience with my refusals, you have decided to *embarrass* me into marrying you?" she demanded indignantly.

Darcy, having already had some minutes to regain his temper and to recognize that he had made a gross error of judgement, did not hesitate to self-criticize, both out of native honesty and a desire to limit the repercussions of his behaviour. "You are quite right," he said penitently. "I had no business behaving in such a manner."

"I *know* you had no business—I am looking, sir, for an explanation!" she cried.

Darcy schooled himself to patience despite a desire to respond as vehemently. "I have no explanation, only a poor excuse—it is hard for me not to feel angry when my cousin flirts so openly with you."

"So you decided to demonstrate to him that I *belong* to you?" she asked acidly.

"I did not *decide* anything; my temper got the better of me, for which I apologize. I must remind you, however, that you have left me with little recourse, since you will not grant me the right to *say* anything to him!" said Darcy, his own irritation rising in response to her challenge. "And I cannot say I saw *you* doing anything to prevent his attentions."

Elizabeth grew white. "I suppose I can blame no one but myself if, after having seen my hypocrisy in accepting your kisses while refusing your suit, you should think I would be hypocritical enough to accept another man's attentions at the same time as well," she said icily, her feelings truly wounded. "Perhaps this will inspire me to overcome that fault. But in the meantime, I fail to see why you could not simply have told him at some private moment that you have intentions towards me, instead of this!"

"I had been of the opinion you wanted no one to know of my intentions," he retorted heatedly.

Elizabeth looked upwards, her foot tapping as she reminded herself unsuccessfully to have patience. "I would imagine Colonel Fitzwilliam would be able to keep the matter in confidence, would you not?" The humour of the situation suddenly became apparent to her, that she should be advising him to tell anyone at all of his interest in her, after having gone to such lengths to disguise it. "Or," she said slyly, "you could simply have told him we have a peculiar understanding that involves stealing kisses in deserted corners, and that you let the tigers feed on any man who dares to flirt with me."

Darcy did not know what to make of this sudden shift in her temper, and did not dare touch her for fear that he would be unable to stop in his present frame of mind. He sank down onto a sofa in deep frustration. Finally he said tiredly, "I *am* sorry, though you may not credit it. I am sorry to be so possessive when I have no right, and I certainly do not suspect you of any interest in other men. It is just this impossible situation where we can neither be together nor apart—and are we still to be stealing kisses in corners when I happen to visit Bingley ten years from now? Are we never to know the happiness of union between us?"

She could not bear the bitter discouragement in his voice. Sitting beside him, she impulsively put her arms around him. He rested his head against hers, accepting her comfort as she stroked his hair, and wishing this could be real and she would always be there for him.

Elizabeth could not decide what she should say—it seemed as if anything she could say to lessen his distress would also be encouraging him. Finally, feeling as if she must say *something*, she said, "I wish I had an answer, for both our sakes. I only wish for you to be happy, and I know that I am making you *un*happy. I wish there were anything I could do to make this easier, but if there is, I do not know what it is." She kissed his cheek as it lay near her mouth, more for reassurance than anything else.

"You could tell me you love me." His voice was muffled.

She took in a sharp breath. "Surely you know that already," she replied, feeling as if even this was more than she was ready to put into words. She was so vulnerable to him already; speaking of her feelings would only make her more so.

Although he said, "Yes, I do," she could feel his disappointment in the tension of his body.

It seemed that his distress made her vulnerable as well. "I do—I do love you," she said impulsively, wanting to ease his pain.

"Oh, Elizabeth," he whispered, gathering her closer to him. "Thank you, my best beloved." His mouth sought out hers, immediately causing a stirring within her as she gave herself over to him. As the familiar waves of desire pulsated within her, she could only think of how much she wanted to be his. She only hoped he would not press her on marriage again now, since she did not know that she could resist him at this moment.

His hand travelled down to explore the curves of her body, leaving trails of fire in its wake. She arched herself against him as her body demanded even more intimacy. His kisses seemed to be drawing her most inner self out, marking her as his forever.

Despite the danger, Darcy let his hands continue to claim her in a way he never had before, stroking and caressing her back, her arms, and going so far as to travel over her outer thigh. He could feel her surrender, and only prayed he would have the strength not to take advantage of it. "My dearest love," he murmured in her ear as he trailed kisses along her face and neck, "if you cannot accept me, at least tell me you will never send me away."

His words cut through the cloud of desire and longing

that enshrouded Elizabeth, bringing her back to reality painfully quickly. She struggled to regain control of herself, even while her body was trembling with need Darcy was all too happy to continue to fulfill. Finally, to be able to think clearly enough to respond, she caught his hands to prevent their roaming. "I cannot promise that, my love," she said, the need to say it paining her as much as she knew the hearing of it would hurt him. "There may come a time when I must do so."

Darcy stilled at her words, his face still buried in her neck. He understood immediately what she meant, and that it was a direct result of how far the passion flaring between them had taken them. He was probably fortunate she had stopped what was between them—he had been at the edge of losing control of himself, and he did not want her ever to know that side of him. What an untenable condition they were in, where each needed the physical reassurance of the other's touch, and desired the natural progression from it enough not to struggle against it, yet knew if it went too far, they would have to separate! He wondered if she had any idea how very badly he wanted her, and what it was costing him to stop at kisses when he suspected she would not demur should he go further. But being able to touch her, even with these limits, and to feel her response, afforded him a release and a reassurance he sadly needed, and he was determined to learn to live within whatever limits she set.

He lifted his face so their eyes met and she could see his

acceptance. "I understand," he said evenly. "Forgive me, I should not have asked it."

She bit the corner of her lip. *If she had any idea how that little gesture impacts upon me, she would never do it again!* he thought with rueful humour, considering the irony of the situation. Seeing her continued uncertainty, though, he added, "I hope you will always tell me when I ask too much of you."

He seemed to have succeeded in his effort to reassure her, for she gave a musical laugh in response. "Sir, if I always told you that, you would not have a moment's silence. I fear it is a natural consequence for me of being in your company, at least in this regard."

His lips twitched, acknowledging the truth of her statement. "Then perhaps it will make no difference if I ask one more thing," he said with a teasing inflection.

She gave him a look of amused suspicion. "What is that, Mr. Darcy?"

"It is exactly that—I think we have gone somewhat beyond 'Mr. Darcy.' Will you not call me by my name?"

Elizabeth hesitated. In one sense, he was asking very little, but in another, it was breaching one of the last barriers which differentiated their relationship from that of a formal coupling. With a spurt of independence, she decided that he was not the only one who could make requests. "If you wish it, I will—but only if you acknowledge that I have some basis for my concern for your reputation."

He grimaced, but not ill-humouredly. *It does me no good,*

*I suppose, to pretend there is nothing to it; it likely only makes her think I am blind to it,* he thought. "Very well, I admit that there is *some* basis, but I think you perhaps overestimate its impact," he said, then added more tenderly, "I do understand you are insisting upon it for my sake, though, and I only love you the more for your concern, even if I disagree with your decision."

"It is not just for your sake, either—your sister could be affected as well. It is not long until she comes out, and what if suitors stayed away from her because of me? It is unfair, but not unrealistic," she pointed out.

Darcy heaved a deep sigh. Shifting himself so her body rested against his chest, he said, "That is a worry unto itself. Sometimes I fear the only way Georgiana will marry is if I can find a trustworthy young man interested in her fortune and simply announce it is to happen. She will never look at a man for herself."

"Because she is so shy?"

"Because she has never been herself again since Wickham got his claws into her," he said with deep bitterness. "She was always somewhat timid, but never like this. You must have noticed—she hardly says a word to anyone, she almost never smiles, she picks at her food and does not sleep at night. All she does is play the pianoforte, and even that she feels as if she does badly. I have kept hoping this would pass, but it has been almost two years now. I could kill him for this."

"I had not realized it was such a change for her," said

Elizabeth, with concern as much for Darcy as for Georgiana. "Does she say what is troubling her?"

"No; whenever I have tried to speak of what happened, she does nothing but apologize for all the trouble she caused, and for being a fool, and she will not listen no matter how often I tell her it was not her fault, and that I do not blame her." He sighed again, tightening his arms around Elizabeth. "I have tried everything I can think of—I have tried keeping her with me and paying more attention to her, I have tried leaving her to herself, thinking that my presence might remind her of Wickham, I have kept her away from people who might accidentally hurt her feelings, even when it has meant offending relations—I have done everything I could think of that might bring her happiness, and nothing has seemed to relieve her grief for more than a day or two. I had hoped she might take a liking to you, but she has been just as quiet as ever since coming to Netherfield."

"I have not made it easy for her to become acquainted with me," said Elizabeth slowly, feeling guilty both for this and for never having wondered whether Darcy might have concerns outside of her. "I thought it a complication we did not need, but if you would like me to try, I will."

"I would be grateful for any assistance or advice," he replied.

She thought he sounded somewhat relieved. Nestling closer to him, she said, "I cannot promise any results, but I will try—William."

"Thank you, my dearest," he said, moved by hearing his

name from her lips. He found her mouth again and soothed himself in the pleasure he could find in her, and she was happy to assist in the process.

# Chapter 7

Darcy was unsurprised to discover Colonel Fitzwilliam waiting in his room for him that afternoon. It did not take any great skill in detection to discern that the usually affable Colonel was furious with him. Darcy greeted him cautiously, already bracing himself for the lecture to come.

He did not have long to wait. His cousin had clearly been awaiting his opportunity. "Darcy, what in God's name is wrong with you?"

Darcy threw himself down into a chair. "You go ahead and tell me—that will save time, don't you think?" he said wearily.

"If you think you can distract me into feeling sorry for you *this* time, Darcy, you are wrong! I cannot imagine what your father would say to you if he were still alive. I am hardly even sure what I am angrier with you about—trifling with a girl like Miss Bennet, humiliating her like that in front of me, or bringing Georgiana under the same roof as your mistress.

Good God, Darcy, what have you been thinking? Is this why Miss Bennet no longer lives with her parents—so that she can be more conveniently *available* to you?" His tone was cutting. "Unfortunately, I cannot do a damned thing about you ruining Miss Bennet, but by God, I am taking Georgiana away from here!"

His cousin's words snapped Darcy out of his lethargy. "She is *not* my mistress, damn it!"

"I suppose next you will tell me there is nothing between the two of you. I did not leave the nursery yesterday, Darcy," said Colonel Fitzwilliam in disgust. "I know what it means when a woman tolerates behaviour like yours."

Darcy closed his eyes. A violent disagreement with his cousin, especially one in which he was so clearly in the wrong, was the last thing he needed at the moment. "I do not deny having strong feelings for Elizabeth, but it is… complicated."

Colonel Fitzwilliam snorted. "*Elizabeth,* is it? And I fail to see what is so complicated about it—if you will not marry her, then leave her alone—do not ruin her life for your amusement!"

Darcy laughed bitterly. "You have this completely backwards, my friend. I *want* to marry her—but *she* will not have *me.*"

There was a moment of silence. Finally the colonel said carefully, "I find this rather difficult to credit—first, that you would consider marrying a woman with no fortune or connections, and if you did, why in God's name would she refuse you?

You are the kind of catch a girl like her grows up dreaming about! I saw how she looked at you. You will have to come up with a better excuse than that one."

"She is not most women, Richard. I will not trouble you with the sad history, but I can assure you that my fortune means nothing to her. As for why she will not marry me, she fears it would ruin me socially."

"Ruin you? Why would she think that? Raise a few eyebrows, I am sure, but no more."

"I tend to agree with you, in fact, but unfortunately she sees it otherwise. It is not just her lack of status which concerns her—she has a broken engagement behind her, and a sister who disgraced herself by running off with none other than our old friend Wickham, and when they finally were married, it was a patched-up affair. *That* is why she thinks I should not marry her."

"I am sorry to say this," said Colonel Fitzwilliam slowly, "but she has a good point."

"Nonsense!" snapped Darcy. "*She* has done nothing wrong, and has behaved admirably throughout."

"I did not say otherwise, but society will not see it so. Marry Wickham's sister? You cannot do it," he said firmly. "I suppose you were involved in that 'patched-up affair'?"

Darcy hesitated, then said, "I was, but Elizabeth does not know, and I would like it to remain that way."

"How much did that scoundrel cost you *this* time?"

"Enough, but I can afford it."

His cousin shook his head.

"And I *will* marry her," said Darcy defiantly.

"Well, I know better than to argue with you when your mind is made up, but for your sake, I hope she stands her ground. I must say I admire her for putting your welfare ahead of her own, though if any woman would, I am not surprised it is her."

"And you wonder why I want to marry her?"

"No," Colonel Fitzwilliam said slowly. "I do not wonder about that at all."

The two men eyed one another for a moment, then Darcy said in a more normal voice, "Do you still object to Georgiana's presence here? I would like her to have the opportunity to get to know Elizabeth."

"Good God, Darcy, are you actually asking my *opinion*? There is a first time for everything!"

Darcy was ready with a heated retort, then thought of Elizabeth. "I am sorry if you have felt as if I do not value your opinion, because I certainly do," he said, as close to humility as he could manage at the moment. "It is not my intention to be arrogant."

The colonel looked askance at him. "Darcy, I did not say you were arrogant, though you *are* in the habit of doing whatever you please."

"You may save your breath—I have had this lecture from Elizabeth already, and believe me, she did not mince her words," said Darcy wearily.

"I already told you not to try to enlist my sympathies—I will *not* feel sorry for you this time, nor will I let you have your way because of it!"

Darcy looked at him in shock. His cousin had never before spoken to him in such a before, nor in such a tone of anger. "Are you suggesting I am playing for sympathy?" he said, his voice dangerous.

"You always do when things do not go your way, and it usually works, though God knows I cannot think of anyone who is less deserving of sympathy! You have everything a man could want in life."

"Not quite—I do not have the woman I love."

"It certainly looked to me as if you had her," snapped his cousin.

"Have we not already had this discussion?" Darcy asked.

"There you go again—so she will not marry you, yet you feel sorry for yourself instead of thinking of how fortunate you are for having won her affections."

"Your point is well taken," said Darcy slowly, "although, believe me, I am far from taking her affection for granted. I expect every day to hear that she has changed her mind and dislikes me again, which is why I do not manage myself at all well when other men smile at her."

Colonel Fitzwilliam looked hard at him, hearing the implicit apology. "You have finally found someone who can make you doubt yourself," he said in disbelief.

Darcy had taken quite enough of this. "*That* is not

news—and, to save you the trouble of saying it, I know perfectly well that I do not deserve her," he said in a hostile voice. "However, I admit I had not known *you* thought quite so little of me. Excuse me." He stood and headed for the door.

"Oh, for God's sake, Darcy," Colonel Fitzwilliam in a disgusted voice. "You know better than that."

Darcy stopped but did not turn around. Closing his eyes, he said in a dangerously level voice, "You have no idea, Richard, what this last year has been like—no idea at all. If I have her good opinion now, by God, she has made me earn it. And I am *not* looking for sympathy; I know I am a better man for it, and have only her to thank."

There was a pause. "I see," said Colonel Fitzwilliam, who had not been oblivious to the frequency of his cousin's black moods in the last year.

Darcy tried to consider what Elizabeth would want him to do in this setting. Finally he turned and said as calmly as he could, "I do not want to be at odds with you over this, Richard. Is it possible for us to agree to disagree on whether a marriage with her is suitable or not? And if you feel it is necessary to take Georgiana away, I will not argue with you, although I do not think there is reason for it."

Colonel Fitzwilliam did not know what to make of this unheard-of capitulation from Darcy. Clearly Miss Bennet had quite an influence on him, to produce such change as this. "Fair enough, William," he said. "I will not stand in your way, but please, be careful with Miss Bennet's reputation. Not everyone knows you as well as I do."

Darcy did not disagree, and they managed to part on a more amicable basis than had seemed possible just a few minutes earlier.

The conversation had left Darcy with a good deal to think about. He was not pleased with the picture his cousin had painted of him, and in that it did not disagree with Elizabeth's judgements of him at Hunsford in describing his arrogance, it was even more painful. He was rather more offended by the description of him as self-pitying; he certainly did not want to be seen as a petulant child, however, he could understand how his cousin would think he did not count his blessings enough. It must be difficult for him to lack the secure future Darcy had by right of birth, nor could he ever have the opportunity to consider marrying for love as Darcy could, and that must be bitter.

The greater problem, however, lay with Elizabeth. This afternoon's events had demonstrated how unstable the situation had become between them. It was past time for patience; they needed a resolution, and quickly. There was only one outcome acceptable to him, and the question lay in how to achieve it. The simplest method would be to allow them to be found in a compromising position—this would be easy enough to manage, and might well happen by itself sooner or later given their relatively unguarded behaviour, especially if his self-control remained as poor as it had earlier. However, that would only cause further harm to her reputation, and, while he was not concerned about it for himself, he had seen how much the events of the last year had eroded her native self-confidence into a shadow of its former self. Further scandal would only add to the burden he wished to lessen.

Less honourable was the possibility of seducing her. Instinctively he knew it was within his power, and the idea certainly had a strong appeal of its own for him, but would it accomplish his goal? Any other woman would feel she had to marry him, but Elizabeth was just determined enough that she might continue to refuse him, even under those circumstances. Then he would truly be caught in an impossible dilemma—he would never be able to forgive himself for treating her as his mistress, nor could he ever imagine abandoning her. No, that plan was too dangerous as well.

He paced the room as he considered how else he might force the issue. Could the support of Bingley or her sister be helpful? Perhaps he should speak to them. Elizabeth would be angry, of course, but he would have to take that risk. But Bingley might also be unhappy about his efforts to pressure Elizabeth.

It occurred to him that he did have a natural ally in this matter though, and perhaps it was time to bring him into play. An idea suddenly came to him, and the more he thought about it, the more certain he became that it was the best course of action for him. It only remained to wait until the next morning to set it into action.

He was looking for Elizabeth, but could not find her anywhere. She was not in the sitting room, the garden, the solarium, or any of her usual haunts. He even became so desperate to see her that he asked Mrs. Bingley if she knew her sister's whereabouts, but that was unsuccessful as well.

Finally he went to his last possibility, and stood for a moment in front of her bedroom door. Perhaps she was resting—he would not wish to awaken her, so he slipped in quietly to the room he had longed every night to enter. She was not in her bed, though his eyes continued to rest on it for a few moments, thinking of all the times he had imagined being in it with her. Then he heard a sound, and looked to her dressing room where he saw the astonishing sight of Elizabeth, sitting in the bath, her back to him, her bared shoulders exposed to his hungry eyes.

She was not aware of his presence. He longed to approach her, but he could not take advantage of her in that way, so instead he spoke her name. She turned her head quickly, looking startled, but her eyes softened when she saw him and a smile touched her lips. He walked towards her and knelt behind the bath, and began to place featherlight kisses along her neck and down the exposed top of her spine.

"William," she whispered longingly. Inspired, he took the soap from beside the tub and lathered his hands, then began to wash her shoulders, moving slowly as he caressed every inch of them. He felt her relax under his ministrations, and he moved his soapy hands down her arms, one at a time, continuing to pay careful attention to his task. His cuffs were wet by the time he had reached her hands, and he did not intend to stop there, so he stripped off his coat, waistcoat, and shirt, and threw them to the side.

He saw a look of hunger in her eyes as she looked at him, and he pressed his chest against her shoulders, glorying in the feeling of his skin against hers. But he wanted more, and he reached for the soap once more. This time his hands started again at her shoulders, but then slid down her chest, thoroughly exploring her tender skin until they began to circle her breasts. Elizabeth lay her head back against him with a sigh of pleasure as his hands circled inwards, delighting in the feel of her. Finally he reached her nipples, already waiting for his touch, and as he began to stroke them, she arched up against his fingers. Her eyes closed, and she began to moan softly as he caressed her.

Soon, soon he would make her his, but first he would have her pleasure. He released one breast and slid his hand downwards, closer and closer until it finally covered her secret places. With a cry, she began to move against him, whimpering with escalating urgency. His hunger for her grew ever deeper as he took in her response, until finally she acknowledged his power by cresting over the final edge. Only then, as her body ceased to tremble, did he take her mouth, plundering its depths for his pleasure.

When she finally lay still, he drew her out of the bath and dried her tenderly with the towel, not missing a drop as he moved from her head to her feet. To his deep delight, she took his hand and led him to her bed. She lay upon it, smiling at him archly, her *body exposed in its entirety to him as he stripped off the last of his clothes and took his place upon her. Finally, at last, he entered her, gently finding his way through her last barrier until he was deep within her, ecstatic in the feeling of her. As she whispered his name, he thrust into her again and again, his body taking over as his pleasure grew beyond reason, and finally, as a wave of infinite satisfaction took him, he spilled his seed within her. His last memory was her voice, whispering tenderly, "How I love you, my dearest William."*

It was a matter of some mystery to Darcy how it was he could sit across from Elizabeth at breakfast, calmly buttering his bread, as if he had not just awoken from a sleep filled with dreams of making love to her in exquisite detail, of taking intimacies even beyond those which passed between many married couples, of exploring the delights of her body, and having her want him as much as he did her. He did not want to imagine what she would think of him if she knew where his thoughts tended. She certainly would not be able to direct her arch smiles in his direction in such an innocent manner.

It was probably just as well they had no opportunity for private conversation, he thought. Directly following breakfast he went riding, determined to lose no time in putting his plans into action. Before he departed, he gave her a long, serious look to which she responded with an impudent smile.

Elizabeth, in conversation with Jane, barely had time

to acknowledge Miss Darcy excusing herself for yet more practice at the pianoforte. *It is easy to see where she obtains her proficiency!* thought Elizabeth with some admiration; she would not have minded having some of the same drive towards perfecting a skill, but her conversation with Darcy had also made her look at Georgiana with different eyes, and she could see why he worried about her.

As she rose from the breakfast table, Colonel Fitzwilliam invited her to take a turn about the gardens with him. She hesitated for a moment, recalling both Darcy's reaction to her spending time with him, and what the colonel must be thinking of her after witnessing Darcy's behaviour the previous day. She reminded herself that she would have to face him sooner or later, and that Darcy had no right to dictate with whom she interacted, and agreed to join him.

The late spring flowers were in their full glory, and she was about to make a comment about them when her companion said, "So, Miss Bennet, why *is* it that you are refusing to marry my cousin?"

She coloured, taken quite by surprise by this indelicate and unexpected question, but finally mustered the composure to say, "Why, I am sure if he has told you that much, he would not have failed to mention my reasons."

"True, but reports at second hand do tend to be distorted," he replied affably, as if this were quite an everyday subject of conversation.

Elizabeth fervently wished she knew the content of his

discourse with Darcy. "My reasons do not reflect ill on him in any way, and that, I believe, is all that truly matters."

"Well, his version is that you are concerned a marriage between you would harm his reputation."

She had to smile at his obvious intention to ignore her efforts to avoid the subject; it rather reminded her of Darcy. "I suppose you are going to tell me it would do nothing of the sort," she said with some amusement. "I must warn you that I will not believe it."

He shook his head. "In fact, I do not disagree with you."

This response shocked Elizabeth, not that he should believe it, but that he would admit such a thing to her face. She rapidly revised the estimation she had made that he was trying to persuade her on his cousin's behalf. She found it surprisingly painful to think that Colonel Fitzwilliam, as a representative of Darcy's family, as well as a man who had formerly admired her, thought her unsuitable.

He continued reflectively, "I do wonder, however, how *relevant* it may be. While his sense of honour is very important to Darcy, what others think of him is less so. In some ways he has always been something of a misfit in the *ton*—he will not practice those little deceits polite society expects of us all. Were it not for his fortune easing his way, I doubt he would have had much social success in Town, and—to speak quite frankly—I doubt it would have troubled him greatly."

Elizabeth, feeling now quite confused, raised an eyebrow to cover her discomfort. "I assume there is a point to this history?"

Colonel Fitzwilliam shrugged lightly. "Just that I do not imagine he would be particularly troubled if it did affect his social status. On the other hand, he seems very much troubled by the prospect of you continuing to refuse him."

She could keep her silence no longer. "At the moment he is, but he is also a man accustomed to having matters arranged as he pleases, and is not used to being denied," she said, surprising herself with her frankness. "Once he has what he wants, it may lose some of its appeal, and the cost might seem more unacceptable."

He seemed to consider this for a few minutes as Elizabeth waited in some anxiety. Finally he said, "He has the means for having his own way, and when means are not enough, he has some skill in persuading people to give him his way in any case. But I have never seen him use his power for ill. As for whether he might change his mind later—well, I am somewhat surprised you would think it, but I forget that you would not have had the opportunity yet to know him all that well."

The shifts in the conversation were definitely becoming disturbing. She decided to retreat, and said politely, "I have no doubt you are right."

He cocked an eyebrow in her direction. "And I should mind my own affairs?"

Elizabeth sweetly denied saying anything of the sort, to which he replied, "I will not press you further, then, except to say that his affections run quite deep. I think you can trust him to know his own mind."

This comment was to stay with Elizabeth for some time. Seeing Darcy so discouraged the previous day had brought home to her the depth of his distress with the situation, and it had troubled her deeply. She realized that she had in fact not trusted him to know his own mind, believing instead that much of his desire for her was because she was unattainable. It was hard to believe he could love her for herself when her own opinion of her worth and discernment had fallen so low. She had assumed he would eventually lose interest in her, and she was embarrassed to realize she had shown so little faith in the man she loved. She had once again deceived herself as well—she had been telling herself she was refusing him for *his* benefit, whereas in truth she was at least as afraid of the consequences for herself. She had been ruled by her fear that, as her father had, he might withdraw his affection for his wife out of regret for an ill-made marriage.

Before this, she had never allowed a man to make her unhappy. She had wanted Mr. Covington's good opinion, but losing it would not have devastated her; the same could not be said for Darcy. She had discovered already more than a taste of the pain he could bring her. It seemed as if her life had become progressively harder ever since his first proposal of marriage, which had so shaken her idea of herself and her faith in her own perceptions. Then she had no sooner found her way to being content with her future as Mrs. Covington than he appeared again, only to cause her to fall in love with him, and as a result to throw away her entire future as well as her good reputation. Now he was back again, tormenting her with hope which she could not bring herself to trust.

Why had he ever returned to Hertfordshire? If he had never come back, she would have been married by now, with a respectable position in society and a husband of whom she was fond. Even if Mr. Covington had never provoked the passion or the excitement which Darcy could so easily do in her, would she have been so unhappy? She would never have known what she was missing, and she would also not have known the pain and hopelessness of the last year. Might not ignorance have been better than this? She felt a sudden surge of anger for his cavalier disruption of her entire life. He had as much as admitted that he had never expected her to break her engagement; why, then, had he come at all to charm her?

Perhaps what Colonel Fitzwilliam said was true, and she did not trust his affection as much as she should. But it had cost her so much already; how was she to have faith that it would do anything but make her as unhappy in the future? He had far too much power over her; it made her want to flee from him despite how much she longed for his company. But were her fears adequate justification for the distress they were both now experiencing? Was she still merely looking for excuses to avoid taking the risk of marriage?

She knew that most of her acquaintance, had they known of the situation, would ask why she should care if his reputation was hurt. They would point out that *he* had injured hers already, even if the cause and effect were not obvious. Why should she not take advantage of the relief from her present situation that marriage to him would bring, allowing her to be mistress of her own home, never to worry about money or her future again? Why should she care what it would mean for him, when he was begging her to marry him? But she would not, could not, think it; he was too dear to her.

An image of Darcy's discouraged face the previous afternoon came before her, and suddenly the fire of her anger sputtered and went out. She knew he had paid as great a price for their love as she, perhaps not as visibly, but real nonetheless. He would never have hurt her deliberately; at worst he was guilty of a thoughtless disregard of the potential consequences of his actions. And she did care about what their marriage would mean for his future, cared more than she wished to admit, because she wanted him to be happy. She knew how much she had come to need his love, and how hard it would be for her to be without him now.

She was so overcome by the pain of these realizations that she sat and cried for half an hour, for all she had suffered and for the ways in which she had yet again failed to understand herself. Her agitating reflections continued until it was time for dinner, and she was required to make herself equal to facing him once again. *At least*, she thought to herself, *now I know what I must do*.

Darcy's ride took him directly to Longbourn, where Mr. Bennet was enjoying a quiet morning in his library when Darcy was announced. It surprised him, but not unpleasantly. "Mr. Darcy!" he said with a smile. "Do come in."

After pleasantries had been exchanged, Darcy went directly to business. "There is something I would ask of you, sir," he said. He was not overly worried about the outcome; he knew Mr. Bennet thought well of him, but he was not yet accustomed to making his feelings for Elizabeth known, and this bore its own anxiety.

"Anything in my power, Darcy. You know you have only to ask," said a curious Mr. Bennet. He could not imagine what he *could* do for Darcy—the man did not want for anything. In truth, it would relieve his mind to have any way to repay the younger man for his generosity, so he settled himself to listen.

"It is my desire to marry your daughter," said Darcy with due seriousness, "and in that I will need your assistance."

Mr. Bennet took a moment to digest this shocking bit of intelligence. In the first moment's confusion, he wondered which of his daughters Darcy meant, but neither Mary nor Kitty could interest such a man, so it must be Lizzy. But Lizzy had always professed such a powerful dislike of the man— though as he thought about it, he had not heard anything of the sort from her in some time. For *quite* some time, in fact—and suddenly certain of Darcy's past actions began to make a good deal more sense to him. Of course, those had taken place while Lizzy was still engaged to Covington, but now she was no longer, and was in fact living under the same roof as Darcy… Mr. Bennet decided he would prefer to follow that particular train of thought no further.

"If it is my consent you are seeking, you have it, of course," he said genially.

Darcy cleared his throat. "Thank you, sir. It is not quite that simple, however; she has not agreed to be my wife. She has, to be quite truthful, refused me."

Mr. Bennet raised his eyebrows. This certainly put him in a spot given what he owed to Darcy, but there was no doubt in his mind as to what he would do. He was surprised, and not pleasantly, that Darcy would even consider it. "I will speak to her on your behalf, if you wish, but if your question is whether I will require her to marry you against her will, my answer must be no. Lizzy is not one to be compelled, not if you value your peace of mind."

"I would not take her against her will," said Darcy instantly, to Mr. Bennet's relief. "No, what I would ask of you is something more… subtle. I would like you to tell her that you are aware of my intentions, and have given me permission to court her."

Mr. Bennet was growing exceedingly puzzled. "That is little enough to ask, though I fail to see what it would accomplish."

Darcy paused, not quite knowing how to explain something he did not himself fully understand. "I find myself in an unusual situation," he began slowly. "Your daughter admits she holds me in a tender regard, and that she would *like* to be my wife, but she will not accept me because she feels it will somehow harm my reputation irreparably if I marry her. She feels that her broken engagement and the status of Mrs. Wickham make her an unsuitable wife for me."

"How very like Lizzy," her father mused. "She can be quite stubborn when she sets her mind to it."

"So I have discovered," said Darcy feelingly.

Mr. Bennet was beginning to see a certain humour in the situation, that one of the most sought after young men in England should be reduced to this state. With a spark of deviltry, he said, "Are you certain you would not prefer a wife of an easier temperament?"

"I will marry your daughter, or I will not marry," said Darcy with finality.

"Are you certain she cares for you? Perhaps she is trying to let you down gently."

Darcy was beginning to regret this interview. "You may ask her yourself, if you like, but she has shown me her regard quite unmistakably," he said, a bit shortly.

Mr. Bennet, well acquainted with Darcy's usual dry sense of humour, was intrigued to discover that on this subject he apparently had none. Innocently he asked, "How has she demonstrated this to you?"

Realizing he had placed himself in a delicate position, Darcy was anxiously attempting to find a safe response to this question when he recognized a look in Mr. Bennet's eye that he knew quite well in Elizabeth. He said distinctly, "I thought you did not want to have to force her to marry me."

Mr. Bennet's mouth twisted with amusement. If any other young man had said such a thing to him, he would likely have been infuriated, but he in fact placed a good deal of reliance in Darcy's judgement and trustworthiness. He had also long suspected that, given Lizzy's passionate nature, she might well go beyond the boundaries of propriety once she finally met a man she could like and respect. And in truth, he had been worried about Lizzy's present low spirits for some time, and the more he considered it, the more likely he thought it that Darcy might be the answer, both in terms of challenging her and in offering her an escape from her present situation. "True—and Lizzy is perfectly capable of exacting her own revenge if coerced. So, what do you plan to do about this, then, Mr. Darcy?"

"Well," said Darcy slowly, "as I said, she is concerned that my reputation will be damaged if I marry her, and will not listen to my arguments on the subject. I propose therefore to remove the stumbling block itself, by making it known as publicly as possible that I intend to marry her. Inasmuch as the intention is as damning as the act in this case, it will demonstrate that she has overestimated society's censure."

Mr. Bennet studied him carefully. "What if she proves to be correct, and your good name *is* damaged?"

To his surprise, Darcy smiled broadly. "That is the beauty of it—if my reputation is sullied, why, then, the damage is done already, and she has no excuse not to marry me."

"You are a very devious young man," said Mr. Bennet with a new respect. "I would not want to be caught between you and Lizzy in a disagreement!"

"You may already have done so," said Darcy bluntly. "Your daughter is *not* going to be happy with me about this."

Mr. Bennet found this prospect highly amusing. "No, I would imagine not," he said with a laugh. "Are you certain you wish to pursue this plan?"

"Have you a better one?"

"No, no, Mr. Darcy, not at all!" replied Mr. Bennet energetically. "What is your next step?"

Darcy shrugged. "I will begin mentioning my intentions in conversation, and wait for the news to spread, I suppose."

"Ah," said Mr. Bennet. "In *that* I might be of some assistance." He excused himself, and returned a few moments later with his wife, who looked quite ill at ease at being introduced into such a conference.

Mr. Bennet addressed her. "I find myself in quite a dilemma, Mrs. Bennet, based on some information Mr. Darcy has given me this morning regarding Lizzy."

"Lizzy!" cried her mother. "What has that wicked girl done now? Oh, Mr. Bennet, I knew we should have sent her back to London straight away."

"It seems she is set on vexing you, my dear. Did you not tell me that Lizzy would never marry?"

"Of course not! Who would have such a girl? So disobedient! So sly!"

Mr. Bennet shook his head gravely. "Therein lies my dilemma, Mrs. Bennet. You say Lizzy shall not marry, but now Mr. Darcy comes asking for my consent to marry her. Now, were it not for your dislike of the idea, I would be inclined to grant his request, as he seems a responsible enough fellow. But it seems I must displease one of you. What do you say, Mrs. Bennet—shall I send Mr. Darcy on his way, and tell him our minds are made up that Lizzy must not marry?"

The effect of this communication was most extraordinary, for on first hearing it, Mrs. Bennet sat quite still, and unable to utter a syllable.

When she made no reply, Mr. Bennet continued, "Of course, having heard the opinion of Lizzy that even her own mother holds, perhaps Mr. Darcy has changed his mind. Mr. Darcy, are you certain you still want to marry such a wicked, disobedient, and sly girl?"

Darcy, finding the spectacle of Mr. Bennet in action to be quite entertaining in its own way, allowed that he thought he would take his chances with Miss Bennet.

His seriousness was sufficient to break into Mrs. Bennet's daze. "Oh! Mr. Darcy, I never meant those things! Lizzy is the sweetest girl! Good gracious! Mr. Bennet, you delight in vexing me! Of *course* Lizzy will marry Mr. Darcy. Oh, Lord! My poor nerves!"

"Excellent; we are all in agreement then," said Mr. Bennet, "all except perhaps the lady. It seems Lizzy has been somewhat remiss about accepting Mr. Darcy's proposal, no doubt because she fears displeasing you."

"Oh, how you go on, Mr. Bennet! Mr. Darcy, I promise you, Lizzy will not give you any trouble—I will speak to her myself!"

"Thank you," said Darcy, who only wished it were so easy. "Perhaps tomorrow, or the next day—I would like to give her some time to think it over."

"Tomorrow—yes, tomorrow, you must come to dinner tomorrow, with Lizzy, and Mr. and Mrs. Bingley, and your family as well!"

Once Darcy had accepted this invitation, Mr. Bennet thanked Mrs. Bennet for sharing her opinion, and suggested she might have matters which needed her attention else-where. A moment later, they heard her calling, "Hill! Hill! I will go to Meryton to tell the good, good news to my sister Phillips. And after I come back, I will call on Mrs. Long and Lady Lucas. Oh, Lord!"

"There, Mr. Darcy," said Mr. Bennet with satisfaction. "All of Meryton will know by nightfall."

"Very efficient," commented Darcy. He added ruefully. "Now all that remains is for me to tell Elizabeth."

"I do not envy you that task," said Mr. Bennet with great feeling.

# Chapter 8

It was not until after dinner that Darcy managed to be alone with Elizabeth, and even for this he had to rely on his cousin spiriting Georgiana away for a time. The chance could not come too soon for him; Elizabeth's spirits had been hard for him to ascertain, as she seemed both unusually subdued yet more tranquil than he had seen in some time, and he was worried about the effects of their conflict of the previous day. To his relief, the others had no sooner departed than she looked up at Darcy with a brief but enchanting smile. Without hesitation he moved to sit by her side, and when she modestly did not look over at him, he began to dust slow, light kisses across her cheek, her hair, and her neck.

"Mr. Darcy, have you no shame?" said Elizabeth, with a laugh which showed she was not displeased.

"None whatsoever," he responded, neatly taking her

embroidery from her hands and setting it aside. He took her hands and placed them around his neck. She looked at him with dancing eyes as he pulled her closer. "I find I am in great need of your kisses tonight, my best beloved."

His lips touched hers lightly, and he nibbled temptingly on her lower lip. She did not hesitate in her response, making evident her pleasure by the way she melted into his arms. Their mouths danced together, giving and receiving pleasure in equal measure.

"Now I am the one who is shameless," said Elizabeth lightly as they paused for breath, her cheeks flushed from the desire he had succeeded in arousing in her. At moments like this, she could hardly recall why she had ever resisted him, when the touch of his hands on her back and her waist was giving her such exquisite pleasure.

"Pray do not change on my behalf!" said Darcy, who was in danger of revising his decision regarding the value of seduction. The feeling of her warmly compliant body in his arms intoxicated him, and to distract himself from the direction his thoughts were taking, he turned his attention to her mouth again, deepening the kiss to express the urgency of his desire for her.

Elizabeth hesitated for a moment, knowing how quickly her desire could spiral upwards; then, feeling the full pleasure of his possession of her mouth, met him halfway until her entire body seemed to tremble with sensation.

Darcy, feeling his passion beginning to run beyond his

control, regretfully released her lips, pulling her head against his shoulder until he felt master of himself once more. He was more certain than ever that his plan to force the issue of marriage was a good one; was she truly so innocent as to believe they could continue to be passionate like this indefinitely without her eventually ending up in his bed?

Elizabeth, who was experiencing a strong response to his proximity, was feeling a disturbingly powerful aching for his touch in the more forbidden parts of her body. *I must not allow this to go so far!* she thought with a little panic, realizing that her revised thinking about their future seemed to put her at more danger from him. Lest Darcy recognize the jeopardy to her self-control his kisses had wrought, she forced herself to say lightly, "What brings on this sudden great need for my kisses?"

"I will not dignify that question with the obvious answer," he said teasingly. "Suffice to say that I fear you will be less willing to give them to me after I have said my piece tonight."

With a look of amused resignation, Elizabeth pulled away and crossed her arms, waiting for the latest iteration in his arguments on marriage. She would hear him out, she decided, and then when he was finished, she would tell him of her decision.

Darcy was reluctant to spoil the playfully flirtatious mood between them, but could see no other choice. "I called at Longbourn this morning when I was out riding," he said carefully. "We are invited for dinner there tomorrow—you, the Bingleys, and I."

Elizabeth looked upwards. "Somehow I doubt the invitation actually included me; my mother would be happiest if I never crossed her doorstep again."

"In fact, I believe you have been restored to your mother's good graces," he said tentatively.

Now she did laugh. "And when did this miracle occur?"

Darcy took a deep breath, then with a slightly horrified fascination noticed that his hand was engaged in playing with one of her hairpins, and had in fact worked it most of the way out of her hair. Surely he had not always had these self-destructive urges? "I believe it followed immediately upon your father informing her that I was asking for your hand—at least, that is when the invitation was extended."

Her smile faded, and he watched the play of emotions across her face, disbelief and anger predominant. She seemed to struggle for self-mastery for a moment, and then finally asked tensely, "Why?"

He did not pretend to misunderstand her. "I have decided to make my intentions towards you public; and it seemed only politic to speak to your father about it first," he said. Seeing the lines of her face tighten, he added cajolingly, "We have been stalemated, and we cannot continue as we are, so I decided to remove your reason for refusing me. Now any damage that may happen is already done, or will be soon enough, and by my own hand, not yours—anyone who would think ill of me for marrying you will condemn me for courting you in the first place. Since I have been unable to convince you that you mean more to me than what others think of me, this is my proof. The only thing which remains to be seen is whether you will make me a laughingstock as well by refusing me publicly." He looked at her hopefully.

Elizabeth was filled with anger, that he should go behind her back like this and involve her family, but she also felt some relief that the decision had been taken out of her hands. She had been expecting something like this sooner or later, though she had not imagined this stratagem—she had thought some effort to compromise her to be the most likely route in forcing her to marry him. She had been doing nothing to prevent that either, allowing him to kiss her freely in the public rooms of the house. It was ironic, though, that he should force the issue just when she was finally ready to concede; and now, since she disliked being coerced, she was vexed with him for it.

"May I ask a question?" Her voice was sharper than she had intended.

"Of course, always," he said, worried by her tone.

"Why did you visit me so often last summer at Longbourn, when I was engaged to Mr. Covington?"

He blinked in surprise. If he had not known what her question would be, he certainly had not expected this, nor could he see its relevance to their current discussion. Still, clearly it was important to her. "I do not have an easy answer for that, since my motivations did not always seem sensible even to me then. At first, I believe, it was because I wanted to gauge whether or not you loved him, thinking it would be easier to forget you if I knew you loved another, but I think very quickly it transmuted itself to being because I simply could not stay away. The idea of you married to another man was more than I could bear, and the only relief I felt was when I was with you, and could pretend nothing had changed, and that you were still free." He looked at her anxiously. "I know it does not make a great deal of sense; I was not in a very sensible place at the time."

She looked down for a moment as she considered this. "And what did you want from me?" she asked seriously.

"Your companionship, your liveliness, your smiles."

Turning to him, she looked deep into his eyes. "Were you hoping I would fall in love with you?"

She had startled him yet again, and with a question he did not particularly want to consider, much less answer. "I do not believe I ever thought of it in those terms," he said slowly, "but I suppose I did, though I am ashamed to admit it. I am, as you have noted before, quite selfish at times."

She reflected that she probably would not have believed him had he denied it. "I see," she said quietly.

Still uncertain of what this turn of the conversation portended, he said, "I expect you are angry with me."

"Angry? That you tried to subvert my affections, or that you spoke to my parents?" As soon as she said it, she knew it was a pointless discussion—she must try to put as good a face on it as possible for both their sakes. Even if she wished to refuse him, he had left her with no choice. "But it does not matter; I accept, in any case."

"You will marry me?"

She sighed. This conversation had not gone at all as she had hoped. "Yes, I will marry you—you have won."

To her surprise, he showed no triumph or even pleasure in her statement. He said steadily, "You are the only arbiter of whether I have won or lost, for without your love this victory is a hollow one. I can understand why you would be angry, and my punishment is in your hands—all you need do is withhold your affection."

"Yet you took that risk," she said, some of her earlier anger at his cavalier behaviour returning to her.

He took her hand in his, and was relieved to see she did not resist. He looked down at their joined hands and said, "Yes—I decided to have faith in you, and to believe that your affection for me could not be so easily diminished."

She was beginning to recover from the shock now, and able to recognize that regardless of his reasoning for taking this action, the outcome had not been truly affected by it. Nothing had changed, in truth, except that he had been more cunning than she had anticipated. He was still the man she loved, despite his faults, and she did not want to quarrel with him. She smiled at him, not failing to note his look of profound relief at her reaction. "Your timing is fortunate, then, sir; for I have been coming to a similar conclusion myself today, and was prepared to accept you tonight in any case," she said, "even without this pretty piece of blackmail you have concocted."

His eyes lit with feeling. "Do you mean that? Or are you merely saying it to make me more comfortable, since I left you little choice?"

She answered him in the currency she knew he would accept, pulling his face down to hers and kissing him tenderly. He was not slow in accepting her overture, and expanding upon it. Elizabeth, feeling a new freedom with their changed status, lost herself in the fulfillment of being in his arms as he kissed her face, her neck, her shoulders before returning again to drink deeply of her lips, expressing a pleasure he could not have put into words. She could not have enough of his touch as his hands roamed through her hair, down her back, and around the curves of her waist. When he finally lifted his head, she was conscious only of a wish that he had not stopped.

He looked at her, his eyes dark with passion. "Can you forgive me, best beloved?"

"I suppose I must, though you are altogether too clever for your own good, my dear; I shall have to remember to be careful of you," she teased.

Darcy, having reversed his previous course, was allowing his fingers to play in her hair, for the simple reason that if he did not find some way to occupy them, they would soon be engaged in discovering how to remove Elizabeth's clothing. Quite intoxicated by having won her, he said unguardedly, "It was better than the other plans I had for convincing you that you must marry me."

She laughed. "Oh? And what were your other ideas?"

To her surprise, his cheeks covered with the deepest blush, and instead of responding to her question, he began to kiss her once more. Before his effect on her could grow too great, she freed herself and said good-naturedly, "You are trying to distract me, sir! I am beginning to grow suspicious."

Without quite meeting her eyes, he murmured something about being caught in a compromising position, and began to place light kisses along the delicate veins of her neck.

"Deceit does not become you," she accused him impertinently.

He suddenly seemed quite absorbed in stroking her hair, which was now in grave danger of coming down. After a moment, though, he met her eyes with rueful embarrassment, then nibbled on her ear. He whispered, "Very well, you minx, if you must know, my other plan was to seduce you."

A wave of heat rushed through Elizabeth at his words, and she became conscious once more of how much she ached for him. The idea of him thinking about her in that way was both embarrassing and arousing at the same time. The fact that he had turned to kissing her slowly and enticingly as soon as he had said his piece did not help, nor did the sensation of his fingers against the back of her head as he disposed of her hairpins. She felt a lurch deep within her as she felt her hair falling loose upon her shoulders, and he wound his hand into the thick mass of it. His kisses became more probing as his finger traced lightly along the neckline of her dress, drifting across the top of her breasts in a manner which seemed to create a sensation of heat in her most secret places.

She felt a moan rising from her lips, and quickly transmuted it into speech. "Is this meant as a demonstration? Because if it is, I can assure you that I understand the meaning of the word 'seduce' perfectly well." Her body craved the return of his hand to her breast with an alarming ferocity. Her fingers, seemingly of their own accord, slipped inside his frock coat to discover a delicious warmth.

He nipped her lip. "Perhaps I am simply enjoying knowing you have agreed to be mine," he said softly before returning to stake his claim to her mouth. In truth, Darcy was in even worse condition than Elizabeth—merely having admitted he had thought about seducing her had taken him beyond the limits of his self-control, and by this point, he had no wish to stop. The feral, insatiable Darcy from his dreams was making the decisions now, and Elizabeth's responsiveness did not help his state. He was far closer than he would ever care to admit to carrying her off to his bed. He longed to make the intimacy implied by her disheveled appearance a reality, and the sooner, the better. Intoxicated with her, he slipped his fingers under the edge of her dress to explore the nakedness of her shoulder. God, but he wanted her as he had never wanted any other woman!

He could hardly believe he had gone this far—if anyone

came upon them now, there could be no denying what had happened. This thought, instead of bringing him to his senses, led him only to free himself long enough to extinguish the lamp beside them before returning to gather her back into his arms and finally, finally allow himself to gently cup the softness of her breast.

Elizabeth felt weak from the waves of desire emanating from the spot where his hand rested. His touch simultaneously relieved her and made her yearn for more. Disturbed by the depth of her own longings and fearing discovery, she spoke his name, but it came out sounding more like a plea for more than a request to desist.

"Yes, Elizabeth?" he said, drawing back just enough to see her eyes.

As she opened her mouth to speak, he drew his thumb lightly across her nipple, and all words failed her as a shock of pleasure ran through her. Darcy smiled slightly, pleased by what he saw in her face, and repeated his action. "You see," he said conversationally, "that plan had its merits as well." He began to move his thumb in small circles.

"William, someone could walk in!" she protested, more weakly.

His dark eyes probed hers. He no longer cared about his loss of self-control; nothing mattered, so long as he could keep touching her. "You think we should stop? If you wish; on one condition." He paused, leaving Elizabeth with wild imaginings of what his condition might be. His voice was low when he continued. "Tell me you want me." He moved to rolling her nipple between his fingers.

"Shall I tell you the sun rises in the east as well?" Her voice was shaky as tremors of feeling she had never imagined possessed her. "Very well—I *want* you, William," she gasped as he intensified his pleasuring of her.

It was fortunate, she reflected, that he chose to keep his word and released her, all but the hand playing in her hair, since saying those words seemed to cause her own resistance to vanish. She closed her eyes, trying to regain her self-possession. After a few deep breaths, she said, her eyes still closed, "I will have to remember in future the danger you have mentioned in feeding tigers."

Darcy was silent as he wrestled with his own demons. He had never intended it to go so far; he knew full well that he would have taken her if she had not asked him to stop. His toying with her responses at the end, provoking her and demanding a verbal submission to replace the physical one he craved, revealed an uncontrolled part of himself he had always harshly repressed. But, by God, it had been gratifying to hear her say she wanted him, and to see her helplessly entangled in the pleasure *he* was giving her. There was, he thought, less of the gentleman and more of the predatory tiger in him than he cared to admit, and he was deeply mortified by it.

His voice was reserved when he finally spoke. "I told you once before that I was not a barbarian; it appears I was incorrect. Thank you for stopping me."

She heard the self-loathing in his voice, and it brought her back to herself quickly as she looked at him in concern. "We are to be married, my dear; and you did stop when I asked," she said gently, a part of her still marvelling that the first part of her statement was true.

His hand tightened in her hair. "Yes, we certainly are to be married," he said, his voice unreadable. "I appreciate your forgiving nature. But you are quite right; someone could walk in. Perhaps I should let you go to deal with some of the damage before that happens." Slowly he loosened his fingers and released her.

"Very well," she said, trying to convey with her voice that she did not blame him in any way. "I will see you soon, then."

She received the briefest of smiles for her effort. As she stood, she leaned towards him and said, "And if I come back to a grim visage, I will take advantage of my new position as the future Mistress of Pemberley and set the tigers on *you*."

He gave a startled laugh, then caught her hand and kissed it quickly before she left.

After all that had occurred, Elizabeth found herself unable to sleep that night, and so was propped up in her bed reading long after midnight when she heard a light rapping at the door of her room. Thinking it must be the maid, she called out to her to enter, and was thus quite surprised when Darcy slipped quietly in and closed the door behind him, clad in his shirtsleeves. Her heart gave a little lurch at the intimacy of his being in her bedroom, and what it might portend, and she clutched her book as if it were a talisman.

"This is indeed a surprise," she said quietly, not wanting to be overheard by anyone passing by.

He came over to stand beside her bed. Looking down at her, he said, "I was taking advantage of the fine weather and walking the grounds, and as I returned, I saw the light in your window, and realized you must still be awake as well."

Her pulses fluttering, she said, "And so I am."

He smiled a little. "You need not worry, my love—I did not come to finish what we started this afternoon; I was merely lonely for your company." He was making a distinct effort to look directly at her face, and not to let his eyes wander down to her nightdress.

She relaxed a little, though conscious there was a part of her that was oddly disappointed. It was uncomfortable having him tower over her, so she shifted to the side of the bed, taking care her bedclothes did not slip. With a warm look, he took her implied invitation and sat facing her, keeping a safe distance between them. She said, "I am always happy to see you."

"Are you?" he asked, then, without allowing her the opportunity to answer, he added, "It has been an important day for us, and there are so many things I did not have the chance earlier to tell you—such as how very happy you have made me by agreeing to be my wife. It has been a long time since I have been able to imagine my life without you by my side, and it is a great relief to know that you will actually be there."

"It has indeed been a day of great changes, and one change to which I will need to accustom myself is to allow myself to be free to say those things I have worked so hard *not* to say until now," said Elizabeth softly. "But I am very happy that we are to be married; I have tried to deny my regard for you for so long, but I hope you know that there is no one I would rather be with than you." A little embarrassed by her seriousness, she added teasingly, "There—are you feeling less lonely now?"

"Much less lonely," he said, his eyes glittering in the darkness. "I am embarrassed to say I even went so far as to concoct an excuse as to why I needed to speak to you tonight, when the truth was that I was finding it hard to believe that you had actually accepted me, and wanted your reassurance you had not changed your mind."

"I have not changed my mind," she said with affectionate humour. "I will marry you, you may depend upon it—especially after having been so unwise as to let you into my bedroom at night!"

"I am not complaining," he replied. Finding his self-control still intact despite the circumstances, he allowed himself to take her hand. "You can always tell me to leave."

She raised an eyebrow. "What, and not hear the excuse you worked so hard to create?"

He laughed. "Very well; I am not averse to having a reason to stay. My excuse was that I realized we had not talked about how to announce our engagement, nor about wedding plans."

"We did not *talk* much at all," she said archly.

His smile was even more devastating than usual in the half shadows of her room. "Be careful, or I may think you are trying to tempt me."

"You come to my room in the middle of the night in your shirtsleeves, and claim *I* am trying to tempt *you*?"

"Minx," he said, rewarding her impudence with a slow kiss which made her question his stated intentions, as well as her ability to resist him. "Much better—I am very partial to the way you look when I have just kissed you."

She gave him an eloquent look. "And how would you like to announce our engagement?" she asked pointedly.

He accepted her redirection graciously. "Whatever pleases you, my dearest—we could tell everyone here in the morning, if you like, and then your family when we go to Longbourn for dinner."

"It would be wisest to mention it before we get in the door, given my mother's likely reaction," she said lightly. "Will your sister be surprised?"

"I have no idea," he replied. "I cannot tell what she thinks anymore; I do not know if she has noticed my interest in you. I think she will be pleased, though."

"I hope she will be. Well, we have concluded the announcement; what shall we do about the wedding?"

He smiled again, and placed a kiss in the palm of her hand. "I favour a short engagement."

She laughed. "I had taken that as a given, my dear. Fortunately for you, I see no reason to wait; I have already left home, and I think a quiet wedding is most suitable under the circumstances in any case."

"I will obtain a license, then we need not wait any longer than you require to make the preparations," he said, looking at her seriously.

She looked at him with some amusement. "I can hardly argue with that," she said.

"Would a week be long enough?" he asked. *It cannot be soon enough for me!* he thought, becoming increasingly aware of her state of undress.

"A week!" exclaimed Elizabeth. "That is a *very* short time. There are farewells I must say—perhaps not as many as there would have been a year ago, but still some—and I must prepare a little at least to leave home! Perhaps... a fortnight?" she offered tentatively, aware that even this represented a rather indecent haste.

Their eyes met for a long moment, then his began to drift downwards. Elizabeth coloured as she realized he was eyeing her nightdress. When he looked up again, only the slightest trace of guilt on his face, he said, "A fortnight. I suppose I can wait that long—if you insist."

She cocked her head. "I thought you said you had not come here to take advantage of me," she said mischievously.

"It is true," he said with mock austerity, "although if you had suggested a six-months' engagement, I might have rethought my position." He had begun to relax his guard a little, now that he had demonstrated his ability to control himself in this most difficult of settings. The sudden increase in the tension between them thus took him by surprise, and he found himself all too aware of how little stood between them.

"You are very certain of yourself, sir," she teased.

*Now,* he thought. *Now is the time to leave.* But her lovely eyes were shining in the light of the lamp, and she wore that impertinent look that always tempted him to kiss her until she forgot everything but him; and he did not leave. "Have I reason to be certain of myself?" he found himself asking.

"Would a gentleman ask such a question?" she responded instantly, her eyes daring him.

A provocative smile grew on his face. "Would a lady be wishing me to do this?" Holding her eyes with his, he reached over and ran his finger slowly under the neckline of her nightdress, then poised his hand on the tie of it. At that moment, he realized he had not come to her tonight to prove his self-control as he had thought, but to look for an excuse to let loose the tiger—and this understanding had come to him just a little too late.

Elizabeth's heart was pounding under the influence of his daring actions and the desire in his eyes. She was not sure to what extent he might be teasing, since his hand had not moved again, and she was equally unsure of what she wanted him to do. Licking her dry lips to moisten them, she said lightly, "I am, of course, quite ignorant in these matters—I have no idea what a lady should wish for in such circumstances."

His eyes flared, and his fingers moved. As the tie gave way, he slid his hand inside to discover the silken skin of her breast. Involuntarily, Elizabeth arched to meet him as his touch sent a rush of heat through her. "William," she said, her voice just above a gasp.

"Just a taste, my love, of what awaits us," he said unsteadily, his fingers finally caressing the flesh he had so often dreamed of.

She reached her hand up to stroke his neck, and tried to pull his head towards hers. He shook his head, not yet ready to satisfy her with his kisses. No, he wanted to leave her wanting more of him. "Not yet, my loveliest and most tempting Elizabeth; not yet."

"Am *I* leading *you* into temptation?" she asked lightly, as if she were not becoming increasingly desirous of more of his touch. The shocking feeling of his hand lightly stroking her breast was exquisite, but she felt a deep need for him to move inward to touch her as he had earlier through her dress. If he did not, if he stopped at this, she did not know how she would bear it.

She need not have worried; as Darcy saw the sultry look of desire take over her face, he bent his head to kiss her neck with tantalizing lightness, gradually moving his lips downward until he reached the edge of her nightdress. Gently he pushed it aside to reveal her breast to his hungry eyes, the touch of his mouth filling her with a surge of excitement deep within. Beyond the point of speech, she bit her lip to prevent a moan from emerging as his lips traced a circle on her breast, then finally came to rest as he ran his tongue along her nipple. She could no longer help herself; a whimper of combined pleasure and desire escaped her.

He looked up for a moment, and said softly, "Am I pleasing you, best beloved?" At her speechless nod of acknowledgement, he turned himself hungrily back to her breast. Savouring the moment he had imagined so often, he slowly drew her nipple into his mouth and began to suckle it, first gently, so as not to frighten her, then stimulating her more potently as he felt the tension of response build in her body.

She could not have imagined the exquisite pulses of pleasure she began to feel as he teased her with his tongue and his lips. She could not control it; she was riding the waves of desire now and ached for more. The fulfillment he was giving her only made her need his touch more elsewhere, wanting him in ways she did not understand.

Darcy knew he had her where he wanted her—moaning with pleasure and beginning to writhe in response to the touch of his mouth. Despite everything, there was still a part of him that was planning to stop before it was too late—but not until he knew he had as thoroughly roused her passion as she did his. The sensation of giving her pleasure was exhilarating beyond belief, and he allowed himself to feel every bit of the gratification of it.

When he was certain he had her in the power of his touch, he released her nipple, and raised his head to look at her face. The sight of the heat of uncontrolled desire in it only raised his own arousal.

As soon as he had stopped, Elizabeth felt a near desperation for him to touch her again. She caught his face and kissed him, not the gentle kisses of their earlier days, but needy, demanding kisses, which he returned with redoubled zeal. It did not remove the ache in her body, but it helped a little. When he stopped again, breathless, he looked into her eyes, his face showing just how much he wanted her. "So," he whispered, "did you like your taste?"

She could see his satisfaction in having gained a response from her, and her lips curved mischievously as, instead of answering him in words, she took a cue from the desires of her body, and pulled her nightdress aside to bare her other breast. She looked at him steadily, knowing he would understand her wordless request.

His eyes grew darker, and a smile of approval grew on his face. "Elizabeth—there is no woman in the world like you," he said as he lowered his head to her breast.

It seemed even more intense this time when he began to suck on her, and she did not know whether it was because she was anticipating it this time, or because he held her other breast in his hand, toying with the nipple. She only knew that she wanted more, and did not know how to get enough to satisfy her.

He took his time pleasing her, and when he finally looked up again, he replaced his mouth with his other hand, and rolled both nipples steadily. "Well, my beloved, what shall it be?" he said, his voice unsteady. "Do I stay, or do I go?"

She knew intuitively what he was asking, but she could not think for the sensation he was arousing in her. "It is not fair to ask… me that when you are doing… such things… to me," she said as coherently as she could.

Regretfully, he ceased his actions and sat back, never taking his eyes from her for a moment. She looked at him, her mind still clouded by the pleasure he had given her, uncertain of what she wanted. If he had not stopped to ask her, she knew she would have willingly given way to anything he wanted of her; but he *had* stopped. An echo of his voice from earlier came back to her: *I did not come to finish what we started this afternoon*, and he had said it as if he meant it. No, if there was uncertainty, they should wait. She closed her eyes for a moment, trying to silence the clamoring of her body for his touch. Finally, she said, "I do not think we are ready yet, William; as you said, it is only two weeks."

She saw the regret in his eyes, but also that he was not seriously disappointed. In fact, although the feral part of him wanted more, part of him was satisfied. He knew he could have had her, and that was enough for now. He acknowledged her with a nod of his head, then said, "Just let me hold you then for a moment, my own."

He retied her nightdress before taking her in his arms. He could feel the racing of her heart, and knew his was not far behind, but he also felt a deep tenderness when she rested her head upon his shoulder as if exhausted. Finally he released her and kissed her lightly on the lips. "Until tomorrow, then," he said.

She smiled. "Until tomorrow."

He rose to leave, but a bit of him would not be silenced, and he turned to her one last time with an enticing look. "By the way, I *very* much enjoyed our taste."

"Incorrigible," retorted Elizabeth affectionately.

He wished he were not leaving, but at the same time took pleasure in knowing he had left Elizabeth in the throes of desire. He was so intoxicated with the gratification of having taught her new ways to want him that he was less careful than he might have been as he left her room. He was only a few steps beyond her door when he heard from behind him Georgiana's voice saying in surprise, "William! What are you doing here!"

He spun around, his mind completely blank as he faced his sister. Had she seen him come from Elizabeth's room? He cursed himself for his carelessness, and the recklessness which had led him there in the first place. "Georgiana," he said, "are you having difficulty sleeping still?" He realized how weak this sounded.

"I was hungry, and went down to the kitchens for something to eat," she said hesitantly, glancing from him to Elizabeth's door and back. "You are awake late as well."

"Yes, I was about to retire," he said lamely.

There was a moment's silence while Georgiana examined the floor around her feet. Darcy could see her distress in the frozen look on her face, and cursed silently. Apparently she had indeed seen him.

He decided in favour of taking the initiative. "Well, since you are still awake, there is something I would like to tell you," he said, striving to sound calm. "My sitting room would be comfortable; shall we go there?"

She nodded silently and followed him, still not looking at him. When they reached his rooms, she sat with her hands folded, looking down, for all the world like a child waiting to be chastised.

"I was planning to tell you this in the morning, but since the opportunity has arisen, I wanted you to be the first to know that Miss Bennet has consented to be my wife," he said, feeling distinctly awkward.

"Your wife?" She seemed hesitant to credit the idea, then, in a small voice, she added, "Congratulations. I hope you will be very happy."

"Thank you. I hope she will be a sister to you as well, and that you will grow to care for her as I do."

"I am sure I will—she is very amiable," said Georgiana woodenly.

There was a pause, and he said, "I imagine you are aware that she has no fortune or connections as the world sees these matters, but her value to me is beyond any of that. This is a marriage of affection, not of practicality. I do not imagine our family will approve."

"William," she said, her voice revealing her distress as she spoke his name, but then her face seemed to close down, and all emotion vanished. "Thank you for telling me. Good night." She bolted from the room.

# Chapter 9

DESPITE HER LATE NIGHT, Elizabeth awoke early as was her habit. Her mouth curved as she thought of the previous night, and the memories of it made her body long for Darcy again. She could not wait to see him again; she was very happy about their engagement, and more secure in it than the previous day, and she wanted to share this with him.

She had already begun to dress herself by the time the maid arrived to assist her. Before anything else, the maid gave her a knowing smile, and said, "Mr. Darcy asked me to give you this, Miss." She handed her a folded piece of paper.

Elizabeth raised an eyebrow, then smiled at her mischievously. She took the note, saying, "Thank you—and if you can keep a secret for a few hours until I have had a chance to tell my sister the news, you may be the first to congratulate me on my engagement."

This was greeted with many happy exclamations and good wishes, as Elizabeth was well liked among the staff at Netherfield. After a minute of this, Elizabeth opened her note:

My best beloved,

I must speak to you alone this morning, before breakfast, about a matter that has arisen. Will you meet me in the library at your earliest convenience? I will be eagerly awaiting you, my love.

Yours, as ever,
FD

She smiled, suspecting that his "matter" was nothing more than a desire to be alone with her again, but she was hardly averse to the plan. She paid a little extra attention to her appearance, but did not want to delay; and had she realized the sparkle which happiness had added to her eyes and smile, she would have known there was no further improvement she could make.

She hurried downstairs and into the library. As soon as she saw him, she felt a rush of affection, and went straight into his arms, grateful she no longer had to disguise or try to suppress her feelings. After a minute of enjoying the blissful feeling of being with him again, she noticed he was holding her more tightly than usual and a new tension in his body.

Recalling his note, a sense of deep misgiving filled her. They had been intending to announce their engagement at breakfast; had he, as she had long feared, changed his mind as soon as she had capitulated? A painful tightness in her throat, she stepped back and said, "Tell me, what is the matter?" She bit off the endearment which had come naturally to her lips; if he was to reject her, she did not want to humiliate herself any further than she already had.

To her great relief, he immediately pulled her back into his arms, but not before she had seen the look of strain on his face. "It is Georgiana—by misfortune, she saw me leaving your room last night, and she is quite distraught. I told her we were engaged, but I think she hardly heard me. She will not leave her room, and she will not allow me to speak with her; her maid tells me she has been crying ever since she first went in this morning."

It was a moment before she could take in this new intelligence, but she quickly realized how deeply distressed he was over this. "Is she troubled about having seen you, or our marriage, do you think?"

"I cannot be sure, but I suspect it is what she saw." Darcy's feeling of guilt was evident in his voice. "She has a tendency to view me as being without failings." It was a view that was far from accurate, he thought. If Georgiana knew half of what was in his mind, she would never trust him again. *He* was to blame for her present suffering; he should never have allowed his uncontrolled side to emerge.

He had spent the last few hours ruminating on how he had lost control of himself, step by step. From the time he had learned of Elizabeth's engagement, each new transgression had paved the way to another, until now his conduct of the previous summer, which had so appalled him at the time, seemed minor in comparison. Well, it was time to put an end to it. He would learn to contain himself again; he had done it all his life. It would be difficult, given the temptation of Elizabeth before him, but if he could only hold himself in check until their wedding, hopefully his animal nature would be satisfied by the more traditional relationship Elizabeth would no doubt expect. His dreams would have to remain just that.

Elizabeth could feel his tension, and worried for him. "My poor love! Is there anything I could do? Would you like me to try to talk to her?"

"Would you?" His relief was clear.

"Of course—I do not know if she will speak to me either, but I will try."

"Thank you," he said. "But let me hold you for a little longer first." He took comfort in the security of her embrace and her love, grateful beyond measure to know she was finally his.

A few minutes later Elizabeth knocked at Georgiana's door.

"Who is it?"

"It is Elizabeth," she said, although she and Georgiana had not reached the point of using Christian names yet. "May I come in?"

There was a hesitation. "Just a minute," said Georgiana reluctantly.

Elizabeth heard rustlings within, and then finally the door opened. Georgiana was still in her dressing gown, and, despite her womanly figure, looked younger than her years with her hair in a braid down her back. Her eyes were tearstained and she looked as if she had slept little, if at all.

Elizabeth smiled warmly at her, recalling how important it had been when she was sixteen to feel as if others were treating her like an adult, and decided to pretend she had seen none of her signs of distress. "Good morning," she said. "I trust you are well?"

Georgiana bobbed her head. "Yes, thank you, and you?"

Without waiting for an invitation, Elizabeth took a seat in the nearest chair. "I am well, although I cannot say the same for your brother. He is very worried about you," she said gently.

"Truly, I am fine; please tell him there is nothing to worry about," she replied quite formally.

Elizabeth could see that the girl was determined not to admit to any weakness, and decided to challenge her. "Well," she said pragmatically, "he feels you were quite distressed earlier, and he does not tend to imagine these things. It seemed to *me* if you were upset about my engagement to him, it would be best for you and I to talk right away to see if we could come to some understanding."

"Oh, no," she cried, her eyes wide. "Please do not think that—I am very happy he has found someone he cares about, and that you will be married. Please, I am not at all upset about that; I am sorry, I should have said something earlier."

*Now we are seeing some real emotion*, thought Elizabeth. "I am relieved to hear it. I care for your brother a great deal, and I know how much he loves you. I would not want to see him unhappy because of any difficulties between us; I had hoped we might be friends."

"Oh, yes, I hope so too," said Georgiana, clearly still worried lest Elizabeth think her against the match. "I am sure we will be. I am so sorry you thought I was upset about that—I would never be, never."

"I am glad, then, that we have cleared that up," she said warmly. "But tell me then, what *was* troubling you so, that you would not speak to him?"

Georgiana looked away. "It was nothing; I was merely tired after a bad night."

"It had nothing to do with seeing your brother come out of my room last night?" she asked gently, wondering what Darcy would think of her raising such a subject with his protected younger sister.

"I…" Georgiana looked around her like a frightened deer hoping for a way to escape. "No, I…" Without warning she sat down on the bed and burst into tears.

Elizabeth looked at her sympathetically, then sat beside her and put an arm around her. "I'm sorry—this must be very difficult," she said.

"I just... never thought he was... *like that*," Georgiana said between sobs. As she realized what she had said, she added almost frantically, "Please, I didn't mean to say... I know you would not... Please, I did not mean that, I just thought he would not... risk compromising... anyone."

"I am not offended," said Elizabeth comfortingly. "I know what happened in my room last night, and which rules were broken and which were not, and I have no concerns about it. I fear it looked worse than it actually was to you, however, and I am worried about *that*."

"But how can you *trust* him, when he does that?" Her voice was so hopeless as to make Elizabeth feel quite protective of her.

"Trust him? That is not difficult," she replied. "Your brother certainly has his faults, but in all the essentials I have found him to be quite trustworthy. He is, however, perfectly willing to break rules if it suits him, and if he feels they are unimportant."

"Men are always willing to break the rules, because it is only the woman who pays for it," said Georgiana with a bitterness that shocked Elizabeth. "What do the rules matter, if *they* cannot be hurt by them? We are the ones who are destroyed by one mistake."

There was more to this than her disappointment in her brother's behaviour, Elizabeth thought. "I should hope not," she said gently, wondering how she could encourage her to talk further. "I have made far more than my share of mistakes, and not been destroyed."

"Not the kind of mistakes I have made," the girl whispered miserably, and began to sob once more.

"Perhaps you should tell me about those mistakes," said Elizabeth gently.

"There was a man… and he told me he loved me, and I believed him, but it was not true, he only wanted my fortune," she whispered, then stopped, all but her tears.

Hoping she was not pressing her too hard, Elizabeth said, "Mr. Wickham?"

Georgiana's head jerked up. "You know about that?" she said, horrified. "He *told* you?"

"Georgiana, did your brother not tell you about *my* sister and Mr. Wickham?"

"No," she whispered, the frightened deer eyes back.

"He should have—you should not have been unwarned; the subject might have arisen here. Mr. Wickham convinced my youngest sister to run off with him, promising to marry her, but having nothing of the sort in mind. It was already too late by the time they were found, but fortunately, he was willing to be convinced to marry her in exchange for a substantial sum of money. For that matter, I myself had met Mr. Wickham some time before that and found him quite charming. He told me some stories which I believed implicitly, to my later regret when I found out they were quite untrue. Your brother knows all of this. So you see, my dear, I am hardly likely to think less of you for believing Mr. Wickham's lies, when I did as well, and my sister did far worse."

Miserably Georgiana said, "I did worse, too."

*Oh, dear,* thought Elizabeth worriedly. "I am sorry—but you know, you were very young, and cannot be blamed for believing his blandishments."

"But I let him kiss me," she said, clearly in agony, yet wanting to confess. "And he wanted to… touch me, and he said if I loved him, I would let him."

Elizabeth felt a surge of fury at Wickham, but pushed it away in order to do what she must. "Just to touch you, or was there more?" she said, trying to put every ounce of understanding and acceptance she had in her voice.

"No, nothing more—he wanted to, but I would not…" She was weeping openly again.

Elizabeth, profoundly relieved, kissed her forehead. "You should be proud of that."

"How can I, when I allowed so much else? I knew better!"

"And you believed you were in love, and that you could trust him," she said soothingly. "Surely you do not think you are the only girl to have made such a mistake? My dear, it is far more common than you think. We all have made mistakes of one sort or another. I had to end an engagement to another man last year, you know."

"You did?"

"Yes, and I will relate the whole sad story some day if you

like, but I will tell you this now, if you can keep a secret—I let your brother kiss me while I was promised to another—does that not equal any of your sins?"

Georgiana's eyes grew wide. "Did he know?—that you were promised, that is?"

"Oh, yes, he knew," said Elizabeth with a smile. "So you see, my dear, it is not all as simple as it sounds in romances. Love is not pure happiness, but more of a two-edged sword, I have found—there is no happiness that can compare to it, but it can also bring terrible pain. When you let yourself love someone, you take on the risk of losing them, to change of heart, to circumstances, even to illness and death. Love and heartbreak go together; you cannot have the one without the risk of the other. You were very unlucky; you learned about the heartbreak very early, but it was just that: ill luck, to encounter a man so well positioned to take advantage of you." It was ironic, she thought, to be presenting lessons she herself had only just learned to Georgiana as if they were well-known wisdom.

"I want to have the happiness your sister and Mr. Bingley have—it just shines out of them. It will never happen for me," said Georgiana sadly.

"Oh, my dear, you see the final result. There was a year, after they fell in love, when Mr. Bingley felt he had to put her aside for a variety of reasons. My poor Jane suffered sadly that year; had you met her then, you would not recognize her in her present happiness. And you *will* have that happiness yourself in time, because to balance your ill fortune, you have the good fortune of having a guardian who is in absolutely no position ever to push you into a marriage you do not desire, nor to deny you the chance to marry for love."

There was a knock at the door, followed by Darcy's voice saying, "Georgiana?"

Elizabeth, with a conspiratorial smile at an anxious Georgiana, called back, "Go away, William. Georgiana is telling me all your secrets. I had no idea you had such a misspent youth."

Georgiana listened with an astonishment bordering on alarm. Elizabeth held a finger to her lips.

"Why do I suspect you are quite encouraging this behaviour in my sister, Miss Bennet?" Darcy said in an amused voice. "I hope I have *some* redeeming qualities left by the time you are done with me."

"Not a one!" called Elizabeth cheerfully. "But have no fear; we will not tell a soul. Well, perhaps only a very few. You could make yourself useful, though, and have some breakfast sent to us—I have to find out a *great* deal more detail yet."

"Your wish is my command," he replied with a laugh, clearly relieved to find her in good spirits. "However, if you are going to persist in impugning my good name, I will feel obliged to ride to Longbourn and inform your mother that you are giving me trouble and that I want her to speak to you straight away."

"Is it threats, now? Did you hear how he treats me, Georgiana?"

"I delight in tormenting you, Miss Bennet. But to show my forgiving nature, I will have breakfast sent to you in hopes it will sweeten your temper. In the meantime, please try to avoid corrupting my sister *too* much."

Elizabeth laughed, and Georgiana went so far as to giggle a little once she had heard his footsteps retreat down the hall. She said in an amazed voice, "I would never dare to speak to him in such a manner!"

"I will tell you a secret, then: your brother enjoys being teased. It is, I am convinced, why he first noticed me—because I was so impertinent to him. But now, you must tell me at least some little secret I can tease him with, some misbehaviour or other."

Georgiana looked at her seriously. "But I cannot—William never does *anything* wrong. That is why it is so hard to know I failed him."

Elizabeth looked at her sympathetically. "You poor girl! What a standard to live up to! But let me assure you, your brother makes quite his share of mistakes; he apparently has had the good fortune to shield you from knowledge of them. He is not without his faults."

"But he would never have behaved as I did…" Her voice trailed off as she evidently recalled that the previous night he had done rather worse. "At least I did not *think* so—oh, I do not know what to think anymore! I know I should not have done it, but he…" She clearly could not go so far as to say that her brother's behaviour was less than perfect.

"Well, I wish I had an easy answer for you. Certainly there are very good reasons for following the rules of propriety, and I recommend them, though I obviously have my own faults in that regard. Still, it is possible to be too restrained, you know— when your brother first noticed me, he was so proper that I had no idea he admired me until he shocked me by proposing to me. I was very rude to him," she said with a laugh, "and I think he learned a lesson about the necessity of showing his feelings. He has, perhaps, overcompensated, but I have no complaints. I hope you will remember, too, that I had already accepted his proposal of marriage—it was not the behaviour of a rake."

Georgiana looked anxious. "You will not tell him, I hope, about what I told you?"

"I see no reason for him to know, or anyone beyond the two of us," she replied comfortingly. She would, in fact, far prefer that he never know; what his reaction would be to knowing what Wickham had done to his younger sister was something she preferred never to discover.

Jane's joy when she learned of her sister's engagement could not be expressed with mere words, and her husband's congratulations to Darcy were of the warmest nature as he expressed his happiness that they would soon be brothers. Neither, however, seemed particularly shocked by the intelligence, leaving Elizabeth to wonder just how much had been guessed already. Colonel Fitzwilliam's welcome of Elizabeth to the family likewise seemed heartfelt, although she could not help but think his reception of Darcy to be a bit cooler. She hoped this did not particularly signify difficulty for the future.

With all the stir, she only had a few brief moments alone with Darcy, just long enough to assure him that her discussion with his sister had proved fruitful and that she seemed on the road to accepting her shock of the previous night. Darcy, although seeming somewhat withdrawn, was touchingly grateful for her assistance in the matter; and expressed several times that he did not know how he would have handled Georgiana without her.

Even with this reassurance, Elizabeth could see his spirits were still somewhat disturbed, and when she saw the opportunity, she suggested that they take advantage of the lovely day to walk to Longbourn for dinner, and then ride home with the others afterwards. He was readily in agreement, and all of the rest of the party forbore to suggest joining them, knowing that the couple would appreciate some time to themselves.

For Darcy, this time alone was a test, a measure of whether he could limit himself to the conduct he felt appropriate to a gentleman with his betrothed. He in fact had little doubt he could accomplish it, having a long history of powerful self-restraint, but controlling his *thoughts* was a different matter. He despised himself for feeling that he was losing something valuable in making himself return to fitting behaviour, and not that he was following the only acceptable course open to him.

They began by discussing Georgiana, with Elizabeth sharing

as much as she felt comfortable of what had been said that morning, and trying to help Darcy understand his sister's guilt and shame over the incident with Wickham, and her fears that she would never be able to love or trust again. He listened with concern, though he appreciated Elizabeth's confidence that she would be on the mend now that she had the opportunity to express some of her worries.

"I hope it will be helpful for her," he said. "It has distressed me to think my improper behaviour has caused her such unhappiness. Had I merely behaved as I should, and never gone to your room, none of this would have happened. And although you have been kind enough not to mention it, I am well aware there are other things which should not have happened, and I regret if my lack of self-control should have caused *you* any distress as well." He glanced at her with some embarrassment to see how she responded to this.

"It seems to me that you spend an inordinate amount of time apologizing for behaviour which is quite to be expected of a man violently in love," said Elizabeth, her tone playful. She did not particularly want to discuss her own role in what had occurred.

She was taken aback by his frown. "I suppose I must explain myself to you, as little as I like the prospect, since it seems from my frequent lapses in your company that you will be forced to deal with the situation on occasion." He paused, trying to think how to express himself to her in such a way as to not appear as ungentlemanly as perhaps he was.

Elizabeth could see how disturbed he was by this. "You need not explain anything, if you prefer not to," she said.

"I would infinitely prefer not to, but I think I must. It is perhaps my most shameful failing. Although my goal is always to maintain my self-control and behave the part of a gentleman, there is a part of myself which I must keep leashed in order to do so." He paused, then continued with a sigh, "You have called me ungentlemanly in the past, and in this regard I truly am. It is a part of me which wants only to listen to my desires, and to ignore the dictates of proper behaviour; and in this case, those desires deal specifically with you. More precisely, with behaving with you in a manner not suited to how a gentleman should treat his wife. You saw some of it yesterday, when my baser instincts came to the fore." He said the last piece in such a tone of abhorrence as to startle Elizabeth.

"Well, I can only say then that I was clearly much less disturbed by it than you," she said gently. "I have always known you were a man of strong passions, and to be quite honest, I would have been surprised had you been completely proper and restrained in your dealings with me. If there is a part of you which is untamed and lives 'in the forest of the night,' well, I can hardly claim you have not warned me of this all along!" She finished with a smile which she hoped would reassure him.

He looked at her unsmilingly. "I appreciate your support, but I fear you underestimate the gravity of the situation."

She was beginning to be troubled. There was a question

which needed to be asked, though she disliked it. "Does this part have to do with... harming me, or other force?"

"Not at all!" He seemed genuinely startled by her question. "No, it is more a matter of... using your... responses to gain what I desire." He glanced at her with an embarrassed smile. "As you may have noticed yesterday. And what I desire is often not... gentlemanly. I cannot tell you how sorry I am—you are the last person in the world I would want to see this side of me, yet it seems you are the only one to whom I show it. I would never want to do anything to hurt you, or embarrass you, or make you unhappy."

"William, I..." She had been about to reassure him once more when she decided to take a different tack. "Has it occurred to you perhaps it might be the other way around—that I might be precisely the person to whom you *should* show it? That it is, perhaps, part of what drew you to me, and to insist on marrying me despite such opposition? My love for you is not restricted to your manners, but is for *all* of you." She paused, then continued daringly, "You also seem to assume I want nothing but propriety from you, but while there is much I am ignorant of, the truth is I find your strength of feeling quite... appealing. The beauty of the tiger does not rest only in its outward appearance, but also in its dangerousness."

"You would suggest that I should *deliberately* let myself behave as if I had no proper respect for your dignity?" he asked disbelievingly. The temptation to take advantage of her generosity was well-nigh unbearable, but it could not be. She did not understand what it entailed.

"Well, propriety has its place, but it need not rule between us when we are alone—I wonder if perhaps you should stop trying so hard to leash the tiger at those times. Perhaps it is not such a fearsome beast as you suppose."

"Elizabeth," he said warningly, "you do not know what you are suggesting."

She smiled at him impishly. "No, I do not, which is half of the allure of it; but I *do* know you will not force me to do anything against my will, and I am not such a fragile flower as to be easily frightened. I have a strong will of my own, you know."

"Indeed I do know," said Darcy feelingly. "But I cannot agree to it. I value your good opinion far too much to risk it lightly." He paused, then added, "Fortunately, we have a fortnight for me to work on my self-control, since I imagine your parents will insist on your returning to Longbourn for the duration of our engagement. Which reminds me," he continued, deliberately changing the subject, "I had meant to ask you what it was that made you decide to accept me, after having withstood all my arguments."

"I doubt it was as simple as any one thing," she replied with a light laugh, still troubled by the lack of resolution in their previous conversation, yet unsure how to address her concerns. "I must confess I had been weakening for some time, and it was difficult for me to watch how much distress I was causing you. The final consideration, however, probably stemmed from a conversation I had with your cousin."

"With Colonel Fitzwilliam?" he asked in astonishment, thinking of that gentleman's disapproval of his plan to wed Elizabeth. "What—did you decide to marry me to spite him?"

Elizabeth shot him a puzzled glance. "I am not certain of your meaning, William—he was very encouraging, even, I must admit, when I kept trying to change the subject."

"He was?"

"You seem surprised!"

Darcy exhaled slowly. "I am," he said. What could it mean, that his cousin had gone from advising him against the marriage to advocating it to Elizabeth, without a word to him? *There is something here I am failing to see*, he thought. "Are you certain he favoured the idea?"

"Yes, quite—he said that if your reputation was harmed, it would probably be of little consequence to you, whereas my refusal was of significant consequence, and he suggested I was underestimating the strength of your attachment, and should have more faith in you. I do not see how that could be interpreted as discouraging me," she said, still perplexed by his attitude.

He did not wish to enlighten her as to his cousin's objections to the match, so he limited himself to saying, "Perhaps I misunderstood him, then. In any case, if he assisted in changing your mind, I am very grateful to him."

She gave him a sidelong mischievous look. "You were more eloquent, though."

They were just then passing a small copse, and Darcy, prepared to prove he could keep himself in check, tugged at her hand with a smile until he brought her into its cover. He took her into his arms and kissed her gently and lingeringly several times, just enough to bring a blush to her cheek and a soft look to her eyes. "There, that is better," he said with satisfaction. He was pleased to see he could still restrain himself to an acceptable level.

She gave him an arch smile. "I am glad you are pleased—and that I have not disturbed your vaunted self-control," she said provocatively.

"Do not mock my self-control, best beloved, unless you are prepared to be quite late for dinner!" he teased, but there was an element of taut restraint in his voice.

She tipped her head to the side, as if she were considering the matter. She could tell he was withdrawing from her; and although she was not sure of the cause, it pained her nonetheless. She had been taken aback by his unusual failure to heed her comments on the question of his behaviour earlier, and it made her suspect that his opinion of her might have been tainted by her permissiveness the previous night. Well, it would have to be addressed; they could not go on like this for the rest of their lives. She said judiciously, "I cannot mock it; I am not as fond of your self-control as all that. After all, I suspect that, had your self-control been flawless, you would never have looked at me in the first place, certainly never proposed to me, and, even if you had come that far, you would have left the moment you learned of my engagement, never to return. I owe *nothing* to your self-control; so far as I can observe, I owe our engagement solely to the lapses in it. But I suspect it is more a matter of your opinion of *my* self-control which presents a difficulty here."

"*Your* self-control?" he asked in surprise. He could see her tension, however, and realized how his words could have been interpreted. "Not at all, Elizabeth, I promise you. You have done nothing wrong, nothing that troubles me in the slightest; the fault is mine."

"It was a *fault* to fall in love with me against your better judgement, then," she said slowly.

Darcy, not wishing to hear her demean their connection, immediately responded, "Not so, my dearest; loving you is by far the most sensible thing I have done."

She raised an eyebrow. "It is no doubt improper of me to argue the point, but I find it difficult to believe you made a reasoned decision to fall in love with an upstart country miss with no fortune or even proper respect for you. No, William, had your reason carried the day, you would never have looked at me but to criticize. Your *self-control* is no friend of mine."

A certain ferocity in her voice made him pause. "Elizabeth," he said finally, "I admit I never planned to fall in love with you, and I cannot deny that in fact I fought it for some time before I recognized only *you* could make me happy, and only *you* could teach me the lessons I needed to learn. It was more a matter of instinct, though, rather than a failure of self-control." This explanation sounded weak even to his own ears.

"And was this *part* of you which you so despise not involved in this instinct?" retorted Elizabeth spiritedly. "Was your *instinct* comprised solely of gentlemanly urges?"

Darcy was silent, all too aware that he had been imagining her in his bed not a fortnight after they met. He could not comprehend why Elizabeth was so insistent on pointing out his weakness in this regard. "Do you *wish* me to be less than I could be?"

"I wish you to be precisely *you*. There is more to you than a proper gentleman, or you should be no different from any other gentleman. I love you because of what sets you apart from all the rest—for your spirit, if you would. Yesterday you asked if I had reservations about marrying you, and I do not; I love you without reserve, for everything which makes you yourself, whether it is a part of which *you* approve or not."

Darcy, moved by these words from Elizabeth, who was usually far more restrained in expressing her affection, put his arms around her, leaning his head against hers. "I do not deserve you," he said, "but I am very grateful for you."

Knowing he had not yet accepted her point, she said earnestly, "Would you have me give up my liveliness, never to be impertinent or teasing? Shall I stop taking long walks, and instead take on a languid and cool attitude so as to be a proper lady?"

"Never," he said instantly.

"Then you do not wish me to be a proper lady?"

"You are everything that is important in a lady to me."

Elizabeth drew a deep breath. "Why, then, do you insist that I would not want *you* to be *yourself*?"

His arms closed around her, and he held her tightly. Such acceptance was a new concept to him, and it was very tempting to give himself over to it, yet the thought of the look on Georgiana's face stopped him. "What will happen, then, when you discover you do not like what you find of me?" he asked, his voice taut.

She caught his face in her hands and kissed him firmly. "Your cousin suggested I should have more faith in you; perhaps he needs to give you the same advice about me." Her voice carried a revealing certainty.

"I do have faith in you," he replied, beginning to despair of convincing her of the seriousness of the problem. "But if you must know why I take this so seriously, I will give you just one example." He paused, closing his eyes for a moment, then said, "Do you know that I would like nothing better than to seduce you at this very moment, to make you mine right here and now, not more than a few feet away from a public road? Do you realize I want to strip away every inch of clothing you are wearing, and taste every bit of you with kisses? *Do you see now why I must control this?*"

A rush of heat went through her at his words, but the pain and hopelessness in his voice kept her focused on him. "Well, I can see your difficulty since, all in all, this might not be the time to be late for dinner," she said, striving for a lightness in her voice, "although I admit the idea has a certain appeal." She smiled up at him bewitchingly.

"God in heaven," he swore feelingly. "Do not say such things, Elizabeth!"

Hearing him sound so much more like himself added to her confidence. "Why should I not?" she asked mischievously, her eyes sparkling. She raised her hand and lightly drew her finger along his neck at the top of his cravat.

His eyes flared. "Because I will take advantage of it," he said, capturing her mouth with an urgent kiss which pressed for far more of a response than his earlier gentle caresses. There was less of seduction or persuasion in it than an expression of raw need, and a passion which could not be satisfied within narrow bounds.

Elizabeth's immediate response to his kisses was in part a relief that he was no longer closing her out, but his urgency rapidly transmitted itself to her and raised a sensation of heated desire within her. She pressed herself against him, wanting only to be closer and to lose herself in the pleasure of his touch. Even more than that, she wanted a response from him, one which would convince her of his acceptance of this bond between them.

Darcy's untempered desire led him to seek relief by letting his hands rediscover the curves of her body, but it was not enough to slake his thirst; and even as his lips were asking ever more of her, he began to crave the greater closeness they had experienced the previous night. It seemed as if there were no going back; that each time he touched her, he needed more of her than the previous time, and after denying himself even the hope of touching her so intimately, he was more desperate for her than ever.

Had they the privacy he would wish, he knew he would not stop, but he could neither still his need nor forget the unpropitious circumstances in which they found themselves. He fought for self-control as his lips ranged freely along her face to the sensitive skin below her ear. Between kisses, he whispered, "Tell me what you want."

Elizabeth, who was beginning to lose herself in her desire for more of him, heard the desperation in his voice, and remembered what he had asked of her the previous day. "I want you," she said softly, not knowing if she could depend upon her voice. "I want to be yours. I want you never to go away from me like that again."

It seemed she had guessed correctly what he needed, for he took in a deep breath, then let it out slowly. His body gradually relaxed within her embrace, and he said, "Oh, my best beloved—you are everything I could desire."

She reached her hand up to caress his thick hair, hoping to transform her own unfulfilled longing into an expression of tenderness. "It frightened me when you were so distant," she said softly.

"It was not my intention to be distant, my dearest, just to avoid falling into temptation," he said regretfully. "But it does not seem to be within my capacity."

"Or perhaps I will not permit it," said Elizabeth cheekily.

He laughed, unable to resist her liveliness. "No, apparently not."

"What was it that was troubling you so, though?" she asked, her voice unwontedly serious. "If it was not my behaviour, then what? Is it Georgiana?"

He nodded silently. "I do not want to hurt her again as I did last night. She deserves better than that of me," he said, his remorse plain in his voice.

"Oh, my love," said Elizabeth patiently, "you are doing her no favours by trying to be perfect on her behalf. Can you not see that part of her distress over what has happened to her in the past is the inability to feel she can live up to your expectations? As long as she sees you as having no flaws, she will blame herself for every failing she finds in herself. You would do well to allow yourself to be a little more imperfect in her eyes."

"But not in this way!"

She smiled. "No, perhaps not; we should be more careful, I suppose, in making certain of our privacy—certainly more careful than we are being at the moment! But still, it is hardly the end of the world that she discovered you last night—after all, it allowed her the opportunity to confide in me, and perhaps gain some bit of confidence in herself. I think perhaps *you* are the one who is suffering more."

Her practicality reassured him as little else could. "Perhaps you are right," he said slowly. "And I certainly did not mean to hurt *you* by trying to exercise self-restraint, but I can see that I may have done so."

"It worried me, perhaps," she said with an impish smile. "I did not know what to make of you, or why you seemed so different, and I am perhaps fonder of this side of you than you know."

"Elizabeth," he said, his eyes travelling down her body, "if you are going to insist on continuing to say such things, we are *never* going to reach Longbourn."

She laughed. "Come, then; I will no longer try your patience, and we shall be on our way."

He gave her a sidelong glance as they found their way back to the road. "It is a pity; I do enjoy it when you try my patience in such a manner."

"You, my love, are beyond redemption," she retorted with amusement.

"And you, my best beloved, looked particularly tempting last night, when you could not have enough of my wicked ways," he said, enjoying the blush which rose immediately to her cheeks.

It was unsurprising that they arrived at Longbourn after the rest of the party. Elizabeth counted this as a blessing, since it meant her mother was already past the first raptures of her joy at the news of their engagement carried by Jane. Fortunately, Mrs. Bennet stood in sufficient awe of her intended son-in-law as to only offer him any civility within her power. Her effusions to Elizabeth could not, however, be prevented, but with the able assistance of Jane and Mr. Bingley, Darcy was brought into the house while she spoke to her daughter.

"Oh, my sweetest Lizzy!" she cried. "Mr. Darcy! Who would have thought it! How rich and how great you will be! What pin-money, what jewels, what carriages you will have! Jane's is nothing to it—nothing at all. How clever you were, to break your engagement to Mr. Covington! You should have told me it was for Mr. Darcy. And to move to Netherfield, so you could be near him—I could not have planned it better myself. Oh, I am so pleased—so happy!"

"Indeed, I am glad you are satisfied," said Elizabeth gravely, amused by her rapid elevation from disgrace to success, "though I did not break off my engagement so that I might marry Mr. Darcy."

"Of course not—but so clever of you to wait so long until he returned here so no one would suspect."

Elizabeth was grateful this subject was dropped by the time they went into the house. The subject soon turned to her wedding, a matter which provoked some conflict, as Mrs. Bennet had quite different ideas as to what sort of event it should be. Elizabeth and Darcy, supported in this case by Mr. Bennet and Mr. Bingley, prevailed in their insistence on a quiet ceremony, with the understanding that Elizabeth's

situation with Mr. Covington made anything else inappropri-
ate. Darcy would not be moved from the idea of the briefest
engagement possible.

"As it is only a fortnight," said Mr. Bennet, looking over
his glasses at Elizabeth, "I think it will not be too great a trial
for you to return to Longbourn for this period. Now that your
engagement is formal, you cannot remain at Netherfield."

"We have your old room quite ready for you," Mrs.
Bennet added. "Tomorrow Lady Lucas is coming to call, and
she will be delighted to see you."

Elizabeth's eyes met Darcy's across the table. He looked
at her to encourage her, clearly in agreement with her parents
in this matter. Turning to her father, she said slowly, "No, I
think it unnecessary. Netherfield is my home now, and I will
be married from there."

She did not dare look at Darcy to see his reaction,
and she knew it would be well hidden in any case for the
circumstances, but she felt his gaze throughout her body. It
strengthened her, and she remained firm as her family urged
her to reconsider. Finally, seeing that she would not relent,
Mr. Bennet noted that Jane and Miss Darcy would provide
adequate chaperonage, eyeing Darcy with a look which could
not be misinterpreted.

Darcy's manners through dinner and afterwards were
impeccable. There was no hint of impropriety in his conduct
towards Elizabeth, even so much as a glance which could be
misinterpreted. This was not merely to satisfy Mr. Bennet,

but also to protect Georgiana; he did not wish to distress her any further, nor give her any more grounds to suspect him. He would have to be much more careful in finding time alone with Elizabeth, but after their earlier discussion, he could not even consider avoiding any intimacies for the next fortnight.

He was so successful in his endeavour as to leave Elizabeth in a certain amount of doubt as to his actual response to her decision to remain at Netherfield. It crossed her mind that he might have preferred to have temptation removed, particularly in order to shield Georgiana, and she hoped he was not angry. If he was, she determined with slight annoyance, she would remind him that all he need do was maintain his reserve, and she would not tempt him.

She was inclined to think he was probably not angry, but was disturbed enough by the possibility as to somewhat avoid his eyes on the carriage ride back to Netherfield. By the time they had arrived, Darcy was not unaware that something was troubling her, and had an unhappy suspicion of what it concerned.

Once they were inside, he drew her off from the others slightly to speak quietly in her ear. "You need not be anxious on my account, beloved. I will accept whatever rules you make without complaint."

"You are not disturbed at my decision, then?" Her voice indicated her worry.

"Disturbed? Not at all. The only thing which is likely

to be disturbed by your presence here is my sleep, knowing you are only a few doors away." He said this last with a slight smile.

She looked down, her cheeks flushed. "If that," she said very softly.

"Elizabeth!" he said, his voice a combination of pleasure, astonishment, and urgent desire. With two words she had completely undermined him; it was all he could do not to carry her away at that moment.

There was no further opportunity to speak; Bingley invited Darcy and Colonel Fitzwilliam to his study for drinks, and he did not dare draw any attention by refusing. Elizabeth, with a last glance at his retreating back, went with Jane and Georgiana to begin discussing the wedding, now that the engagement was official. The occasion could not seem to take on any reality for her, though—it was as if the important event had already occurred in her finally accepting him, and all the rest was detail. She wished she could be with Darcy; even in such a brief separation as this, she missed him with what felt like a painful urgency.

The gentlemen returned just as the ladies were preparing to retire for the evening. Darcy continued to appear composed and collected, but when he took her aside under the pretext of saying a private good night, it was clear his appearance did not reflect his state of mind. His eyes caressed her as he murmured, "If you choose to let me into your room tonight, my love, I will not be leaving."

Elizabeth's eyes widened slightly. She had not quite intended *that* in her earlier suggestion, having thought more of a repeat of the previous night. "I… will keep that in mind, should I be faced with the decision," she delayed, the rush of heat through her body seeming to interfere with clear thought. "And would this be the gentleman or the tiger?" she asked with an arch look.

His eyes drifted slowly downwards, taking in her figure. "The gentleman would never have made such a suggestion," he said suggestively.

"I see," Elizabeth replied, a bit breathlessly.

"You did suggest that I allow that side of me freer rein, as I recall." His dark eyes were intense. "I warned you that you might not realize what you were taking on."

"So you did." Her mouth was dry.

"You can always reconsider," he said, in a voice which suggested he certainly hoped she did not. Then, in a more normal voice, designed to be overheard, he added, "I will bid you good night, then."

She gave him a mischievous look. "Good night, William. I hope you sleep well."

His eyes seemed to imply he would be exacting revenge for that remark later on, but he merely kissed her hand lightly.

Elizabeth was unsure how serious Darcy had been about coming to her room, and equally unsure of what she would do if he did. She had only just changed into her nightclothes when a knock came at the door. She certainly had not been expecting him yet—the household was still awake, but her heart was pounding as she went to the door, and opened it to find Georgiana.

"I am sorry to disturb you—I had hoped you were not asleep," said the girl anxiously.

"No, not at all," replied Elizabeth, struggling to regain her equanimity after finding the wrong Darcy at her door.

"I was wondering… well, I was wondering if I could talk to you for a few minutes."

"Of course," Elizabeth said warmly. "Shall we go to your room? Mine is quite chilly, I must admit, and only bearable when I huddle under the covers." *And your brother is unlikely to walk into your room*, she thought.

When they had reached Georgiana's room and were well settled, Georgiana, after thanking her repeatedly for being willing to talk to her, said, "I wanted you to know… well, I was thinking after we talked this morning that you must think me a fool for… permitting Mr. Wickham's advances. I did not want you to think I was like that—I do know better, and I do not know what came over me to allow him to… I am so very ashamed of it." She looked beseechingly at Elizabeth.

"I assure you, I thought nothing of the sort," replied Elizabeth kindly, as it was clear Georgiana had been feeling ashamed all day of what she had confessed. "I have no doubt it was quite out of character for you, and could only happen because he could be so charming, and he knew how to manipulate you so well. And you were very young, and unprotected—it would have been a miracle if nothing had happened."

"I should never have permitted it," she said sadly.

This was clearly not going to be a brief discussion, and Elizabeth settled herself in for an extended period of reassurance, not without wondering what Darcy might be doing at the same moment.

# Chapter 10

ELIZABETH EASED GEORGIANA'S SLEEPING head off her shoulder and slipped out of the bed. Tucking the bedclothes around the girl, she took the lamp and left as quietly as she could. She was halfway to her own room when she remembered Darcy. Had he come and found her gone? Or thought she was refusing to answer the door to him? Or had he never come at all?

She opened the door not to find the expected darkness, but instead the light of another lamp. It rested on her bedside table, illuminating the shape of the man sitting on her bed, reading her book. She started at the sight, then her pulses began to flutter as Darcy looked up at her, an unreadable expression in his dark eyes.

He said conversationally, "I was beginning to wonder when I might see you."

A saucy smile curved her lips. "I apologize for keeping you

waiting, sir. I hope you found some way to amuse yourself in my absence."

He looked down at the book in his hand as if uncertain how it had found its way there. "Not as well as I should have liked to have been amused."

She raised her eyebrow at his remarkably level tone, wondering what he was thinking. "You were preempted by your sister, I am afraid, who asked to speak to me. I went to her room, just *in case* any gentlemen might turn up at my door, which could have been a most embarrassing circumstance. As it happened, she had a great deal to say. She just fell asleep in my arms after a long bout of tears."

A light flickered in his eyes. "*I* was planning to fall asleep in your arms tonight," he said. "How fortunate that you have a reasonable excuse to present for your absence. So, what did my dear sister have to say that was so urgent?"

She smiled at his combination of seductiveness, petulance, and concern. "We covered a rather extensive range, I must say, starting with a very detailed account of what happened at Ramsgate, with a discourse on Mrs. Younge, and then moved on to your mother's death and her loneliness when she was sent off to school, and I believe we had reached her fears of living in London when she finally fell asleep. When your sister decides to say her piece, sir, she does not do it by halves."

"I am," he said, standing and walking over to her, "astonished."

"And, were it not for your other agenda for the evening, you might even be gratified," she teased.

"I have not given up on my agenda for the evening." His hands busied themselves with the belt of her dressing gown.

Elizabeth's knees seemed to grow weak. She could think of nothing to say, but merely looked into his eyes. She did not know how it had come to pass, but in the last day, since she had at last accepted him, she had taken him into her heart to an extent she could barely begin to comprehend. Perhaps it was because she had struggled against caring for him for so long, or because she had despaired of ever having him for so long, but once she had given way, she had done so completely, leaving no part of herself uncommitted to him.

He held the ends of her belt in his hands. "I was worried about you, Elizabeth," he said, his visage serious.

This was not what she had expected to hear. "Worried about me? Why?"

"I had every reason to think you would be here when I came, and you were not, and then you did not return for a long time. I could not imagine where you might have gone to, or what might have happened to you."

"What could possibly have happened to me between the drawing room and here that could cause you worry?"

"You might have decided to take a walk in the moonlight, and become lost, or hurt. And I could do nothing about it—I could not start a search for you, for how would I explain knowing you were missing? Or perhaps you were avoiding me—perhaps you could not tell me what you truly thought." His voice was very controlled.

"William," she said, with just a touch of exasperation, "did it not occur to you there was likely a perfectly reasonable explanation for my absence?"

He crushed her into his arms. Burying his face in her neck, he said, "Of course it did. But I have waited for you for so long, and I am so afraid of losing you, or that you might have a change of heart about me—I could not bear it, Elizabeth."

She put her arms around him comfortingly. "I know—I feel the same," she said softly, kissing his shoulder. "I will not have a change of heart, you know—my heart has been yours for a very long time now. You may depend upon it."

She could feel the tense muscles of his back through the fine lawn of his shirt. Never before had she been able to sense his body as well as she could now in the absence of his coats, and she stroked his back slowly, appreciating the shape and closeness of him. He seemed to relax somewhat under her ministrations, and she enjoyed the comforting feeling of having her head against his shoulder.

It was not clear to her when it changed to something else, when his warm breath on her neck turned to kisses so light she did not at first recognize them as such, nor when his hands first began to move along the silky fabric of her dressing gown. Her body recognized it almost instinctively, as she began to feel the heat of his body against hers. It was unmistakable, though, when he released her momentarily, only to slip his hands inside her gown and recapture her, but with only the thin barrier of her summer nightdress between his hands and her. She shivered at the intimacy as his hands travelled first up her back, his fingers exploring, then back down to discover the curves of her hips, stroking gently, then, as he felt her response to his touch, pressing her against him.

His kisses became more assertive as she arched herself against him, craving the pleasure of his body against hers. There had never before been so little between them when he held her, and she could feel his warmth against her breasts, making her long for his touch there as well. As an unbearable tension developed within her, she knew she would have to make her decision soon, or it would be made for her by her own desire and the ache in her secret places.

His lips were exploring the sensitive hollow at the base of her neck as she said shakily, "I thought you said you would stay *if* I made the choice to let you in my room; yet you made that choice for me, it seems."

He raised his head to look at her, his eyes dark with passion and his hair disheveled. "So I did," he said in a low but unrepentant voice. He drew his hand upward until it cupped her breast, then, as he felt her quick intake of breath, stroked her nipple lightly with his thumb. He smiled as her eyes closed in response to the sensation. "Well, loveliest Elizabeth, will you let me in?" He brought his fingers together so as better to toy with her sensitive flesh as he nuzzled her ear.

Elizabeth, overcome with the heady delight coursing

through her at his touch, only knew she could not bear for him to stop yet. A soft moan passed her lips as all coherent thought fled her.

He was in no hurry, and the sound of her quick breaths and sighs of pleasure was music to his ears. As her excitement began to rise, and she pressed herself against his hand as if asking for more, he judged it was time. Seductively he said, "What is it to be, then? Should I stop—" he paused his action for just a moment, "or would you perhaps like my mouth there instead? You will remember that I did warn you I would use your own responses against you."

She could not stand for this pleasure to end, not when her other breast ached for his touch as well and an unmistakable sense of heat built between her legs. "Please," she whispered, "do not stop."

A smile of triumph crossed his face. Ever since Elizabeth had suggested he might let loose his self-control when with her, it was as if he had just been biding his time for this moment when he could avail himself of her sanction. He no longer cared that it was not how a gentleman would treat a lady; all he wanted was to have her, but not until he had given her as much pleasure as she could bear and brought her to the heights of wild passion of the Elizabeth of his dreams. No, she would not be a lady tonight, lying passively beneath him; he had something quite different in mind.

He found a sense of release in giving up the last vestiges of his self-control, in finally allowing himself to be gripped by urges so forbidden to a gentleman, in calling a halt to any pretense that he wanted nothing more of Elizabeth than a kiss on the hand. He did not know how he would ever regain that restraint, but for the moment, he did not care.

He dropped to one knee in front of her. "Such an excellent attitude must be rewarded," he said as he drew her nipple into his mouth through the fabric of her gown. He was not ready to give her everything she wanted, not yet, but he stimulated her with his lips and his teeth until her body was no longer steady under his ministrations and she leaned her hands upon his shoulders for support. He dropped his arm to bunch the hem of her nightdress in his hand until he could reach under it easily to stroke the forbidden skin of her leg, gratified as her hips involuntarily pressed forwards against him.

With a last taste, he withdrew from her breast and stood. In her face he could read the untamed desire he had waited so long to see. He kissed her lightly, then penetrated her mouth with his tongue, exploring her thoroughly until she clung helplessly to him, meeting his invasion with her own.

God, he wanted her, but even now she was not yet enough his. "More?" he asked thickly, and as she nodded dreamily, he moved behind her and lifted her dressing gown from her shoulders. Once that obstacle was removed, he pulled her back against him so that she could feel his arousal, and caught her breasts with his hands once more for another round of pleasuring. She leaned her head back against him, and his hands moved up to the ties of her nightdress, disposing of them quickly until he could push the garment down over her shoulders to reveal her rounded breasts.

She caught the nightdress at her waist, and he heard her sharp indrawn breath as he inserted his hands beneath it to caress the tempting curves of her hips. She had allowed him more latitude than he had expected, but not yet as much as he hoped. "Elizabeth," he murmured in her ear, "I want to see all of you." At her moment of hesitation, he added, "I told you I would be no gentleman—I want far too much of you to settle for what a gentleman takes from his wife." He let his hand slide down toward the juncture of her thighs, deliberately tempting her. "And before we are done, you will want more of me than a lady expects from her husband. Oh, yes, you will want more."

Elizabeth struggled to catch her breath against the sensations he was creating in her, not just with his touch, but with his voice. She knew that her native modesty was losing the battle against the lure of the forbidden, subverted by the pleasure of his touch. In sudden decision, she released the fabric, and the last barrier fell to the floor.

She felt his lips on her neck once more, and his hands crept down to her thighs. "*Very* nice," he breathed. "Unfortunately, you know what they say about feeding tigers—it only makes them hungrier, and I am... very hungry."

"Shall I stop feeding you, then?" she asked with a smile, to prove she was still capable of speech.

"Do not even suggest it, my love. I enjoy being hungry in

such a good cause." He slid his hand between her legs, bringing it slowly up to rest over her most secret places.

Elizabeth shuddered at the burst of sensation which ran through her. She would not have imagined she could feel so much, and the feeling did not stop, but grew as she pressed herself against his hand. "Oh, William," she sighed.

He rubbed his hand back and forth, thrilling in the pleasure he was giving her. He could not quite believe he truly had her in his arms in this state, and that she did not seem disturbed by it. "Come to bed, my love, and I will show you even more," he said.

His words seemed to bring back some of her modesty, for she stilled and coloured slightly, embarrassed by her uncovered state, especially since he was still clad. She turned in his arms and pressed her hands against his shirt, in part hiding herself against him. "Not until you remove this," she said, her eyes daring him.

A new light appeared in his eyes, and a pleased smile crossed his face. "As you wish, my dearest," he said, bending his head to taste her lips evocatively before complying with her request.

Elizabeth hardly knew what to do with the sight before her, since it went beyond her imagination. She ran her hands lightly up the defined muscles of his chest, then pressed her body against his, aroused by the feeling of his skin rubbing her breasts as she swayed towards him. She closed her eyes to savour the experience and turned her mouth up to his.

He caught it in a kiss of deep passion, exploring the confines of her mouth as he stroked her back, pulling her tightly to him. Her conduct was feeding the fire within him until it blazed with almost unbearable heat, and he wanted her with a fierceness that surprised even him. Without breaking contact with her lips, he swept her into his arms and carried her to the bed. He lay down beside her, skimming his hand over her breast until he was satisfied with the look of desire in her eyes, then he drew her nipple into his mouth, gently teasing it until she writhed against him. He slid his hand once more down to the juncture of her legs, feeling her arch to meet him.

He had been waiting for this moment. He lifted his head, watching her until she opened her eyes, and with his gaze fixed on her, he finally slipped his fingers into her folds to discover her place of pleasure. Her expression of surprise and arousal was all he had hoped it would be. He showed her a new level of excitement, stroking her in tiny circles until her low moans became more frequent and higher, her head moving from side to side with the fierce pleasure rushing through her. With a satisfied look, he bent his head to her breast again, and added the tantalization of his mouth to the activity of his fingers until he felt her reach her crest. The sound of her soft cries satisfied his deep urge to take her pleasure, and he prolonged the moment as long as he could. When her tremors finally ceased, he kissed her gently.

"William," she breathed in astonishment.

His voice was self-satisfied. "As I said, before I was done, you would want more than a lady receives from her husband."

She smiled at him archly. "I cannot say, since it seems to be my fate that I shall never know what a gentleman gives to his wife."

"Is that a complaint, my love?" he asked lazily, letting his fingers begin to move against her again.

Her eyes widened. "Not at all," she said, a bit breathlessly, as his touch revived her earlier pleasures.

He enjoyed watching her rising passion for a few minutes, then paused to strip himself of his remaining attire. With the sensation of finally finding the place always meant for him, he situated himself atop her, his legs parting hers.

Elizabeth, perhaps more startled by his appearance than she cared to indicate, pulled his head down to hers for a kiss. As she did, his hips began to undulate against her, his arousal stimulating her as his fingers had done earlier. It gave her exquisite pleasure, and without a thought she spread her legs wider to permit greater contact. She arched against him, gasping, and her movement clearly fired his desire even higher, for he returned to her mouth demandingly, as if he required even greater dominion of her. As their mouths intertwined, he pulled his hips back and slowly but without hesitation entered her, pushing his way past her last barrier to take final possession of her.

She flinched in a brief moment of pain, trying to incorporate this new experience as he began to move gently within her. It was only a brief interval before she could feel a new kind of pleasure growing within her at his actions, and she opened her eyes to find him looking at her questioningly.

"Am I hurting you, best beloved?" he asked with concern.

She shook her head. "Only for a short time," she said with a distracted smile.

This last reassurance was all he needed, and he thrust himself deep within her, letting instinct take over. Feeling the consummate joy of being fully accepted at last by the woman he had loved for so long, he found a rhythm which seemed to draw the greatest response from her. He felt her wrap her legs around him, pulling him deeper within her, and her moans of pleasure only fired his desire yet further. As he moved within her, he let the supreme delight of her body around him wash over him and build to ever greater heights until he released himself in a pinnacle of superb pleasure.

Sated, he collapsed in her arms, marvelling at the softness of her body beneath him and the gentle touch of her hands on his back. He felt a deep contentment, a sense of finally coming home, and took his ease in the comfort of loving and being loved. Soon, though, a cognizance of Elizabeth's situation entered him, and he moved off her to lie beside her, his hand moving as if by instinct to cup her breast tenderly.

He kissed her gently, and was relieved to see her smile at him. "I hope I did not hurt you, my love," he said.

She shook her head, still too far caught up in the intense emotion of the moment to speak. The mild ache she felt did not compare to the power of the closeness she felt to him, and the freedom that had come from both seeing him in total abandon and her discovery and sharing of her own pleasure. She nestled closer to him, kissing his shoulder.

With slightly greater uneasiness, he said, "Are you disturbed by this, by what has passed between us? I hope you will feel you can tell me."

She looked up into the shadows of his face. "Oh, no. No. I am perfectly well, and content to be here with you," she said, hoping to reassure him.

"Then I am happy," he said, but there was a look in his eye which made her doubt his words. She waited to see if he would say more, but in his silence she read more concern than ease.

She reached up to trace the line his hair made as it fell against his face. "Is something troubling you?" she asked simply, not wanting to lose the precious sense of intimacy with him she felt.

His mouth moved in a mirthless smile. "I am caught," he said, "in the bitter dilemma of being quite ashamed of myself for taking advantage of you, and at the same time, wanting nothing more than to do so again as soon as possible. As I told you earlier, I am not reconciled with the part of myself that is so selfish as to think only of my own desires."

She nibbled his neck playfully. "Well, you may believe what you like, but it certainly seemed to me that you were doing a great deal of thinking about me."

"You give me too much credit," he said seriously. "I take pleasure from *your* pleasure; it is far from selfless of me."

She bit her lip, her contentment fading away. "I am sorry if you regret what happened," she said, feeling the beginning of a deep mortification building within her.

Her troubled tone did not pass by unnoticed by Darcy, and he kissed her earnestly. "Oh, my best beloved, that is exactly my problem: I do *not* regret it, but I think that I *ought* to, and I do not know how you can forgive me my selfishness."

She forced herself to relax, not as simple a matter as she would have wished, once she had begun to feel uncomfortable in her exposedness. "You are the only one here worried about this, my dear," she said. "I have learned a great deal in this last year, not the least of which is the price of being condemned as shameful, and what it is to have nothing left to lose. I know what it is to have my name fall into ill repute, and what it means to feel that censure, and to take it onto myself; and I *will not* feel ashamed any longer for loving you, or for acting on the natural consequences of that love. We are betrothed and soon to be married, and it is no one's business but our own how we celebrate that fact, just as it is no one's business but our own whether or not we behave as *they* think a lady and a gentleman ought in the privacy of our own rooms." Her voice had become fierce by the time she finished.

He took this in quietly, then raised an eyebrow. "I had not realized I was marrying a tigress," he said mildly.

"The more fool you," she retorted in delight at his changed mien. "I had assumed that was *why* you were marrying me."

He smiled at her arch look, and kissed her thoroughly. "I

am marrying you, if you must know, because I finally realized under your tutelage that what was important was not rank, or privilege, or reputation, but only the knowledge of loving and being loved. I cannot tell you what an education it was for me when I first went to your uncle's house in London, and saw, in a place I would have once never deigned to enter, a kind of warmth and affection throughout that I lacked and wanted dearly; and I realized how much better it would have been for Georgiana if, instead of growing up with my rigid ideas of what was right and proper, she had spent those years with your aunt and uncle and knowing what it was to be loved and accepted for what she was."

Elizabeth traced her finger along his cheek, moved by his words. "I do love you, William."

"That means the world to me, my dearest." He ran his fingers through her hair, thinking of how often he had imagined this scene, but he could never have guessed at the contentment he felt, holding her in his arms so intimately.

She became still as a thought entered her mind unbidden. "William," said Elizabeth with sudden suspicion, "when were you at my uncle's house?"

How had he managed to forget himself enough to have mentioned he had been there? He had not wanted her to know, but he would not dissemble to her, especially not now. "It was when your sister disappeared," he said with a sigh. "I knew Wickham's companions of old, and was able to offer your father some assistance in locating her."

She looked at him searchingly. "Why has this never been mentioned to me, by either you, or my father, or my uncle for that matter? Why the secrecy?"

He looked uncomfortable. "I asked your father, and your aunt and uncle, not to tell anyone of my role in the matter. I did not want you to feel any obligation to me."

"You are too kind," she said with a laugh, then, at his serious look, said suspiciously, "What is it, William? What are you not telling me?"

He looked away. "I felt a responsibility; I had failed to expose Wickham for what he was out of my own unwillingness to lay open my actions to the world."

"Must I ask my father?" she asked archly at his obvious evasion.

He kissed the tip of her nose. "You know me too well, my love. Very well, if you must know, I went with your father to retrieve your sister; and, having greater experience in dealing with Wickham, negotiated the bargain with him—I am assuming you *do* know their marriage did not take place without money changing hands. And I returned for their wedding, to make sure he kept his word, because Wickham knows to be afraid of me, and he does not fear your father."

"I still fail to see why you would keep this a secret from me," she said, with a good suspicion as to what he was leaving out of the story. "Unless, perhaps, you had some *financial* role in this you are conveniently forgetting to mention."

He looked so much like a child caught in misbehaviour

that she could not help but laugh. He replied with as much dignity as he could manage, "As I said, I felt some responsibility for the matter."

She shrugged teasingly. "If that is to be your story," she said.

He smiled and kissed her neck softly. "Very well, minx; I did not like to see you so unhappy."

She paused for thought, or as much thought as she could manage with his lips trailing along her collarbone. "But then you left," she pointed out.

Gathering her into his arms, he said, "Pray do not remind me of that time; it was as dark a one as I have known. I thought you loved Covington, and I wanted you to be happy; that seemed to require your sister's marriage and my departure, so that is what I arranged for. I was selfish enough to come to see you that last time, knowing I should stay away, simply because I could not bear for my last sight of you to be in tears in *his* arms."

"Oh, William," she said softly, tears rising to her eyes as she recalled the moment, "and I was crying because I wanted *you* to comfort me, not him, and it could not be."

"Is that what it was?" he asked reflectively. "I wish I had known, though perhaps it is just as well I did not; I would have been all too tempted to do something foolish." In an attempt to remind himself all this was in the past, he allowed himself to caress the curves of her body. He still could not credit how very generous and free she had been with him; he counted himself extremely fortunate to have found a woman who could match him in that regard.

She smiled mischievously. "Yes—you were never at your best when he was present." She could see by the look on his face, though, that this was still a bitter memory and not a teasing matter, and she hastened to amend herself. "Even so, you were the one I wanted—and how angry that made me!"

He looked at her seriously, trying to still the part of himself which was still ferociously jealous that another man had ever had a claim on her. "You did not want to love me?"

She laughed. "No, I most certainly did not! You completely disrupted the calm path of my life."

His hand strayed along her flanks, intimately reacquainting him with her shape. "You could have made it so much simpler by accepting me last April."

"*You* could have made it simpler by not waiting nearly half a year to follow up on your letter!" retorted Elizabeth good-humouredly, finding it impossible to ignore the effect his explorations were having on her.

He cupped his hand around her breast, rubbing his thumb across her nipple. He had an intense urge to take her again, but he knew it was for the wrong reasons; he wanted their lovemaking to be characterized by passion and laughter, not to come out of jealousy and a need to stake his claim to her once more. Still, the liberties he was taking soothed him to some extent in reassuring him that she was his.

Although distinctly aroused by his fondling, Elizabeth

was discovering that, outside of the heat of the moment, these intimacies came as more of a shock, and she realized just how far they had altered their relationship that night. Impulsively, she hugged him close and said, "Oh, William, what a difficult course we have taken! I wish I had known last April what I know now, and not had to learn so much in the hardest possible manner."

He heard the confusion in her voice, and it brought out his protective instincts. He moved his hand to her hair and began stroking it gently. "I wish neither of us had suffered the way we did, but I know for my part there were lessons in it I needed to learn. Before I met you, I had the good fortune never to lack for anything I wanted, and it had never occurred to me that I *could*. Even after you refused me, I kept in the back of my mind the idea that if you knew the truth, it would be within my ability to change your mind, should I decide to try. It was not until I went to Vienna that I finally acknowledged that you were what I wanted more than anything in life, and I never would have you. I cannot tell you what that took, but it was important for me to realize I could not have whatever I wanted merely for the wanting of it."

"But you ended up winning me in any case," she pointed out with a smile.

"Yes, but only after I admitted to myself I could not," he replied. A thought crossed his mind of something he had long wished to know, but never felt able to ask before. "When was it that you decided to break off your engagement?"

There was a pause before she spoke. "It was shortly after you left for the final time," she said slowly. "I had considered it earlier, while you were away in London, but not seriously; it was not until the last time I saw you that I recognized I would not be able to forget you, no matter how hard I tried, and that I could not marry him, feeling as I did about you, even if it was my only chance for an independent future. And with Jane's engagement, the pressure to safeguard my family was no longer there."

"To safeguard your family? What do you mean by that?"

She sighed. "It was one of the reasons I agreed to marry him—to protect my mother and sisters from an intolerable situation after my father's death. I could not justify sentencing them to near penury when there was a perfectly agreeable gentleman who wished to marry me, and could provide for them in the future."

Darcy frowned, unable to forget that *he* had proposed to her not long before, and *he* would have been in a far better position to provide support to her family. "Surely your father would not leave you in such financial straits as that," he said with some authority.

She tilted her head back to look at him, surprised to find him unaware of her family's financial situation. "My father settled 5000 pounds on my mother; there are no savings apart from that, and neither my mother nor my younger sisters would do well in straitened circumstances," she said with some apprehension for his reaction. "I had always thought

Jane would marry, and I would not need to worry, but when I returned from Kent and saw how out of spirits she remained, I knew I could no longer depend on that, so the responsibility fell to me."

She could not have guessed how relieved he was by this intelligence regarding her motives in accepting Mr. Covington's offer. He could not fault her for taking on the responsibility, and in fact could only blame himself that the necessity had arisen at all; had he not endeavoured to separate Bingley from Jane, Elizabeth might have remained free. It only convinced him further of her worth to know she had refused both him and Mr. Collins under circumstances which would have caused any other woman to accept any suitor of means, no matter how distasteful. Yet still he could not free himself from the thought of her with Mr. Covington, and he said impulsively, "Yet you refused me—there must have been some difference."

"Oh, William," she said, distressed to realize he was still pained by her decisions. "That was a *completely* different circumstance; I had such a grave misunderstanding of you. It would have been completely reprehensible for me to consider marrying you then, given what I thought I knew of you. He was someone I had known for years; I knew him to be amiable, and I felt a certain affection for him which I hoped might grow someday into love, but I admit I accepted him with reservations—he was not the man I had dreamed of marrying. I might have been content with him, had I never known anything different, but he would never have been able to stir me the way you do." She looked at him earnestly in the flickering light of the lamp.

"You had reservations about accepting me as well," he said uncomfortably.

"That does *not* compare—they were not about you or my affection for you, but only about the consequences of our marriage. It was completely the opposite situation. I loved you enough to deny myself for your benefit." She was beginning to understand how much uncertainty underlay his confident manner. She could not comprehend how he could be insecure of his place in her affections, but if he needed reassurance, she was not loathe to give it. "You are everything I dreamed of," she said seriously; then, her high spirits unwilling to be subdued for long, she boldly ran her hand down his body and added teasingly, "And quite a few things I never began to dream about as well."

Darcy had a potent reaction to both her words and her unanticipated forwardness. Putting his hand over hers, he wordlessly encouraged her to continue her explorations. It was a suggestion she was not averse to receiving, both to fulfill her own curiosity and for the heady pleasure of watching his response to her touch. She had never before had the opportunity to touch him when he was not making equal inroads upon her body and her peace of mind, and she found quickly how very much she enjoyed the intimacy of the warmth of his skin under her fingers. Even beyond that, her sense of playfulness was engaged by discovering what manner of touch pleased him the most, what made his eyes darken with desire, and what made him groan with pleasure. As she approached his arousal, he pushed himself against her until she brazenly took his hint. She was too astonished by his response to feel much shock at her discoveries there, and she found herself both aroused and satisfied by reducing him to the same level of distracted, moaning excitement that he had induced in her several times in the past.

Finally he removed her hand, his breathing uneven. "If this is an example of what you can do to me when you are merely improvising, I hesitate to think what it will be like when you know what you are doing to me. You will be quite dangerous, my love."

She smiled at him mischievously. "I certainly hope so!" she said.

Her unabashed comment made Darcy feel an almost irrepressible urge to make love to her without delay. He had not allowed himself to hope she would want to please him in such an active manner, and he was profoundly aroused by her clear enjoyment of her success. He captured her mouth, trying to relieve himself by taking every bit of pleasure he could from it. She had taken him remarkably close to the edge of his control—*perhaps beyond it!* he thought as his hand, apparently with a mind of its own, travelled directly to her most private parts, where his fingers slid deep inside her.

Involuntarily she raised her hips to meet him, the

intimacy of feeling his fingers within her further arousing her desire. Darcy made an inarticulate sound as his lips travelled hungrily down her neck and then her body until he captured her nipple in his mouth. She moaned as the current of pleasure began to run through her, only intensified by her greater knowledge of what was to come.

His fingers touched a tender spot on her as they moved, and she flinched slightly. Darcy stopped immediately, and looked at her in concern. "Should I stop, my dearest? I do not wish to hurt you," he said, his effort to hold himself back visible.

She smiled at him mischievously. "Well, now that I know what is to come, I might as well put my knowledge to good use," she said archly.

His fingers gently found their way to the spot which could most readily arouse her desire, and busied themselves with drawing as much response from her as she could give. "You may think you know what is to come," he said seductively as she began to moan beneath his touch, "but I have plans for you which go well beyond what you have discovered so far."

She opened her eyes to look at him in question, already beyond the point of speech, her hips moving against his fingers in search of even deeper pleasure.

He smiled in satisfaction at her state. "I warned you I had many improper desires—and I intend to ensure you enjoy them all," he said as he lowered his mouth to her breast once more.

# Chapter 11

ELIZABETH FELT UNACCOUNTABLY SHY as she went down to breakfast the next morning. It was not so much a matter of regretting the previous night as being embarrassed to now know herself capable of such wild and wanton behaviour, and to have it known as well by Mr. Darcy. He had not been exaggerating when he had warned her that he had even more improper designs on her. She flushed as she recalled the previous night's activity, the agonizing pleasure of his mouth at her most secret places, and how he had encouraged her to set her own demands by taking her place atop him as they joined together. While she did not believe he was truly disturbed by her conduct, she worried a little that his calmer and more controlled side would disapprove.

She greeted the others as she entered. Darcy appeared sedate, but she was unable to gauge his mood. He was at the side table helping himself to breakfast, and she walked over to join him.

After the conversation at the table resumed, he leaned toward her and said quietly, "So, are you still willing to speak to me, my love?"

Although his words were spoken jestingly, she could hear his very real concern, and she realized that he was even more worried what she was thinking of the previous night than she was. "Well, our days would be very long indeed if I were not," she said, looking up at him with a smile, then adding in a much softer voice, "though I do not expect it would have so much impact on our nights."

His eyes flared. "I can recommend these rolls, Elizabeth; they are delicious," he said, indicating a plate of pastries before her. As she took one, he whispered in her ear, "Though nothing is as delicious as you when you are taking your pleasure."

Her cheeks covered instantly with the deepest blush. She could not believe he had said such an intimate thing to her in front of others, even if they were quite unable to hear. When she finally looked up at him with amused reproach in her eyes, she saw a look of distinct satisfaction on his face, and realized he had thoroughly enjoyed discomfiting her.

She debated making a retort, but instead murmured, "William, a remark like that will not go unrevenged." She gave him a bright smile and turned toward the table.

She seated herself next to Georgiana, having noted that

the girl appeared about as embarrassed as she herself had been earlier, and surmised she was worrying about having confided so much in her the previous night. Feeling for her discomfort, Elizabeth forcibly tore her thoughts away from Darcy and set herself to the task of easing Georgiana's worries. It was as good a distraction for her as it was for Georgiana, and by the time she looked up at Darcy again, she could meet his eyes without her earlier discomfiture.

After breakfast, Jane asked Elizabeth for her assistance with some matters of the household. Elizabeth tossed a saucy glance in Darcy's direction before going with her sister, knowing full well he would have preferred to have her company himself.

Darcy, finding himself at loose ends while Elizabeth was with Jane, decided to play billiards, only to discover his cousin had already had the same thought. On finding him at the billiards table, he challenged him to a match, to which Colonel Fitzwilliam readily agreed. He seemed quieter than was his wont during the game, causing Darcy to wonder if he might not have recovered from their recent quarrel. It disturbed him to think such a thing could come between them after their lifetime of friendship.

In an attempt to broach the subject, he said, "I understand that I am in your debt for speaking to Miss Bennet on my behalf. She has told me your arguments had quite an influence on her in making her decision."

Colonel Fitzwilliam glanced up at him sharply, then

returned his attention to the table where he neatly sank another ball. "If it helped to persuade her, I am glad; though it was not on your behalf that I spoke to her, but in her own interest. I would not want to see her suffering a lifetime of poverty and spinsterhood because she was too considerate to risk causing you a little discomfort. God knows it is unlikely she would receive any other offers; certainly not from anyone who has as much to offer her as you do." He eyed the table closely, apparently pondering his next shot.

Darcy was somewhat taken aback by this summation, which seemed to make no room for tender sentiments. Recovering, he said, "Well, whatever your reason, I appreciate the result."

"Yes, I imagine you do," his cousin said dryly. He cursed as his carefully placed shot missed the mark.

Darcy fell silent. It was a novel and disagreeable sensation to find himself so ill at ease with his cousin, and without a clear understanding of the reason. He was all too aware that the previous night he had committed the very sin of which he had been falsely accused during their argument, and although he recognized Colonel Fitzwilliam could not possibly be aware of what had transpired, his guilty conscience had difficulty believing it.

They took their turns at the table in an uncomfortable silence until finally Colonel Fitzwilliam asked, "What are your plans for after the wedding? Pemberley?"

Grateful for the opening, Darcy said, "Yes, I think so,

although I have not discussed it with Miss Bennet as yet. I would like to show her Pemberley."

"It is one of your more attractive assets," said Colonel Fitzwilliam coolly. "It will no doubt make an impression upon her."

Darcy paused and, without moving from his position over the cue, looked up at his cousin. "What is it, Richard?" he asked mildly. "You are not yourself—I have never seen you so."

The door opened to reveal Bingley. "Darcy, Fitzwilliam, is this where you have been hiding yourselves?" he asked cheerfully, oblivious to the long, serious look between the two men.

Darcy returned his attention to the table and made a successful shot. Straightening, he said, "Yes, Elizabeth is off somewhere with your wife, talking about whatever it is women talk about." He wondered with a little embarrassment just what she might be confiding in her sister.

Bingley's face broke into a wide smile. "Dearest Jane," he said fondly. "She is dreading losing Lizzy's company, I must say, and I imagine she will want to steal all the time with her she can before then."

A flash of humour showed in Darcy's eyes. "She may find some competition from me—I am not so ready as that to spare Elizabeth from my side."

"Is it not amazing, Darcy, how very necessary those lovely ladies have become to us?" said Bingley.

Colonel Fitzwilliam made a noise of disgust and rolled his eyes, clearly impatient with this fulsome talk.

Darcy looked at him with amusement. "Just wait, Richard; some day it will be your turn to be enslaved by a pair of bright eyes."

A look of sharp anger, usually foreign to the colonel, flashed across his face. "Don't be insufferable," he snapped. As Darcy and Bingley looked at him in surprise, he racked his cue and abruptly departed the room.

"He has been in an odd mood of late," said Darcy finally. "I would not worry about it too much; I am sure he will be back to himself soon."

"I hope so," said Bingley, his voice expressing confusion and doubt.

❧

Elizabeth's thoughts had not travelled far from the events of the previous night, and when she saw the opportunity while she was alone with her sister, she said carefully, "Jane, do you remember a time, some years ago, when you and I were at Aunt Phillips's, and she had tasted a little too much of the wine?"

"I remember several occasions of the sort, in fact, Lizzy," replied her sister with an affectionate smile.

Elizabeth's expression became mischievous. "I refer to one particular time, when she took it upon herself to enlighten us as to the mysteries of the marriage bed." She had a vivid recollection of her own carefully hidden fascination as her aunt had described the fumbling under nightclothes leading directly to a then improbable-sounding event in which a wife's duty primarily consisted of lying still.

Jane flushed delicately. "Oh, yes, *that* time." She looked at Elizabeth with some concern. "You need not worry, dearest Lizzy—there truly is nothing to fear. I am sure Mr. Darcy will be gentle with you, and I daresay it is a happy thing to be able to give your husband such pleasure."

Elizabeth, finding it somewhat difficult to reconcile this description with the events of the previous night, asked, "But for you, Jane—is it pleasant for you?"

A slight frown line appeared between Jane's eyebrows. "I do not think it is meant to be *pleasant* precisely, but it is not *unpleasant*, and perhaps there are even moments when… but in any case, it is over quickly, and afterwards it is enjoyable to lie together." She blushed slightly at this admission.

"I see," said Elizabeth, who could not have described her time with Darcy as either "not unpleasant" nor "over quickly." With amusement she thought, *Well, if we are to spend half the night in such activity, I should be grateful it is pleasurable to me, at least!* It did not seem, however, that her dearest sister was likely to prove a confidante in these matters.

❧

The following morning Elizabeth found herself wondering if she was doomed to forever meet Darcy over the breakfast table with the deepest of blushes. *No*, she quickly amended her thought with amusement, *once we are married, I will have the opportunity to blush as soon as I see him on awakening!* The idea caused her to feel even greater embarrassment, and she turned her attention to her breakfast in an attempt to avoid Darcy's gaze. His eyes reminded her far too much of the last time she had seen him, when he had once again came to her room late in the night.

She had been uncertain as to whether he would take the risk of coming to her again so soon, and after the loss of sleep the previous night, had fallen asleep. She awoke some time later to find him sitting on her bed, shirtless, with one of her feet lying in his lap, the other cradled gently in his hand. His lips were tracing their way up the inside of her leg, pushing aside her nightdress as he went. He was partway up her calf when she awoke, and the intimacy of his appearance took her breath away.

On seeing him, she awkwardly struggled to raise herself to a sitting position, but he silently pressed her back with one hand, his dark eyes glittering at her as he moved his mouth upwards to delicately caress the soft skin of her inner thigh. Taking his time, he watched her arousal build, his lips approaching close to her secret places, then dancing away to explore the lines of her hips. By the time he was making himself free with the taut skin of her torso, her breath had been coming rapidly and she tangled her hand in his hair, moaning his name and seeking to bring his face up to hers. He would have no part of it, though, pausing only long enough to murmur, "Not yet, my love," as he extricated her from her nightdress, leaving her exposed to his appreciative eyes. She waited for him to touch her with his hands, but he did not, only letting her feel the sensation of his lips and his tongue against her as he continued to move upward to place kisses on the tender flesh of her breasts.

Elizabeth, afloat upon a sea of need for him, wriggled, trying to bring his mouth to her nipple, but a low laugh from Darcy told her she was not likely to succeed. "You are trying to torment me!" she accused, her voice trembling with desire.

He moved on to her shoulder, not failing to dust her neck with kisses along the way. "You are quite correct, my best beloved," he whispered between kisses. "I want to torment you, to tempt you, and to tantalize you, until you are as hope-lessly desirous of me as I am of you." His mouth continued on its journey down her arm, pausing in the hollow of her elbow, then again in the palm of her hand until he took her fingers one at time into his mouth, nibbling and sucking at them as his tongue danced against her fingertip.

The ache in her body was building to an almost intoler-able level, and her desire to touch him and to bring him to touch her where she needed him most had gone beyond the rule of reason. "William," she pleaded, again trying to bring his face to hers. He was clearly unready to hurry his enjoy-ment of her, though, and he set a leisurely pace, moving his lips back up her arm to her shoulder, the little hollows at the base of her neck, and finally up to her face. He paused with their faces just inches apart, delaying allowing her the satisfaction of their lips meeting at last as he whispered, "Do you want me?"

"How can you doubt it?" she had gasped as she finally pulled him to her, her hands insistently exploring the warm muscles of his back as she kissed him with all the desperate need he had awoken in her. He met her with an equal hunger, drinking deep of her desire for him and trying to sate himself momentarily with her kisses, because he was not yet ready to give up the pleasure of tormenting Elizabeth into wanting ever more of him, despite becoming increasingly distracted by the feeling of her hands upon him.

The ache Elizabeth felt in those sensitive parts of herself he had so deliberately ignored took on new power as his mouth returned to her breast, only to circle her nipple again and again. She involuntarily arched against him, arousing him by her insistence, until finally he barely skimmed her nipple with the tip of his tongue. She took in a sobbing gasp at this, and he looked at her for a moment in deep satisfaction before at last taking her into his mouth and suckling her. She could not help crying out at the sudden, intense pleasure of it, and his fingers travelled to her lips to quiet her as he continued to stimulate her, the movements of her body against his filling the deep need he felt for her desire and pleasure.

She caught his fingers between her lips, attempting to maintain some last trace of self-control, and rapidly discovered the impact she could have on him by teasing his fingertips with her tongue. Before she could enjoy her discovery for long, though, he withdrew his fingers and released her breast from his mouth. Their eyes locked as he spread her legs wide and settled himself between them.

This was the one thing which had shocked Elizabeth the previous night; she had been otherwise quite willing to follow his lead, but had been taken aback by the prospect of his mouth on her. It had taken a certain amount of persuasion and reassurance on his part to convince her to lie back and close her eyes, but it had been quite worth the effort. He had been extremely gratified by the intensity of her response when she finally was able to relax and allow herself to enjoy the pleasure he was giving her. Now he just looked at her and whispered, "May I?" as his fingers opened her to discover her deepest secrets.

Elizabeth hesitated a moment. She had not quite got past the shock of that first time, and was quite sure that in this they had crossed over the boundary into deeply improper behaviour. She could not forget either the exquisite and intense delight he had sent coursing through her body, and struggled with the even greater impropriety of not only having allowed it, but finding herself *wanting* him to do it again, and to transport her into the realm of pure pleasure and satisfaction. Without giving herself time to reconsider, she nodded quickly, then gasped as his tongue discovered and made free with the spot where all her pleasure began. She lost all compunction, all awareness of anything but him as he stimulated her into higher and higher levels of pleasure, until she was overtaken by pulse after pulse of deep satisfaction, drawn out and intensified by the continued gentle probing of his tongue.

He wasted no time in taking possession of her, his deep thrusts wringing further pleasure from her. She clung to him with her arms and legs, enjoying the feeling of him moving inside her, until he found his own oblivion and collapsed in her arms.

And now she faced him at the breakfast table. She could tell from the look in his dark eyes that he knew just what she had been thinking, and that the knowledge of the secret between them pleased and aroused him. She smiled at him sweetly, suspecting it would provoke him, and indeed his eyes flared at her. She found it quite difficult to concentrate on her breakfast.

During breakfast, the housekeeper came and asked to speak to Mr. Bingley privately, and shortly thereafter, Bingley returned and rather brusquely requested his wife to join him in his study, where they were closeted for some time. This unusual event did not pass unnoticed by either Elizabeth or Darcy, but neither commented on it owing to the presence of Georgiana and Colonel Fitzwilliam. Still, they exchanged a questioning glance when Mrs. Bingley returned, her usually peaceful countenance showing some signs of distress. Darcy, who was already feeling a certain amount of guilt about how much he had deprived Elizabeth of sleep in the previous three nights, made his excuses and went to seek out Bingley in hopes of gaining some insight to alleviate the concern he saw on Elizabeth's face when she looked at her sister.

He found his friend still in his study, looking uncharacteristically gloomy. He hesitated slightly to interrupt him; he knew he had little of Elizabeth's ability to elicit confidences, nor the capacity for appearing cheerfully oblivious when he was not. Still, he felt an obligation to Elizabeth, so he entered and asked Bingley if he could join him.

Bingley appeared startled at his appearance, but recovered and welcomed him. Without transition, he abruptly asked if Darcy had obtained the marriage license yet.

"Not as of yet," said Darcy easily, feeling secure on this subject. "Elizabeth is awaiting her mother's final decision between two dates, but I hope to secure it later this week."

Bingley seemed to ponder this more than it perhaps deserved, then said in something of a rush, "I think tomorrow would be an excellent time for you to marry Lizzy."

Puzzled, Darcy said, "Why? Is this a jest? I cannot think Mr. and Mrs. Bennet would be pleased by such a hurried wedding, nor to bid their daughter farewell so quickly."

"Damn it, Darcy!" Bingley exclaimed plaintively, clearly uncomfortable with his situation. He hesitated, then added, "You have put me in a very difficult position. Until you place that ring upon her finger, *I* am responsible for Elizabeth's well-being. God knows I have turned a blind eye often enough in hopes the two of you would come to an understanding, but there is only so far I can go!"

Darcy flushed as he looked at Bingley in sudden comprehension. He was silent a moment as he attempted to collect himself, finding to his surprise that, faced with this moment, he had no regrets whatsoever apart from having placed Elizabeth in an embarrassing position by having the misfortune to be caught out. He had become accustomed to the idea that they made their own rules to suit themselves, yet he understood Bingley's point quite well. "There seems to be little I can say, then," he said, his voice controlled, "beyond that I am far from having any objection to an immediate marriage; but I must warn you, Elizabeth may not be in accord with this."

"Oh, for heaven's sake, Darcy, do not hide behind that one!" exclaimed Bingley in some annoyance. "She placed herself under my care when she came to live with us, and if she has some objection, I am sorry for it, but I was not planning to offer her a choice."

It did not come as a surprise that his friend looked for a traditional response from the women of his household, but Darcy had spent sufficient time with Elizabeth for his own expectations to have altered somewhat from necessity. He considered his words carefully, with concern for the conflict already present between Bingley and himself. "I will speak to her, and will certainly make the strongest case possible for it, but I am not prepared to insist if she refuses."

"You do not seem to have been so loath to impose your will upon her last night!" said Bingley resentfully.

Darcy was sufficiently angered by this implication that he came close to retorting without thought, but he stopped himself just in time. The passion he appreciated in Elizabeth could cause her irreparable harm in her brother-in-law's eyes; and if the only alternative was for Bingley to believe he would have used Elizabeth to that degree, he would not argue the point. Still, he felt the keenness of the cut that his dear friend would jump to such a conclusion about him, and he said stiffly, "I do not believe Elizabeth holds anything against me; she is very generous."

"Well, I hope for your sake that she is," said Bingley. "I am sorry, Darcy; I do not want to quarrel with you—but you must see my position." He looked at Darcy in a silent appeal for his understanding.

"Yes, of course," said Darcy, feeling once more in control of himself and the situation. "I bear you no ill will; and I will speak to Elizabeth directly."

Bingley looked enormously relieved to turn over the responsibility of facing his spirited sister-in-law. "Thank you, Darcy," he said. "Do let me know if there is anything I can do to help."

"I will," said Darcy, irony heavy in his voice.

❧

He found Elizabeth in the garden with her sister, and indicated his need to speak privately to her. It was clear Jane was not prepared to leave them alone together—plainly the need for constant chaperonage had been discussed. Darcy was less than pleased with the idea of having this conversation under her watchful eye, but tried to make the best of it by taking Elizabeth off to a far corner of the garden where at least their words could be not be overheard.

Despite his forebodings, Darcy lost no time in acquainting her with the results of his conversation with their host. "I seem to have created a great deal of trouble for you by my own impetuosity. Bingley is insisting we marry immediately," he said quietly, hoping she would not be too angry.

She looked at him in confusion for a moment, then her brow cleared and she laughed. "Poor Bingley!" she exclaimed. "The embarrassment he must be suffering! He does try so hard not to offend anyone, and I imagine he has not the least understanding of our predicament. I do not think he shares your nature, and I know Jane does not share mine."

He was relieved she was taking this intelligence so lightly. "I am glad to see your only concern is for his embarrassment," he said dryly, "but I certainly did not want to put you in this position."

"Well, it is somewhat embarrassing for me as well," she allowed, "but I have become rather accustomed to being embarrassed, and at least in this case it is for a sin I did commit, rather than one I did not! No, my dearest, I am not upset—except perhaps that it will make our nights more difficult," she added in a teasing whisper.

He felt a surge of desire at her words. "Elizabeth—if you are attempting to distract me, you are doing an admirable job," he said, allowing his eyes to drift down her form. "Our nights together are one of my very favourite subjects, but I do not believe your sister would be happy about the direction my thoughts are tending. Perhaps we should return to the subject at hand."

She gave him an arch look, amused at the degree to which he could arouse her simply with a look and a few words. "Very well, I will attempt to behave, if that will make you happy. What is it you would like to discuss, then?"

He drew a deep breath. "You have not yet told me what you think of Bingley's request. I am aware you would prefer to wait a little longer before marrying, and I do not know if you are willing to do so this soon," he said carefully.

She looked at him, seeing his concern for her, and thought of what revising their plans would mean—the rushed packing, the abbreviated farewells to her family—and then she thought of how it would feel to formalize their marriage, and experienced a rush of warmth at the idea of being his wife. *It would give us freedom to be together again*, she thought, glancing at Jane. In sudden decision, she smiled up at him brilliantly. "Although it may not be the most practical approach, I would be well pleased to be married to you as soon as may be."

His expression evinced not only relief but a heartfelt delight. "My best beloved," he breathed, with a look in his eye which told her that he would like to be expressing his feelings in a much more direct manner. "I can think of nothing that would make me happier than to tell the world you are my own, and I am yours." Unconsciously he shifted his body closer to hers.

She took the pleasure of losing herself in his dark gaze for a moment, but before the connection could become unbearably close, she said lightly, "Then it would seem we have a great deal to accomplish rather quickly."

A smile grew on his face as he traced her beloved features with his eyes. "Yes, it would seem so," he agreed.

# Chapter 12

WITHIN A BRIEF SPACE of time they settled the question of the order of the day. Darcy was to call on the curate regarding the ceremony, while Elizabeth oversaw the preparations for their departure. Afterwards, they would go to Meryton together to obtain the license, then call at Longbourn to announce the change of plan. First, though, it remained to inform the other inhabitants of Netherfield of their intentions, and they began with Jane, who expressed a slightly reserved pleasure in their decision. Bingley in turn responded with the greatest of relief, his reaction making clear how difficult he had found it to confront his longtime friend from whom he was accustomed to seeking advice rather than offering it.

Telling Georgiana and Colonel Fitzwilliam proved a little more complex. Georgiana, though not displeased, was clearly taken aback and did not know what to make of the alteration in arrangements. "I am very happy for you," she said hesitantly, "and I am happy for myself that I will have my new sister even sooner than expected."

Elizabeth, seeing that she still seemed worried, asked gently, "Are you concerned about this change in our plans?"

"No," said Georgiana shyly. "Or perhaps yes… I just do not know whether I should stay here without you, or go back to London, or…" Clearly neither of those options appealed to her, but she would not suggest joining the newlyweds at Pemberley.

Colonel Fitzwilliam shot Darcy an uncharacteristically grim look. "I have a thought, Georgiana," he said. "I need to return to Matlock soon—why not come with me? My parents would be very happy to have you to visit for a few weeks. Then, if you wanted, you could go to Pemberley." He turned to Elizabeth, and his look softened. "Though I should ask first if that arrangement would suit you, Miss Bennet."

"I think it would work admirably," said Elizabeth warmly to Georgiana. "Would it please you?"

At Georgiana's silent and tentative nod, Elizabeth turned back to Colonel Fitzwilliam with a smile. "Thank you for such an excellent solution to our dilemma, sir." It was strange, she reflected—although she had never before been able to perceive a family resemblance between Darcy and his cousin, somehow today she could see a familiar likeness in the set of his jaw and his expression.

After a few minutes of polite conversation, Darcy excused himself, pleading the necessity of finding the curate, but

Elizabeth decided to remain a little longer to be certain Georgiana was adjusting to the idea of her changed plans. She asked her a little about her aunt and uncle, and Colonel Fitzwilliam, seeming back to his usual affable self, told several amusing stories about them.

Elizabeth was still puzzling a little over the rapid change in his demeanour when she abruptly realized what had seemed familiar in him earlier—his expression had reminded her of how Darcy used to look the previous summer when she was with Mr. Covington. In sudden comprehension, she thought back over the events of the previous weeks, seeing how very difficult the situation must be for Colonel Fitzwilliam. She wondered if Darcy knew, but decided almost immediately that he could not; it was not the sort of thing he could keep to himself, and in any case, he had shown no objection to her being in his cousin's company despite what she knew to be a rather powerful propensity to jealousy.

She could not help but be saddened by the state of affairs; she was fond of Colonel Fitzwilliam, and at one point had been prepared to be more than fond, and she certainly had no wish to pain him in any regard. Feeling somewhat subdued, she excused herself in order to begin her preparations, with much to think about regarding the complexities of life.

Elizabeth had fortunately recovered her usual good humour by the time Darcy returned, and the sight of his high spirits as he told her about the plans for the following day cheered her immensely. To know his joy in their marriage was a pleasure for her, and helped her put her more poignant thoughts behind her.

They set off for Meryton, where they were to obtain the license, and Elizabeth was to purchase a few last items for the wedding and her departure. She was glad to be in the company of her betrothed, and it showed in her sparkling eyes and lively attitude.

Darcy's mood could not be better, but he still had a little concern about Elizabeth. Finally he broached the subject, asking, "Are you in truth not dissatisfied with these new arrangements? I know that you wished to wait, and I feel as if I somehow selfishly got my own way at your expense."

She smiled at him. "Truly, I am not dissatisfied. I think I am more prepared for it than I was when we first discussed when to marry, and it does not seem so huge a leap." She looked up at him through her lashes. "After all, I have been getting in *practice* to be married," she said provocatively.

His eyes grew dark. "Just think how much more pleasant our *practice* will be when I need not leave you, but can hold you in my arms the whole night through," he said. He did not know how he had torn himself away from her these last two nights.

"Perhaps I will have the opportunity for a little more sleep, then," she teased.

With a slow smile, he said, "I would not count on that— no, I would not count on that at all, my best beloved."

They had reached the edge of Meryton, and as a result began to restrict their speech somewhat, but the affectionately teasing tone of their conversation continued. Elizabeth was not in a humour to fret over how the inhabitants of the town might see them on this, her last full day in Hertfordshire, so she did not attempt to disguise her happiness or to hide the warmth in her countenance when she looked at Darcy. She was gazing up at him with a happy smile when Darcy's face grew abruptly serious, and when she looked to see what was concerning him, she saw that their path was about to cross with that of Mr. Covington.

He was coming out of the milliner's shop, and clearly had not seen them until he was nearly upon them, so the meeting between them could not be escaped. The greetings between them were uncomfortable, and Elizabeth felt painfully embarrassed.

"I understand I must offer you both my congratulations," said Mr. Covington in a stiff voice.

"Thank you," said Darcy evenly.

Elizabeth looked away in discomfort. She felt for Mr. Covington's position. She knew they were no doubt under observation by curious passers-by, and he could not afford to be as cavalier of their opinion as she, so for his sake she wished this encounter to go well. She did not particularly trust Darcy's temperament where her former fiancé was concerned, yet hardly dared to look up at him either. After a brief, awkward silence, she said, "How is your mother,

Mr. Covington? It has been some time since I had the pleasure of seeing her."

"I am sorry to say her health is not of the best at the moment, although we are hoping it will improve with the warmer weather," he said, perhaps slightly more gently.

"Please give her my regards, and tell her I have been thinking of her." Elizabeth did not know how to extricate them from this situation, and when she finally glanced up at Darcy, she saw he was looking thoughtful.

"If you will be so kind as to excuse me for a moment, Miss Bennet, Mr. Covington, I have some business in the shop here," said Darcy. "I will return shortly." He bowed and made his way inside, leaving the two of them on their own in the midst of the public street.

Elizabeth looked after him in shock. This was the last behaviour she would have expected from him. She struggled to gather her wits, and said weakly, "I hope her health will return soon." There seemed to be an embargo on every subject.

There was a moment of silence, and she still could not bring herself to meet his eyes. At last he said, in a tone of reproach, "You might have said something, Lizzy."

She looked at him, startled. In her confusion, she did not even think to rebuke him for his familiarity. "I beg your pardon?" she asked.

"I wish you had told me, when you broke off our engagement, that it was because of *him*, rather than leaving me to believe it was on account of your sister. Or did you think I would not be able to make the connection? Perhaps no one else would be in a position to guess you made your decision for other reasons, but I have not forgotten how he behaved when I visited you last summer." Mr. Covington's voice was level, but he could not completely disguise the bitterness behind his words.

Dismayed by the conclusion he had evidently reached, she replied falteringly, "But it was not... I fear you are under a misapprehension; at that time I had no expectation of seeing Mr. Darcy again. I did not believe he would ever consider such an alliance; it was not part of my reasoning at all."

"You will forgive me if I find that somewhat difficult to believe," he said, with a hardness in his voice she had never heard before from him.

She had not expected forgiveness from him, but it pained her to hear the resentment in his voice, and to know she was responsible for its presence. She could certainly understand the injury to his pride, and she cast about for a way to relieve it. "I am sorry you do not believe me, sir. The truth of the matter is that while I was aware Mr. Darcy was unhappy about my engagement, I had no expectations of him at all. However, you may not be aware that my family owes him a great deal more than we could ever repay—he laid out a substantial sum of money to bring about my sister Lydia's wedding." She waited anxiously to see if he would draw the hoped-for conclusion from these two unrelated facts. It would be easier for him, she was certain, if he believed that her family's debt was the cause of her defection from him, rather than a matter of her preference.

He drew in a deep breath and let it out slowly. "I... see," he said. Then, straightening his shoulders, he added with a surprising formality, "I will have to ask you to excuse me, Miss Bennet. I had promised to call on Miss King this afternoon, and I do not want to keep her waiting."

Elizabeth stopped herself before she could raise her eyebrow at his implication, and instead forced herself to say in a serious tone, "Of course. I had not realized Miss King had returned to Meryton; I am pleased to hear it."

"I will bid you good day, then, Miss Bennet." The tone of farewell in his voice was unmistakable.

She curtseyed. "Good day, Mr. Covington." She looked after him for a moment while he strode away. *Mary King will be good for him*, she thought. *They both deserve greater happiness in love than they have found in the past.* This reflection brought her mind back to Darcy, and she entered the shop in search of him.

He was apparently negotiating with the shopkeeper over a pair of silk gloves. She felt a brief moment of hesitation before approaching him, suspecting he would be less than happy about their chance meeting with Mr. Covington; but when he sensed her drawing close to him, he turned to her with an unexpected look of vibrant happiness in his eyes. She could not but smile in response; it was as if he was offering her a glimpse into his soul, and the joy he found in her. She felt an intense longing to tell him she loved him, but under the circumstances, gazing at one another was all that was possible, and even that almost unbearably intimate.

Darcy concluded his purchase, feeling suddenly grateful to Bingley for insisting upon this change of plans. He could not marry Elizabeth soon enough to suit him—so much of his happiness rested in her, and this meeting with Covington had only confirmed her worth to him.

He had been surprised on encountering Covington to find that he no longer felt the jealous rage he had long harboured towards the other man. It had been a revelation to discover that he no longer feared losing Elizabeth to him somehow; that the very freedom and joy with which Elizabeth had finally given herself to him both in spirit and in body had convinced him of her commitment to him, and, oddly enough, the sight of Covington had proved to him the truth of her love.

Until then he had not realized, or perhaps had not allowed himself to think of, the fact that Covington was in many ways a better match for Elizabeth than he was. Covington would not have taken her away from her family and the society she had known her whole life, and he would have offered her a comfortable life in a sphere to which she was accustomed, instead of asking her to take over a position as mistress of an estate whose size was completely foreign to her. Darcy could not deny, either, that Covington's behaviour was superior to his—not only had he never required instruction in civil conduct such as Darcy had received at Hunsford, but Covington had, even in times of difficulty, acted the part of the perfect gentleman to Elizabeth, a claim Darcy could not even begin to make. No, the only thing Darcy had to offer that was superior to Covington was his fortune, and as he knew all too well, his wealth was meaningless to Elizabeth.

Yet she had denied Covington for his sake, denied him even when she did not believe he would return for her, despite his incivility early in their acquaintance and his disdain for proper behaviour during her engagement. She had loved him, even though a marriage to him would mean leaving behind her home and her beloved sister, and despite all the challenges it would offer. She had continued to love him as he methodically ignored every precept of propriety in their relationship. The more he considered it, the more he realized that there could be no explanation for her choice apart from a pure, unreasoned love for him which transcended all his faults. It was a realization which had brought him a sensation of enormous liberation.

There was no room for him to speak his feelings nor to demonstrate them at Meryton. Applying for the license for the morrow could not help but be a pleasure in the confirmation it held for their upcoming union. It was not until they were out of Meryton and on the road to Longbourn that he felt he could begin to express his feelings, but, as was often the case, Elizabeth reached that point first.

"So, sir, you seem in particularly fine spirits today," she said with an arch look.

"Should I not be? After all, tomorrow is the last day I will have to awaken without you in my arms," he said boldly.

She coloured, knowing from his look that his thoughts ranged well beyond the realm of merely awakening together, and that her own wanton desires pleased him greatly. Trying to distract herself away from the tingling sense of excitement he had created in her, she said, "I was surprised you were willing to leave me alone with Mr. Covington."

"I have the greatest of faith in you, my best beloved," he replied with a smile.

"I am glad you recognize that you need have no concerns on his account," she said, still surprised to find him so free of jealousy.

"He would have been a better match for you, you know," he said, stealing a glance at her.

"That, my dear, does not even merit a response!" she said with a laugh.

"But it is true nonetheless," he insisted. "I have nothing he lacks but money."

She stopped and turned to him with a saucy look. "You have tigers, unicorns, and a phoenix, which happen to be my precise requirements in a husband."

He understood her meaning, for he felt their bond went beyond the everyday as well. Nevertheless, he raised an eyebrow, and said, "So you only love me for the wild animals?"

She glanced at him archly. "*Wild* animals? Mr. Darcy, you assured me the tigers of Pemberley were tame!" she said with a mock formality.

The road was then passing through a small thicket, and he took advantage of the privacy to take her into his arms and kiss her until her eyes were soft and her cheeks becomingly flushed. "And you believed me?" he said in her ear, with the supreme lightness of spirit that comes only with loving and the knowledge of being loved, despite all of the attendant fears and risks. "That was foolish—everyone knows tigers cannot be tamed."

"In truth, I would not have them any other way," said Elizabeth contentedly.

*Epilogue*

ELIZABETH PAUSED ON THE landing of the great staircase at Pemberley, looking down to where Georgiana, dressed in a gown of the finest silk and lace, was in happy consultation with Mrs. Reynolds, no doubt over some last-minute detail. She smiled at the liveliness evident in the quick movements of Georgiana's graceful hands and the animation of her voice as she spoke, and she could not help but contrast this happy and elegant woman with the somber and quiet girl she had first met four years previously. What a change time had made! Time, the love of her family, and most especially the tender affection of the young man who would be taking her as his wife later that morning—all had combined to transform her into the joyful and lovely bride she was today.

It had been a long road; despite everything Elizabeth had done to try to help her sister-in-law to heal her wounds, there had been times when she had despaired of ever seeing the sadness in her eyes lift. But persistence had proved the key, along with the unconditional adoration of her niece and nephew. *It will be hard for them to accept that Aunt Georgiana is not available for their every whim anymore!* she thought, knowing perfectly well that nothing would keep Georgiana away for long.

She was so caught up in her thoughts that she did not hear footsteps approaching behind her until a pair of familiar arms stole around her waist. With a contented sigh, she leaned back against her husband, feeling his warmth infuse her.

"My best beloved," he murmured, nuzzling her hair. Looking downstairs to see what had caught her interest, he said, "Does this bring back memories?"

"Well, not of our wedding day," she said with a laugh. "That was far too disorganized an affair—Mrs. Reynolds would never have permitted it, had she been there. But of how we began—yes, a little." Their marriage, though, had led directly to this day; had Darcy not married her, without fortune or connections, he would never have considered approving Georgiana's choice. Although her betrothed was gently bred—he was, in fact, a distant Fitzwilliam connection who had become Darcy's protégé—as a third son he had no fortune of his own. Ironically, Georgiana had come to know him after Darcy bestowed on him the living at Kympton, which was once destined to be Wickham's; but a more dissimilar soul could not have existed. Mr. Wagner's gentle nature and cheerful outlook made him a perfect match for

Georgiana, and it had been he more than anyone who had drawn her out of her shell.

She realized Darcy had grown very still, and she knew him well enough to be aware that this signified serious thoughts. "What is it, my love?" she asked, turning her head to kiss his cheek lightly.

"Oh, I was thinking how close I came to never having you," he said, and she could hear, even after all these years, the distant echo of that pain in his voice. "Thank you for being willing to take the risk of accepting me."

She turned in his arms until she could hold him, pressing her head against his. "My love, I cannot imagine my life without you," she said. "And the risk was yours, as you know well."

"Minx," he said affectionately, recalling her fears for him. They had not proved to be completely unfounded; once word of her past had leaked into London society, there had been a definite chilling of the atmosphere there, and invitations which once would have been forthcoming slowed considerably. Their first, and only, Season in London had not been a particular success, at least not until the arrival of Darcy's aunt and uncle in Town. He had not minded, however; he far preferred being at Pemberley with Elizabeth to being in London without her, and there had been no difficulty with her acceptance in Derbyshire society—Mrs. Darcy was the mistress of Pemberley, regardless of whence she had come. The matter of her past still worried her upon occasion, but she could not deny his contentedness with his situation, nor his reliance upon her.

Their marriage, as it happened, had not been completely without benefit to Darcy's family. By an odd twist of fate, that same loss of social status inflicted on Darcy by his marriage had proved an unexpected boon to his cousin. Lord and Lady Matlock, unlike Lady Catherine de Bourgh, had decided they were above acknowledging that there was any fault in Darcy's choice of bride. They had welcomed Elizabeth into their family circle, and, as prominent and influential leaders in the *ton*, tolerated no slights to either her or Darcy at social events they hosted or attended. More than one socialite had discovered the price of angering Lord and Lady Matlock, finding themselves excluded from many further invitations.

This had not gone unnoticed by the clever mind of Sir Thomas Carlisle, who had parlayed an interest in textile production from a beginning in penury to one of the greatest fortunes of the age. Although as a tradesman he would never be accepted in the *ton*, he was not afraid to part with a great deal of that fortune to allow his only daughter to make her way into the kind of society he himself would never be allowed to enter, and he saw in Lord and Lady Matlock's treatment of Elizabeth a possibility for his daughter's future. It was not long before an approach was made, and Colonel Fitzwilliam was brought to trade the prestige and protection of the Fitzwilliam name for the extensive fortune of the former Miss Sophia Carlisle.

Although Darcy and Elizabeth had not seen a great deal of them since their marriage, Elizabeth was fond of Sophia, finding her both amiable and unpretentious. While no one could claim it had been a love match, there was a clear amicability between her and her husband, and they shared a fondness for society which made their townhouse a center for many gatherings. Richard, who had resigned his commission on his marriage, often tried to convince Darcy to join them in Town for the Season, but Darcy would always refuse, claiming to prefer to enjoy Pemberley with his family.

Elizabeth felt a shift in his body and realized he was no longer thinking about the past but about the very present moment. She smiled at him in amusement as he pressed himself against her in an unmistakable manner. "I believe we have a wedding to attend, my dear," she said lightly.

"I hope it will be over soon, and the wedding breakfast *very* brief, because I have some *urgent* business to discuss with you," he said, with that look in his eyes that could still awaken her desires.

"Well, perhaps it would not have been so *urgent* had you not stayed up half the night drinking with Richard!" she said tartly, but with a smile which removed any sting from her words.

He gave her an intent look. "Why, did you miss me?" he asked teasingly.

She snuggled against him. "Of course I did," she said.

He leaned over to whisper intimately in her ear. "Well, I

shall have to make it up to you then, my best beloved, as soon as our guests leave. Fortunately, that gives me some time to think over the question of how best to satisfy you. Shall I use my hand first, or my mouth to please you? Or perhaps both. I may not be able to wait as long as it takes to get to our bed-chamber; we may have to make do with the study, because I am very hungry"—he paused to nibble her ear delicately—"to hear you cry out in pleasure at my touch."

The past four years had taught Elizabeth how much her husband enjoyed saying such forbidden things to her, and how exciting he found it to whisper intimacies like this to her when they were in a public setting, yet still she coloured lightly. She could not deny that she found his behaviour arousing, as a familiar feeling of liquid heat began to build within her, and she gave him a wicked look, because she also knew that part of his pleasure came from seeing her response to him.

"And you want that too, do you not?" he continued to whisper as she fixed her eyes on the scene unfolding in the hall below, where Richard and Sophia had joined Georgiana. "You want me to touch you again and again until your pleasure takes you, and I want to see your face as it happens, because you are so very beautiful at that moment."

She looked down at the floor, reflecting with a smile that she would never have thought that the staid Mr. Darcy she first met would have such a taste for skirting the edges of for-bidden territory, nor that she could ever find it so appealing.

She very properly said nothing, though, knowing he was fully capable of reading her reaction from her body.

"In fact, my loveliest Elizabeth, I find I am far too impatient to wait until after the wedding breakfast."

She raised an eyebrow. "We do have a wedding to attend," she pointed out, with a look that expressed her certainty that he would ignore that fact, and that she would follow his lead willingly.

His eyes flared. "That means only that we must not linger," he said softly as he released his hold on her, only to take her hand and direct her back along the hallway to the study.

He locked the door and led her to a chair, where he lost no time in arranging her across his lap and moving directly toward his goal. He smiled broadly and nipped at her lips as his fingers discovered the incontrovertible evidence of her arousal. As she arched in pleasure at his intimate touch, he said seductively, "I can see this will not take long at all, my love." Her only reply was a moan as he used his knowledge of her body to rob her of any remaining coherent thought.

He was right; it did not take long for him to bring her to the limits of her pleasure, nor did it take long when she exacted her revenge by opening the front of his breeches and straddling him with a boldness which would have shocked her in the earliest days of their marriage. It was a boldness which her husband appreciated and encouraged, and she did not hesitate to show him her enjoyment in bringing him to his own peak of pleasure.

They enjoyed the comfort of being in one another's arms for a short interval, and then Darcy said reluctantly, "Though I would love to stay here, we must go; I would not want to shock Georgiana with our absence."

Elizabeth laughed. "Georgiana is completely shock-proof after living with us so long, my love." Though Darcy often worried about his sister discovering evidence of their intimate activities, in her own mind, Elizabeth thought it had done his sister a world of good to occasionally run into proof that joyful passion could be part of a happy marriage.

She took a few minutes to restore her appearance to a public standard, then held out her hand to her husband. "Shall we go, then?" she asked.

He kissed her lingeringly before agreeing, appreciating the particular look of softness Elizabeth's eyes always held after they had made love. "I will go anywhere with you, my love," he said.

"The church would seem to be a good place to start," she teased. Darcy unlocked the door, and the two made their way down the stairs hand in hand until they came within sight of the others, then reluctantly released their hold on each other.

"Good God," Richard said in an amused voice when he spotted them. "If they are not every bit as insufferable as they were as newlyweds!"

"Yes, we certainly are," said Darcy, his tone daring anyone to challenge him.

Elizabeth looked at the two men affectionately. "Insufferable or not, I believe we have a wedding to attend, gentlemen," she said lightly. She shared a smile of amused understanding with Sophia, silently acknowledging the occasional challenges of dealing with the Fitzwilliam men, then each woman took her husband's arm as they left for the church.

# Acknowledgments

This book could not have been written without many people, most especially the online readers who loved it and commented on it as a work in progress. I'm much better at writing books than at titling them, so longtime reader Leslie Emer has my thanks for coming up with the perfect title when I was stumped for one. My fellow writers at Austen Authors have provided support, friendship, and a lot of much-needed silliness. My fabulous editor, Deb Werksman, and my fantastic agent, Lauren Abramo, helped this edition into the world. Last, but never least, my dearest husband, David, and beloved children, Rebecca and Brian, for support, understanding, and lots of chocolate.

www.pemberleyvariations.com

www.austenauthors.com

# About the Author

Abigail Reynolds has spent the last fifty years asking herself what she wants to be when she grows up. This month she is a writer, a mother, and a physician in a part-time private practice. Next month is anybody's guess. Originally from upstate New York, she indecisively studied Russian, theater, and marine biology before deciding to attend medical school—a choice which allowed her to avoid any decisions at all for four years. She began writing *Pride & Prejudice* variations in 2001 to spend more time with her very favourite characters. Encouragement from fellow Austen fans convinced her to continue asking, "What if…?," which led to seven other Pemberley Variations and two modern novels set on Cape Cod. Her most recent releases are *What Would Mr. Darcy Do?*, *A Pemberley Medley*, and *Morning Light*. She is currently at work on some book or other, and will let the world know if she ever figures out what it is. She is a lifetime member of JASNA and lives in Wisconsin with her husband, two teen-aged children, and a menagerie of pets.

# Mr. Fitzwilliam Darcy:
## THE LAST MAN IN THE WORLD
### A *Pride and Prejudice* Variation
### ABIGAIL REYNOLDS

***What if Elizabeth had accepted Mr. Darcy the first time he asked?***

In Jane Austen's *Pride and Prejudice*, Elizabeth Bennet tells the proud Mr. Fitzwilliam Darcy that she wouldn't marry him if he were the last man in the world. But what if circumstances conspired to make her accept Darcy the first time he proposes? In this installment of Abigail Reynolds' acclaimed *Pride and Prejudice* Variations, Elizabeth agrees to marry Darcy against her better judgement, setting off a chain of events that nearly brings disaster to them both. Ultimately, Darcy and Elizabeth will have to work together on their tumultuous and passionate journey to make a success of their ill-timed marriage.

*What readers are saying:*

"A highly original story, immensely satisfying."

"Anyone who loves the story of Darcy and
Elizabeth will love this variation."

"I was hooked from page one."

"A refreshing new look at what might have
happened if…"

"Another good book to curl up with… I never wanted to put it down…"

978-1-4022-2947-3
$14.99 US/$18.99 CAN/£7.99 UK

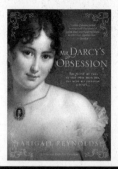

# MR. DARCY'S OBSESSION

~

## ABIGAIL REYNOLDS

"*[Reynolds] has creatively blended a classic love story with a saucy romance novel.*" —Austenprose

"*Developed so well that it made the age-old storyline new and fresh... Her writing gripped my attention and did not let go.*" —The Romance Studio

"*The style and wit of Ms. Austen are compellingly replicated... spellbinding. Kudos to Ms. Reynolds!*" —A Reader's Respite

*What if...* ELIZABETH BENNET WAS MORE UNSUITABLE FOR MR. DARCY THAN EVER...

Mr. Darcy is determined to find a more suitable bride. But then he learns that Elizabeth is living in London in reduced circumstances, after her father's death robs her of her family home...

*What if...* MR. DARCY CAN'T HELP HIMSELF FROM SEEKING HER OUT...

He just wants to make sure she's all right. But once he's seen her, he feels compelled to talk to her, and from there he's unable to fight the overwhelming desire to be near her, or the ever-growing mutual attraction that is between them...

*What if...* MR. DARCY'S INTENTIONS WERE SHOCKINGLY DISHONORABLE...

978-1-4022-4092-8 • $14.99 U.S./$17.99 CAN/£9.99 UK

# THE MAN WHO LOVED PRIDE & PREJUDICE

~

## ABIGAIL REYNOLDS

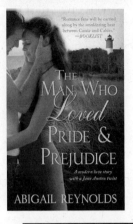

**A modern love story with a Jane Austen twist...**

*"A wonderfully fresh retelling of a perennial classic."*
—BOOKLOONS

*"As enjoyable and sensual as any of Reynolds's novels."*
—LIBRARY JOURNAL

*"This modern romance is by far her finest yet. I read it from cover to cover in one night and I simply could not put it down."*
—AUSTENPROSE

Marine biologist Cassie Boulton has no patience when a modern-day Mr. Darcy appears in her lab on Cape Cod. Proud, aloof Calder Westing III is the scion of a famous political family, while Cassie's success is hard-won in spite of a shameful family history.

When their budding romance is brutally thwarted, both by his family and by hers, Calder tries to set things right by rewriting the two of them in the roles of Mr. Darcy and Elizabeth Bennet from *Pride & Prejudice*...but will Cassie be willing to supply the happy ending?

978-1-4022-3732-4 • $6.99 U.S./$8.99 CAN/£3.99 UK

# *In the Arms of Mr. Darcy*
## SHARON LATHAN

### *If only everyone could be as happy as they are...*

Darcy and Elizabeth are as much in love as ever—even more so as their relationship matures. Their passion inspires everyone around them, and as winter turns to spring, romance blossoms around them.

Confirmed bachelor Richard Fitzwilliam sets his sights on a seemingly unattainable, beautiful widow; Georgiana Darcy learns to flirt outrageously; the very flighty Kitty Bennet develops her first crush, and Caroline Bingley meets her match.

But the path of true love never does run smooth, and Elizabeth and Darcy are kept busy navigating their friends and loved ones through the inevitable separations, misunderstandings, misgivings, and lovers' quarrels to reach their own happily ever afters...

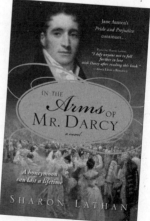

"If you love *Pride and Prejudice* sequels then this series should be on the top of your list!"
—*Royal Reviews*

978-1-4022-3699-0
$14.99 US/$17.99 CAN/£9.99 UK

"Sharon really knows how to make Regency come alive."
—*Love Romance Passion*

# Mr. Darcy Takes a Wife

## LINDA BERDOLL

### The #1 best-selling Pride and Prejudice sequel

"Wild, bawdy, and utterly enjoyable." —*Booklist*

### Hold on to your bonnets!

Every woman wants to be Elizabeth Bennet Darcy—beautiful, gracious, universally admired, strong, daring and outspoken—a thoroughly modern woman in crinolines. And every woman will fall madly in love with Mr. Darcy—tall, dark and handsome, a nobleman and a heartthrob whose virility is matched only by his utter devotion to his wife. Their passion is consuming and idyllic—essentially, they can't keep their hands off each other—through a sweeping tale of adventure and misadventure, human folly and numerous mysteries of parentage. This sexy, epic, hilarious, poignant and romantic sequel to *Pride and Prejudice* goes far beyond Jane Austen.

What readers are saying:

"I couldn't put it down."

"I didn't want it to end!"

"Berdoll does Jane Austen proud! ...A thoroughly delightful and engaging book."

"Delicious fun...I thoroughly enjoyed this book."

"My favourite *Pride and Prejudice* sequel so far."

978-1-4022-0273-5 • $16.95 US/ $19.99 CAN/ £9.99 UK

# Mr. Darcy's Diary

## AMANDA GRANGE

"A gift to a new generation of Darcy fans
and a treat for existing fans as well." —**AUSTENBLOG**

### *The only place Darcy could share his innermost feelings…*

…was in the private pages of his diary. Torn between his sense
of duty to his family name and his growing passion for Elizabeth
Bennet, all he can do is struggle not to fall in love. A skillful and
graceful imagining of the hero's point of view in one of the most
beloved and enduring love stories of all time.

---

What readers are saying:

"A delicious treat for all Austen addicts."

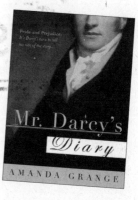

"Amanda Grange knows her subject…I
ended up reading the entire book in
one sitting."

"Brilliant, you could almost hear Darcy's
voice…I was so sad when it came to an
end. I loved the visions she gave us of
their married life."

"Amanda Grange has perfectly captured all of Jane Austen's clever
wit and social observations to make *Mr. Darcy's Diary* a must
read for any fan."

978-1-4022-0876-8 • $14.95 US/ $19.95 CAN/ £7.99 UK

# WICKHAM'S DIARY

## AMANDA GRANGE

Jane Austen's quintessential bad boy has his say…

*Enter the clandestine world of the cold-hearted Wickham…*

…in the pages of his private diary. Always aware of the inferiority of his social status compared to his friend Fitzwilliam Darcy, Wickham chases wealth and women in an attempt to attain the power he lusts for. But as Wickham gambles and cavorts his way through his funds, Darcy still comes out on top.

But now Wickham has found his chance to seduce the young Georgiana Darcy, which will finally secure the fortune—and the revenge—he's always dreamed of…

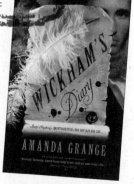

Praise for Amanda Grange:

"Amanda Grange has taken on the challenge of reworking a much loved romance and succeeds brilliantly." — *Historical Novels Review*

"Amanda Grange is a writer who tells an engaging, thoroughly enjoyable story!"
—*Romance Reader at Heart*

Available April 2011
978-1-4022-5186-3
$12.99 US